CHILDREN OF THE DETERRENT

IAN W. SAINSBURY

Cover design by Jacqueline Abromeit

For Ruth

1

Daniel

I'M STANDING on a cliff edge, watching a woman fall. She falls backwards away from me, her eyes never leaving mine. There is very little wind, but as she spreads her arms, it's as if a breeze has caught her, twisting her body around like a leaf in autumn.

She's naked, her dark skin silhouetting her against the turquoise waves.

I think of my father, and of my dead friend. I think of the future and wonder, for the first time, if it might be utterly unlike my expectations. I wonder what this feeling is, this feeling that has crept up on me and finally surfaced; fresh, unknown, and impossible to ignore.

As she drops towards the rocks, I start smiling.

～

I WAS BORN WITH SUPERPOWERS, but you wouldn't have known it. Nothing kicked in until late puberty. I was a chubby baby, a plump toddler, a corpulent child then, finally, a fat adolescent. I never felt the urge to race an express train, leap a building or punch through a wall.

I flew once—briefly—according to Piss Creature. Piss Creature was our collective name for Pete and Chris, the nastiest, meanest kids in my class when I was thirteen. They were twins; big, loud, scary. Every school year has a bully or two, as sure as there'll be a kid whose glasses are held together with tape and a girl whose breasts grow faster than the rest of her body.

The other kids referred to them as Crete and Piss and some point that was amalgamated into Piss Creature, which fitted so well that it stuck until they were expelled four years later after setting fire to the gym.

Piss Creature had nudged me out of a classroom window while I was opening it. We were only one floor up, but I was pitched through at an awkward angle. The ground rushed towards me, and for a horrible moment, I thought I would hit it face-first. Somehow, I twisted my body in the air so my shoulder took the brunt of the impact. My collarbone snapped and, a fraction of a second later, white-hot pain flashed through my shoulder. As I lay on the grass moaning, I heard Piss or Crete shouting, "You see that? Pigs *can* fly!"

I spent the rest of that summer in a cast. I knew better than to rat on Piss Creature. No one ratted on anyone, ever. Funny how that rule was inviolable, but 'do to others as you would have them do to you' never caught on. The head teacher asked me what happened. I even had a hospital visit from the school counsellor while the cast was fitted. My mother didn't ask. Someone had dragged her out of the pub in the middle of the afternoon to take care of me, and the only emotion I could detect in those dull eyes was resentment.

I slipped and fell out the window. No one bought it, but they all accepted it. The teacher and the counsellor because it reduced paperwork, Mum because it absolved her from taking any action on my behalf, or acknowledging my existence.

We were never close, Mum and I.

There was another expression I'd always liked - 'don't get mad, get even.' All that summer, while the other kids played football, swam, or just hung around the town centre, I stayed home; hot, uncomfortable, sweating underneath the plaster, dreaming up ways of getting even. I told myself I would have my revenge. Meanwhile, the enforced lack of exercise and the ready availability of Curlywurlies meant I added a few more inches to my waistline.

The cast came off on the last day of the holiday. First day back, I ran straight into Piss Creature at the school gates. One of them squeezed my newly healed shoulder, eliciting an involuntary gasp of pain. The other knocked my bag into a puddle and slapped my ear hard.

Four years later, about two months after they were expelled, I pulled a balaclava over my head one night and visited Piss Creature's house. They had bought a car together, something sporty with blacked out windows. It was parked round the back. Their parents were away. I had checked.

I gave the car a hard enough nudge to set the car alarm screaming. A light went on in an upstairs window, and a face appeared. As well as the balaclava, I'd gone for black jeans and a bomber jacket. I was carrying a baseball bat.

The pair of them appeared in the garden about thirty seconds later, one carrying a crowbar, the other a rifle.

Specifically, an air rifle. This was suburban Britain, not the wrong side of New Orleans.

The twins ordered me to put down my baseball bat. "If you want to live." I managed to put it down without laughing. They realised I wasn't going to run and advanced on me, slowly. I stood my ground.

When they were about ten feet away, I held up a hand.

"Far enough."

They stopped automatically for a second or two. Then the one with the rifle lifted it towards me, while the other began walking again, swinging the crowbar.

I placed my right hand on the roof of the car and pushed down. There was a brief, unexpectedly loud shriek of twisting metal mixed with an explosion of glass as the windscreens and side windows blew outwards. I pushed steadily until I felt the roof of the car reach the gravel of the drive.

I was on one knee, the car still making strange metallic noises as it adjusted to its new form. It looked like an elephant had sat on it.

The twin with the crowbar dropped it. His brother pulled the trigger of his rifle. It must have been some kind of automatic response, because the pellet hit the right buttock of his twin, who jerked a little, went white, but made no noise. His eyes were fixed on me. His brother's, too. Terrified, the pair of them.

It felt good. Really good.

"Leave town, boys," I said. This was improvised. I hadn't thought beyond wrecking their precious car. I hoped I sounded like a grizzled cowboy when I said it, despite the fact that this was Essex, not Arizona. My voice had finally broken fully, which helped. Piss Creature left the area the next day. Never came back. I felt just a little pang of disappointment that they hadn't guessed my identity. It took a bit of enjoyment out of my revenge. Even without the balaclava, though, I wonder if they would have known me. During the previous six weeks, I had added eight inches to my height, and all that pale, sagging fat had become dense, hard muscle.

As I walked home, I realised flattening their car had only taken the edge off the high I was on. I wanted more. No, it was more powerful than that. I absolutely had to have more, and I absolutely had to have more immediately. The sudden loss of control that followed was as unexpected as it was frightening. I ran, heading out of town. Every parked car I passed, I swung a fist. I left a trail of damage the local paper didn't shut up about for weeks, blaming it on travellers, although none had been seen anywhere near the village.

I woke up a few hours later in the middle of a field, starving and weak, my fists aching. I stared at my hands for a few seconds, trying to piece together what had happened. Then I stood up, washed in a stream and was home just after dawn, shaking and sweating. I ate a loaf and a half of bread and crawled upstairs to bed.

That was nearly twenty years ago. The summer I got superpowers. Yeah, I know. Most people still don't believe in halfheroes. Those that do think we're all either dead or institutionalised. Trust me, I'm lucky I'm still able to walk and talk. I was one of the first not to self-destruct. Maybe the first. There was no advice available back then, no one knew the danger we were in. No one knew what we were.

My name is Daniel Harbin. I'm thirty-six years old, and I'm a child of The Deterrent.

∾

In November, it'll be twenty-six years since my father

vanished, died, went into hiding, returned to his home planet, discorporated, ran out of batteries, took up a life of crime, became an ascetic hermit in Tibet, went into the movie business...Pick the one you like the sound of. There's no shortage of theories out there. But I'm the only person alive who knows the truth about why Dad disappeared.

And how to find him.

I know, I know. I'm not the first to go looking for The Deterrent, but I'll be the last. Besides probably being his oldest surviving child, I also have a totally unfair advantage. I have the words of Cressida Lofthouse. You've almost certainly read the book based on her notes, written under the name HT Bowthorpe.

Hey. I can almost hear the scornful laugh from here. But hold on a second there. When I talk about her words, I am not referring to *The Deterrent: The Inside Story Of Britain's Superhero*, which is, undeniably, an interesting tale, supposedly based on information gathered by Ms Lofthouse during the years she observed my father.

The Bowthorpe book is so far removed from what happened it should be shelved in the Fiction, rather than Modern History, section of your local library.

Luckily for me, as well as that heavily censored version of events now accepted as canon, Cress wrote a candid account, which Station would torture, maim, and kill to keep out of the wrong hands.

My hands, for instance.

Sorry, Station, I have bad news for you.

I have Cressida Lofthouse's diary.

And it's a hell of a read.

2

Cressida

March 22nd, 2013

To whom it may concern.

The notebooks you are holding comprise the diary I kept during the years since the discovery of Abos - The Deterrent. Much of this story is now public knowledge, but there are certain facts that never emerged from the morally suspect secret government department known as Station. My goodness, I sound as bad as the conspiracy theorists. But I have one advantage over them. I knew The Deterrent personally, I worked at the secret government department in question and, God help me, I kept an official record. A record I doubt will ever find its way out of the reinforced room containing Station's filing cabinets. Filing cabinets! I know, how quaint.

So much disinformation has appeared on the internet over the years that I've begun to wonder if Station itself isn't planting some of the sillier theories and is actively encouraging the more extreme views.

Back in 1969, I had to sign the Official Secrets Act. I understood the value of discretion when dealing with a discovery that forever changed humanity's understanding of our place in the universe, but I was also cognisant of the fact that no one country, not even my own, should keep back knowledge that might benefit our species. So I asked a few careful questions about the Act and my responsibility towards it. The gist of what I was told was that any records I kept belonged to the government, would be kept on site, and must always be read and approved by Colonel Purcell's office, as commanding officer of Station. Purcell himself told me this in a horribly patronising manner as if he were addressing a silly schoolgirl. Well, I decided there and then I'd keep a diary at home. Not just because I felt a moral obligation to record what really happened, but because I'm fed up with being underestimated and talked down to by pompous men. The world is changing, chaps!

Father died in 1985. Hopkins and Carstairs were still running Station when that happened. As far as I know, they still are. Carstairs is a nasty piece of work. As for Hopkins, he was even worse than Purcell to work for. Still patronising, but cold and callous with it. I didn't like his moustache, either.

I've recently been told I only have a short time to live. A bit late for regrets, but isn't that generally the time regrets make themselves known? At least it's not too late for me to conceal this diary. They still watch me, albeit sporadically. I suspect the house is bugged. That's one hazard of being involved with a secret government department; no one can ever afford to trust anyone, so loose ends such as myself have a habit of disappearing once we're off the payroll. I'm told my blood disorder is extremely rare, incurable and fast-acting. And Station employs so many scientists, geneticists, and specialists in human biology. Perhaps you will think me paranoid. Perhaps not, if you know anything at all about my former employers.

Enough. Lately, I have come to the conclusion that I did not spend my time on this planet wisely. Now that my time is up, however, I can make partial amends by telling the truth about the superhero the world knew as The Deterrent. Particularly the information only I know about his actions just before he disappeared.

As for my role in his life, it was mainly as an observer. These pages might suggest otherwise, but you and I would do well to remember what Abos was. And what he wasn't. I know right from wrong, and, even though it would have meant defying my father, I could have blown the whistle when I saw what they were doing to Abos. That I didn't do so is my most enduring regret.

Abos, wherever you are, I am sorry.

CRESSIDA LOFTHOUSE

~

August 31st, 1969

I don't think I've ever seen Father so excited about anything. It's hard to know where to begin. The most exciting part of all, for me at least, is that I am to be allowed to assist him and make notes. I am to delay my first year at Durham University, and instead, help Father with his new project. He says we'll be working weekends, nights, whatever is necessary. He couldn't tell me anything about it.

Goodness only knows how I am supposed to sleep tonight.

September 1st, 1969

Father's new office is impressive. The government has certainly taken this discovery very seriously, setting up a new department within an existing organisation hidden alongside the Underground at Liverpool Street Station. There are offices, a large dining hall, even dormitories down there. There are also lots of areas we were politely, but firmly, steered away from. The laboratory itself is modern, well-equipped, and huge. I shouldn't wonder if Station itself hasn't been there since before the war, though. I had no idea such places were hidden in our home city.

Station. A very unimaginative name for a top-secret government department, but perhaps that's clever in a way. After all, if someone working there were to say in public that they work for Station, it would just be assumed that he was referring to the railway or the bus station.

Actually getting into Station, though is far more exciting than the name suggests. I certainly felt like a spy doing it. You enter a hideously ugly concrete office building next to the train station. If you're driving, there's an underground carpark and an enormous goods lift.

The reception area above has secretaries, desks, telephones, security guards, and a bank of lifts. We all have name badges, and our credentials and photographs are kept on a database, to be checked every time we clock on.

Once through security, one enters the lift. Father and I have been issued with keys that open the emergency panel in the lift, behind which is a single button. The lift then goes down to Station. The rooms above are, apparently, completely unused.

All very exciting.

Father has a nameplate on his door. I must admit that 'Professor Graham Lofthouse, Chief Scientist' sounds far more grandiose than 'Head of Chemistry.'

After I fixed him a J&B this evening, he told me to pour one for myself. I could hardly believe it! He proposed a toast to our bright new future, then another to the future of humanity. He even hugged me. The first time since Mother's funeral. I waited until I was back in my room before I cried. I know he can't bear to see me cry. He's happy. That's the most important thing.

September 3rd, 1969

Today, Father showed me what all the fuss is about. It was difficult not to admit to a feeling of anti-climax. Perhaps, if I were a scientist like him, I would be more excited.

He ushered me into a small room where I had to wash my hands, put my hair in a net (very glamorous) and don a pair of surgical gloves. Then we went through to a much bigger room where Father introduced me to the scientific team.

Peter McKean is a geneticist like Father. They've worked together before. I remember him coming round for dinner when Mother was still alive. He's short, serious, taciturn. He always struck me as a man who would only read books that he considered 'improving,' and would avoid fiction entirely. I may be doing him a disservice, but he does seem awfully lacking in imagination.

Roger Sullivan is an American, so, naturally, I expected him to be brash, loud and insincere. Well, shame on me for my uptight English preconceptions. Roger is a softly spoken, polite man who has the knack of making you feel as if you're the only person in the room when he talks to you. Oh, all right, he's handsome too. I'm gushing. How ridiculous. He's there because of his knowledge of metallurgy, although he seems to be an expert on comets, asteroids, and meteorites, judging from the briefing today.

Sandra Hodge is a government scientist. She wasn't particularly forthcoming about her speciality, and she has a forbidding glare that discourages asking questions. She's as old as Father, if not older. Mid to late fifties would be my guess. She dresses as if her gender must be disguised, or subdued, at all costs. Underneath that lab coat, there's an awful lot of tweed. Her chest is large and, apparently, solid. She's terrifying, frankly. I found myself wondering if she'd ever had sex. Does she know it's 1969, not 1939? Still, I'm hardly one to talk. It's not as if I embraced the sexual revolution. I'm not sure that a few half-hearted fumbles in nightclubs count, do they?

Oh, dear God, I sound as if I'm sexually frustrated. Perhaps I am. Not much chance of changing that around here. Unless Roger...

Oh, stop it, Cress.

Mike Ainsleigh is my age. Lanky, hair down to his shoulders (I noticed Captain Hopkins giving him a disapproving look), a droopy moustache, and round wire-rimmed glasses. I think he would like to believe he looks a little like John Lennon, but he's too gawky and unsure of himself to pull it off. He's clumsy, too. Dropped his tea down his front when I asked him the time and he checked his watch with a full cup in his hand. Father says his thesis was outstanding, and he'll undoubtedly be one of the pre-eminent scientists of his generation. If he ever stops wearing his cardigan inside-out, that is. He may be outstanding, but he seems to be here to perform the dogsbody duties that no one else wants to do.

Once the introductions were over (leaving Mike mopping his soaked shirt with a napkin), Father showed me the cylinder. It was in the middle of the room on a large metal table.

While I stared at the thing and tried not to look under-whelmed, Father told me the story behind its discovery.

It was found in the foundations of one of the new build-ings going up in Marsham Street, in Westminster. I've seen the buildings Father was referring to - great concrete monstrosities. I know we have to move with the times, but honestly, is there any excuse for such ugliness? It's only a few streets away from the Tate Gallery, which has long been a favourite haunt of mine. Imagine coming out after gazing at those beautiful pictures and being confronted with that horror on the skyline.

I digress.

The construction workers turned up to work one morning and, about an hour into their digging, uncovered something strange. It was an odd looking thing, and it only took one of them to say the words 'unexploded bomb' for the site to be cleared and the foreman to telephone the police. The police called the army, the army came in, took a look and sent a query up the ranks to their most senior scientific officers. That was how Colonel Purcell got involved. After taking a look himself, he ordered the item be brought here.

Station is Purcell's department, and I think he's been

here a good while. I can't say how long, because if he doesn't like the sound of a question, he doesn't answer it. When I asked him directly, he gave me the silent treatment. The same as when I asked what else went on at Station. He knows I'm here to document our findings, but he does nothing to conceal his distaste at the idea. It was obviously foisted upon him from above, and he resents it. The man is profoundly unhelpful.

Apparently, the construction company was told that it was indeed an unexploded World War Two bomb: an experimental weapon, which explained its unusual appearance. I doubt the workmen who found it were convinced by this story, but Purcell seems certain that no mention of this will ever appear in the press. How he can be so confident, I have no idea. I imagine a government department that has remained hidden in an underground building near the centre of London without a single mention in the newspapers knows one or two things about secrecy.

Once the item arrived, Purcell assembled the scientific team. From the little that Father has let slip, they were recruited by appealing to their scientific curiosity and their patriotism. That, and a salary they would never get close to in academia. Despite Father's enthusiasm, this seems a little too much like bribery or hush money to me. I wonder what they would say if he wanted to leave the project? Or if I changed my mind? There's a kind of institutional ruthlessness about Purcell and his team that I don't much care for. In the interests of trying to be thorough, I will list them here, but as they have made it clear they will not be fraternising with the 'civilians', I only have my first impressions to go on, and they weren't good. To a greater or lesser degree, they all make me feel uncomfortable. There's Colonel Purcell, Lieutenant Colonel Ferriday, Captain

Hopkins (worst of the bunch), and Captain Mansfield. Various uniformed underlings scurry about obeying their orders, but they appear to be nameless and inter-changeable.

The item itself is, as I said, a little disappointing. It's cylindrical, six feet, four inches long, fifty-eight inches wide, four feet deep, tapering at both ends. It's transparent and hollow - approximately six inches thick. I had once seen a German bomb in a museum on a school trip. It was ten feet long and weighed more than a ton. It scared me half to death. In contrast, the cylinder I saw today, supposedly heralding a new scientific age for Great Britain and the world, looks more like a school science experiment.

Inside the container, occupying about a third of the space available, is a blue-green substance. It's a thick liquid. I heard Miss Hodge refer to it as semi-solid. To me, it looks like nothing more than mushy peas. If you can imagine mushy peas with a blue tinge on the surface. Doesn't sound very appetising, does it?

Two facts about the item have caused an immense amount of excitement and led to this vast secret place being re-organised to study it. Firstly, the transparent material is not, as one might suppose, made of glass. It's some kind of metal. Don't ask me how - that's Roger's field of expertise, and he's convinced we're in the presence of the single most important scientific discovery of the century. He looks even more handsome when he's passionate about something.

I just had a little giggle to myself at the thought of mixing up my official record with this diary. I can't begin to imagine Colonel Purcell's face if he was reading this!

The second fact that has everyone freaked out is the goo inside. The mushy peas. Whatever it is, it displays what Mr McKean called, "an undeniable homeostatic condition observable under changeable conditions, combined with, theoretically, some kind of circulatory system."

I must have looked blank, because Roger leaned over and whispered, "He thinks it's alive."

No one's said it aloud, but I imagine everyone must be wondering the same thing as I am.

Can this really be a coincidence? Some kind of unknown device, constructed of material beyond our capabilities, containing—possibly—something that is, in some sense, alive, appearing in the middle of our capital city in August 1969?

One month after humans first walked on the moon.

3

Daniel

MY EARLY CHILDHOOD WAS UNREMARKABLE. Abnormal things started happening to me in 1998. George said I should write it down, all of it. Re-live it once, only once, by writing it the way I lived it, then read it back with the perspective I have now. Now that I know what really happened. Now that I know the lengths Station will go to. The lengths they were always prepared to go to.

George was right about everything else. She's probably right about this.

January has turned out to be unseasonably warm this year. Or perhaps it's just this part of the country. It's certainly warm enough for me to sit outside with the laptop, occasionally looking up across the fields to the sea.

Right. The story of my life so far - at least, the bits that need telling.

Who, where, when, and what - is that what journalists say?

In which case: me, a small Essex town, 1998, and my balls.

It all started with my balls.

THE SUMMER before my eighteenth birthday, my balls finally dropped. They did so in dramatic fashion. I was woken by a loud noise one Saturday morning. The dream I had been ripped away from was generic in nature, familiar to anyone who is, or once was, a teenage boy. It involved teenage girls. I think I'll leave it at that.

I had been asleep in my customary position: on my back, one hand down my pyjama bottoms. I knew immediately something was different, and a quick fumble around my genitals confirmed it. When I realised what it was, I wept with joy. Literally. I lay in bed, one hand checking my chin for anything that might be described as stubble, the other cupping my undeniably saggier testicles, heaving out enormous sobs as tears of relief ran down my face.

I doubt there's ever been another adolescent male more prepared for the onset of puberty. I had spent hours in the local library, squirrelled away in the corner, reading every book on male development. I'd studied the diagrams, made notes about the changes that might occur. I knew the signs and had been checking myself daily since I was thirteen.

It's hard to explain how terrible it was to be a late developer in an Essex comprehensive school in 1998. After PE, there were communal showers. *Communal showers.* What oafish, unfeeling, ignorant twat thought that was a good idea? Communal showers at the stage when the majority of teenagers—other than the lucky few who somehow moved directly from childhood to adulthood—were desperate for privacy. Communal showers. Unbelievable.

As well as having a hairless chest, armpits, and groin to hide, I also had a pair of breasts some of the girls would have envied, perched above rolls of fat. Half of my classmates called me Danielle, asked my bra size, and generally derived a great deal of enjoyment from my physical appearance. I learned to say nothing. My voice was high, fluting. Hard to deliver a withering riposte asserting my masculinity when I sounded like Barbara bloody Windsor.

If I'd been intellectually gifted, artistically talented, or even the class clown, I might have found some respite from the taunts of my peers. But I was average in every sense other than my size. Try fading into the background when your arse hangs over the sides of your chair, and your thighs can barely squeeze under a desk.

School was a living nightmare, a torturous, endless endurance test. English was the only lesson I enjoyed. I had a little aptitude, and some feeling for the subject. When we studied Shakespeare, and I first heard Shylock's speech in The Merchant Of Venice, I felt—for the first time—that sense of awe when someone reaches out from the pages of a book and, across centuries, speaks directly to you.

"I am a Jew. Hath not a Jew eyes? Hath not a Jew hands, organs, dimensions, senses, affections, passions; fed with the same food, hurt with the same weapons, subject to the same diseases, heal'd by the same means, warm'd and cooled by the same winter and summer, as a Christian is? If you prick us, do we not bleed? If you tickle us, do we not laugh? If you poison us, do we not die?"

I was no Jew, just a painfully shy obese kid. But when Mrs Hargreaves read that speech aloud to a class of bored fifteen-year-olds, I was transfixed. And when she read the next line, I was aware of Pete and Chris in my peripheral vision.

"And if you wrong us, do we not revenge?"

If I had known then what I would become, I might have derived some comfort from it. Then again, maybe not.

That summer morning, balls in hand, tears wet on my cheeks, I became aware of an anomaly. I reached out for the glass of water I kept on my bedside table, only to find it wasn't where I expected it to be. The table itself wasn't where I expected it to be.

I dried my eyes on the pillowcase. Something was wrong. It was a question of perspective. I squinted at the ceiling. The dusty Airfix Spitfire dangling from the light looked further away. The water was unreachable because the table was now a couple of feet higher than it should have been. Either that, or—

It was at that moment that my mother opened the door. Unusually, she didn't knock. It wasn't that she had a greater regard for my privacy than the architects who design school showers, it was more that she feared seeing my corpulent form before I'd covered it.

"What the hell was that?" she said, as she walked into my room. An unlit cigarette dangled from her lips. She looked older than her thirty-eight years. I imagine an impartial observer might have put her in her mid-fifties. Sustained alcohol abuse will do that to a person. She was wearing makeup, but it was the remnants of the previous night's slap, the black trails of mascara making her look like a melodramatic actor on a daytime soap.

"What was what?" For one crazy moment, I thought she was referring to my testicles.

She looked at me in disgust. Since that was my mother's

default expression when in my company, I paid it no mind, but I did take my hand out of my pyjamas.

She was waving a finger, indicating the bed. Her mouth was working, the cigarette clinging to her lower lip as she made sounds, but her brain had not yet provided her with enough horsepower to put together a comprehensible sentence. I was used to this. Children of drunks generally are. I waited for the sounds to resemble words. Eventually, she managed one of the clearest sentences I'd ever heard from her before midday on a weekend. Or a weekday, to be fair.

"You...can pay for this out of your pocket money, you lazy, fat bastard."

I didn't respond, even to point out that she had never given me any pocket money. Most the money I had saved came from my Sunday job stacking shelves at the supermarket. I supplemented this meagre income by stealing from her. The money went on school clothes and books she'd forgotten to buy. Or groceries. Sometimes her need for booze was so strong she forgot to shop for anything else.

She backed out of the room and shut the door. Quietly. She never slammed doors in the daytime. Too hard on the hangover. It was only when she'd drunk away the previous night's damage that she would happily slam doors and kick things. Me, mostly.

I sat up fully. That's when I realised what had happened. Rolling off the bed, I looked back at the damage. The crash that had woken both me and my mother had been caused by the bed collapsing, depositing me onto the floor. All four solid wooden legs had snapped like matchwood. There were splinters on the carpet. It looked as if someone had taken a sledgehammer to them. It wasn't a particularly sturdy bed, but even so.

Briefly mourning the world-class collection of video-taped pornography that had been crushed, I felt the excitement that had arrived along with my freshly dangling testicles begin to diminish. I might be on the cusp of adulthood, but I was still obese. What kind of kid lets himself get so fat that his bed can't bear his weight?

I stood up slowly, looked at myself in the mirror, and got my third shock of the morning.

I moved closer to make sure I wasn't imagining things. My face looked back, and my eyes were drawn to the faint beginnings of stubble (yes!). I doubted anyone would have spotted any other changes. My mother had noticed nothing, but that didn't count for much. I could have shaved my head and painted it bright orange without her commenting.

But I could see the difference. I looked at my flabby face and, hesitantly, an unfamiliar smile crept across my features.

There was no doubt about it. I had lost one of my chins.

4

Cressida

A visit from the top brass today. I suspected something out of the ordinary was on the way because of the amount of cleaning and tidying that's gone on in the place in the last few days. No one said anything though.

I was writing up my notes when they arrived. Not that there's much to write up these days. But I try to make some kind of effort to earn the very generous pay cheque they give me every month. There are only so many ways one can state the same thing: "day fifty-four, no change; day eighty-one, condition of item unaltered; day two hundred and sixty-seven, tests on the item yield no new knowledge about its nature."

Miss Hodge has seen her hours reduced to seven or eight per week. McKean and Roger still come in, but their shifts are shorter. Even Father has reduced his working hours, arriving later in the morning and leaving mid-afternoon most days. I seem to replace his bottle of J&B far more often than I used to. It's hard not to worry about him. I don't know what he expected from this project, but I am sure it wasn't boredom. Only Mike keeps up his regular full-time schedule.

Purcell himself greeted our visitors and showed them into the lab.

Father shook some hands and mouthed some social niceties. I watched through the glass from the office next door, all the while, ostentatiously writing notes. We'd all been told to look busy, and I didn't intend to let the side down.

As he waved his arms around in full professorial fashion, no doubt dropping in impressive technical jargon (the lab is all but soundproof so I couldn't make out what he was saying), the small party of besuited men ignored him and went straight to Abos.

Oh. I've just flicked back through the pages and realised that I've yet to explain our subject's nickname. For months, it was 'the item,' until I overheard Mike talking to it while he mopped the lab. He didn't hear me come in and was chatting away as if to a friend.

"And then Phil Spector was brought in to produce it, and to me, it sounds like a mess. I mean, it just isn't The Beatles anymore. You know what I mean, Abos?"

I was right behind him by that point.

"Abos?"

He dropped the mop and jumped about three feet into the air.

"Miss Lofthouse. I was just—"

"Keeping the item abreast with current popular music trends, yes, so I see."

I couldn't resist teasing Mike. Although we are the same age, there's something young and puppy-like about him, and I know I act much older than twenty. I've run the household since I was fourteen. I often feel socially awkward or inadequate. But I can relax around Mike because he's even more inept than I am.

"Why Abos?"

Mike blushed and pushed his glasses up his nose.

"It's just a, well, it's silly. It's a nickname, really. Um, you know, just something..."

I waited. Eventually, he came to the point.

"One night, I called it an amorphous blob of slime, and the name stuck in my head. Like I said, silly."

"Abos. Amorphous Blob Of Slime." I considered it for a few moments and realised I liked it. If McKean was right, and the sludge inside the cylinder was alive, it was only right to give it a name.

"I like it," I said. "Abos it is."

As impossible as it sounds, I believe Mike managed to blush a little more.

Anyway, the visitors clustered around Abos and didn't seem to pay Father very much attention at all. As they were peering at the cylinder, Miss Hodge bustled in with some paperwork and wrote some figures on the blackboard in the corner. Before she had been there two minutes, the door swung open again, and McKean and Roger came in carrying instruments I hadn't seen for months. Once Father had introduced them to the suits, they started taking measurements, recording temperatures, comparing readings, and so on.

At that point, I understood what was going on. Father was putting on a show. Nothing has changed since we first saw Abos a year and a half ago. We've learned virtually nothing apart from the fact that it is impossible to gain access to the contents of the cylinder. Nothing will cut, dent, or even slightly mark that transparent surface. Every known chemical combination has been tested, along with extremes of temperature. Because of McKean's insistence that Abos is alive, a television and radio were wheeled in, and educational programmes played. English language lessons, basic biology, that kind of thing. No response from Abos, but a gradual deflation of excitement for all of us.

When I caught a glimpse of the bearded man at the centre of the small group, I understood what the visit was about and why Father was so desperate to impress them. Even I, with my feeble grasp of politics, was able to recognise the Chancellor Of The Exchequer.

They stayed for five minutes, then went straight to Purcell's office. I saw Father's shoulders slump as the door closed behind them.

Oh dear.

March 15th, 1971

They're not quite closing us down, but feels like it.

Father called a meeting this afternoon after spending much of the morning with Purcell. He came straight to the point.

"Our funding is being cut by ninety percent."

The silence was grim after that bombshell. McKean broke it.

"Bloody politicians. There's an election coming, and they

want to protect their skins, find some extra cash to bribe the electorate with. Scum."

Roger was upset, too. His eyes actually blaze when he's angry. I may have flushed a little.

"Idiots! How can they turn off the tap now? I know we haven't been able to get into the cylinder, but it's not as if we can drop a bomb on the bloody thing, is it? There are new technologies being developed which could change everything. I was in Cambridge last week, watching gas-assisted laser cutting tools go through steel. In the States, my old team are working on—"

Father cut him off with a weary wave of his hand.

"There's no point, Roger. It's over. The decision has been made. We will meet here once a quarter. If there is any change in the item's status, we will be recalled. But for now, we all need to find alternative employment. We can expect glowing letters of recommendation, at least."

No one responded. A good job in a university science department could hardly replace the possibilities lying there in the lab. But everyone present understood we'd run out of options. No progress had been made.

"So what happens to Abos, er, the item?" Mike rarely spoke up in meetings and, when everyone swung round to look at him, he stared at the floor.

"It stays right here," said Father. "The new budget means I will be here one day a week. Mike, if you can find a part-time job that will allow you the time, I'd like you to come in every morning and keep up regular observation."

Mike nodded. Funny. I almost fancy he thinks of Abos as his friend.

The rest of the meeting involved a few half-hearted complaints, some fruitless speculation about the next election, and a great deal of bitterness.

Father told me later that I can continue to keep records, accompanying him once a week. I have been offered a secretarial position in a nearby government department for the other four working days. If I want to take it. Instead, he encouraged me to go to university as a mature student. He knows that's what I've always wanted.

I took a long look at Father's tired eyes. I'm convinced that, were I to leave home and pursue my studies, he would be utterly lost without me. So I lied and said I wanted nothing more than to stay in my favourite city with my wonderful father and continue to help him with Abos, despite the funding cuts.

He didn't even try to hide his relief.

So, no university degree, then. And a menial dead-end career for life. Not a good day for anyone. It ended even more badly.

Roger made a pass at me. I know, I know, it's what I wanted. We've been flirting for months, but I wasn't sure it would be a good idea to mix work and pleasure. Besides, he'd never yet even asked me out for a drink after work. Recently, I've started to think I must have been misreading the signs.

We all went to the Mason's Arms this evening. Even Sandra Hodge, although she only stayed long enough to sip primly at a bitter lemon before saying a curt goodbye and leaving.

Roger had squeezed in next to me on the bench, and I was extremely aware of his leg pushing against mine as we sat there. Roger and Father were talking about microprocessors, an innovation I had never heard of and was struggling to understand. Why on earth would anyone want a computer in their home? They'd have to set aside a whole room for it. Roger seemed enthusiastic, anyway. I was unable to contribute much, partly because of my ignorance of the subject, but also because of that leg. McKean was drinking pints of stout, one after the other, saying little.

While Father was at the bar, Roger slipped an arm around me for a moment and whispered something. I have no idea what he said because all I was aware of was the fact that he had gently licked my earlobe. After nearly spilling my drink, I managed to compose myself, although I was convinced my face must be broadcasting my feelings.

Which were what, exactly?

Shocked? A little. Annoyed? No. Turned on? Yes, very. No point denying it.

So when Roger was at the bar and Mike said something to me when he stood up to leave, I had to make him repeat it.

"I said, did you know Roger's living with a girl?" Mike held a cloth cap between his fingers and was kneading it nervously. He looked miserable.

I felt a stab of anger. Just behind it was a flood of understanding because I knew it was true. It explained why Roger had never asked me out., The fact that he had never mentioned this girl also spoke volumes. At that moment, however, I was too upset to think straight, and I'm ashamed to say I took it out on poor Mike. I told him to mind his own business, reminding him it was the nineteen seventies, not the nineteen thirties, and who I choose to sleep with was my concern.

No, I don't understand why I said those things. The only male I've slept with is Mr Tedkins, the bear I've had since I was tiny. My decision to stay in London felt like I'd just turned my back on three years away from home, a chance to embrace my womanhood, lose my virginity, "fool around," as Roger charmingly puts it. And now Mike had spoiled this little glimpse of sexual freedom by telling me what, deep down, I already knew: Roger is a cad. It's an old-fashioned word, but, when it comes right down to it, I'm an old-fashioned girl.

It happened when I was coming back from the toilet. The Mason's Arms is one of those pre-war pubs where the toilet is still outside. I'd just stepped out when a shape emerged from the darkness. I think I shrieked a little, then giggled at my nervousness.

It was Roger, of course. I'm not going to go every detail here, as I intend to forget what happened as quickly as possible. Suffice to say, he had made a unilateral decision that we were going to have sex, right then and there, against the wall of the pub. As if I was a cheap whore. He had his hand up my skirt and was kissing me before I knew what was happening. Apparently, being pushed away and told, "no" over and over is meaningless to him. He treated it like foreplay.

A swift knee to the genitals did the trick, though. I walked back to the pub, leaving him vomiting in the gutter.

Father was just standing up when I got back in.

"Shall we call it a night, Cress?"

I nodded mutely at him. He was so wrapped up in what had happened that he didn't really look at me. I wonder if he would have noticed anything if he had. When we got outside, Roger was just coming back in. He held the door open for us.

"You look peaky, Sullivan," said Father. "I suggest you call it a night."

"I think you're right, sir." Roger smiled at him, and winked at me. The nerve of the man.

"Goodnight, sir. Goodnight, Cressida."

"Goodnight." The word was out before I could stop it,

and as we walked to the tube station, I knew I would never mention what Roger had done. After everything that's happened, I wouldn't want to do that to Father. I know Roger's a key member of the team.

At least I'll only have to see him once a quarter.

5

Daniel

THE SUMMER of '98 was the best of my life right up to the day when it all turned to shit.

At first, I assumed the changes in my body were part of puberty. All the books mentioned a timeframe during which puberty would begin, and I knew I was at the far end of late. What the books didn't do was detail any unusual changes late developers might experience. For all I knew, what was happening might be commonplace in those who nearly made it to their eighteenth birthday before their voices dropped.

I assumed I had been suffering constitutional delayed puberty. It was inherited from one, or both, parents. I was still weeks away from the revelation about my father's identity, and there was no way I was going to ask Mum when she'd first grown pubic hair.

So when, just over a week after I broke the bed, my head

brushed the lintel of my doorframe, I put it down to a growth spurt, which might be common during constitutional delayed puberty.

I had developed the kind of obsessive relationship with my mirror associated with narcissists. I spent far too long looking at myself, my gaze wandering from my face to my chest, stomach, groin, legs, and—thanks to a cunningly positioned second mirror propped against the cupboard —my arse.

I had a better excuse than most for my fixation. My appearance was changing daily. A fortnight after the incident with the bed, I was down to just two chins. I'm not sure how many seventeen-year-old boys have whooped and fist-pumped the air on discovering a double chin, but I danced around the room when I saw mine.

From five chins to two in fifteen days. By the following weekend, I was down to one.

The changes in my body were even more remarkable, but, since I could conceal them by continuing to wear baggy clothes and making sure I slouched, I didn't attract any unwanted attention. I had just left school forever, it was holiday time, and, since I didn't have a single friend, no one witnessed my impossible transformation. Mum was around every day but it was easy to stay out of her way. I left the house every morning and didn't return until late afternoon, by which time, she was drunk enough not to notice me. Even if she did, she was unlikely to remember it the following day.

I had been accepted at a North London college to take a degree in English. The college in question called itself a university, but we all knew you only went there if you couldn't get in anywhere else. I didn't care. I was finally getting away. I had applied for a student loan, I'd be able to rent a room in a shared house. I could escape. And, since no one at university was likely to know me, my changed appearance would go unnoticed. Although, as I admired the slabs of muscle where my sagging breasts used to hang, I dared to hope I might attract a little female attention.

It's difficult to look back without pitying the optimistic young man I briefly became that summer. I might have gone to university. I might have got a degree, a job, a normal life. A girlfriend. Kids, maybe, one day.

But even then, even as I posed in front of the mirror, I think there was part of me—the part that had got used to the hundred insults every day—that knew there would be a price to pay.

I just didn't know how high that price would be.

I TOOK the bus to Harlow every day. I'd told Mum I had a summer job, but that was just to stop her asking questions. Not that it was likely she would. That would mean taking an interest in my life.

Tilkley business park stood in an undeveloped waste-land three miles out of town. Built in a flurry of early eighties economic optimism, its developers had hoped to entice companies from London's booming financial services industry. The timing couldn't have been worse. Before the park was even half completed, the economic crash sucked away all the interest along with all the cash.

There had been a few unsuccessful attempts to reverse the site's fortunes over the years. Now, the few completed buildings gave the otherwise empty landscape an eerie atmosphere, like a nineteen seventies science fiction film with a tiny budget. A cheap, man-in-a-rubber-suit monster wobbling around the cracked-concrete roads wouldn't have looked out of place.

For a few weeks, I had the place to myself.

My first visit was the most memorable.

I got off the bus at the stop after Tilkley, jogging the mile back. Jogging was a new experience, and I relished it, feeling no pain in my legs, no slap of fat against fat, no burning lungs as I casually ran along the road to the entrance. I didn't realise how fast I was going until I caught up with a cyclist. Not wanting to draw attention, I backed off. I couldn't stop smiling.

When I reached the park, I didn't slow, just turned into the curving entrance road leading to its chained gates, then followed the metal fencing to the left, where a forest butted up against the southern perimeter. I ran a whole circuit of the site. The back entrance was locked. At one point, the trees grew as close as three yards to the fence, and it was here that I left the path and headed into the cool shade of the forest.

From there, I climbed a tree and had a good look at the site. Despite the prominent signs on the gates and fence, I doubted Tilkley Business Park was "patrolled twenty-four hours a day, seven days a week." The whole place was surrounded by an unbroken, twelve-foot steel chain-link fence topped with razor wire. Why pay for a security company too? There were signs with pictures of video cameras on them, but no actual cameras. The place was too far out of town for local teens or druggies to hang out. There was graffiti, but it was old.

The place was deserted. It was perfect. I just had to work out how to get in.

I inspected the fence. Right at the top, just under the razor wire, it looked like it might be possible to peel back the metal links, which were rusting. Over the course of the previous week, I had started getting stronger every day. There were three bent forks, a crushed tin of cat food and a telephone book ripped in two to prove it. If my half-baked plan of becoming a freelance writer failed, I could always enter The World's Strongest Man competition. I squinted at the top of the fence. I was sure I'd be able to bend the metal. If I could get up there.

I decided to take a run-up, jump as high as I could, grab the fence and climb the rest of the way. Every kid has climbed a chain-link fence. It's easy when you're eight years old and weigh very little. It's a different story when you weigh...well, I have no idea what I weighed. I'd stood on a big pair of scales at Boots the week before, and they'd broken. I had no desire to find out what effect that kind of weight might have on my fingers if they were the only things supporting me as I hung from the fence.

I took ten paces backwards, eyeing the area I hoped to reach when I jumped. I decided that if it was too painful to climb the fence, I'd just have to find another way in. That proved to be unnecessary.

About six steps into an explosive run-up, I pushed down into the dirt as hard as I could with my right leg and propelled my body upwards. My fingers formed claws ready to grab the chain links.

I missed the fence. It passed under me. I was at least five feet above the razor wire as I soared over it, my mouth open in surprise and delight. I had about a second to panic about landing before my feet hit the concrete. There was no grace in the manoeuvre that followed. I rolled six or seven times in total before coming to rest in an untidy heap, face down in a nettle. Weirdly, my face didn't hurt at all.

I sat up and crossed my legs underneath me, taking

stock. My fat had turned to muscle, I was now over six feet tall, I could jump about fifteen feet into the air, and my face could withstand the sting of a nettle. Does resistance to nettle stings count as a superpower? I like to think it does.

I don't know if anyone will understand this, or believe it, but I didn't spend much time wondering what was happening to me. I didn't care. I was alive, strong, fast. Unstoppable. I sat there and laughed at the sheer joy of being alive.

It was a great moment.

I came up with a daily routine. I'd arrive at Tilkley and jog around the site. The first couple of laps to make sure I was alone before upping my speed. I discovered I could run fast - how fast, I couldn't tell, but I guessed my pace was somewhere between keen amateur runner and professional athlete. I wouldn't be outrunning a car anytime soon, but I was respectably quick. I could sprint very fast but only over short distances. About a hundred yards before my lungs started to burn and my legs couldn't take any more punishment.

That lick of speed was surprising considering my size. My incredible growth spurt had settled down a little. It looked like my height would top out at about six-three or four. Being tall made me stand out a little, but it was my bulk that drew nervous, side-long glances on the bus. I'd taken to sitting on the back row, taking up half of the available space. No one came near me.

I had drawers full of tracksuits at home which still fitted. Back when I was fat, they were snug around the middle, and I'd have to roll up the cuffs at the wrists and ankles. Now they were too short, and I had threaded new elastic through the waist to stop them falling off. I'd trawled the charity shops and soon had a utilitarian, if ugly, wardrobe.

Away from Tilkley, I formed a habit of walking with shoulders hunched, legs slightly bent. This gave me an odd rolling gait, not unlike a slowed-down Charlie Chaplin. I'd noticed steroid-pumped bodybuilders walking the same way, so I hoped people would assume I was spending too much time in the gym. It seemed to work; the looks I got now were often a mix of guarded amusement and pity.

My morning run was followed by the leap over the fence. I was getting better at landing, often coming out of a roll with my momentum pushing me back onto my feet. I sometimes imagined how good that might have looked had there been anyone around to see it.

There were three buildings in the park, ugly eighties-designed plasticky offices. On the second day, I broke into all of them. I'd packed a hammer and nails along with my sandwich so that I could put back the sheets of wood I removed from the windows. At the end of the third day, I found that I could push nails through wood with my thumb. I stopped bringing the hammer.

All three office blocks smelled bad, but one of them had fewer rats, so I used it as my base. It was also useful due to some of the items left behind. There was a pallet stacked high with bricks and twenty bags of hardened cement. The stairs were bare concrete, and led up to three further floors, all empty.

I'd spend twenty minutes every morning running up and down the stairs as a warmup, three bags of cement across my shoulders.

The best room in the building was just off the reception area. Behind a closed door, with a sign saying *Manager*, was a carpeted, furnished office. When I first opened the door, I couldn't understand why it was there, in an otherwise bare and unfinished building. It was carpeted, for a start. There was a large desk, a faux-leather director's swivel-chair, two other chairs, curtains, three lamps, a telephone, ancient computer, fax machine, filing cabinet, and hat stand. When I looked closer, I discovered the room was the Tilkley equivalent of a show home. It was supposed to sell the business park to prospective companies. I'm sure the reception area would have been next on the list for the tarting-up treatment. The computer, a massive block of a thing, was a fake, as was the fax machine. The telephone handset was glued to the base. The desk drawers didn't open.

I only sat on the chair once. It collapsed.

The metal filing cabinet was the best find. I carried it out of the office and set it down in the middle of the reception area. It was empty, but the drawers still opened and closed. I could lift it easily over my head. I made it harder for myself putting two bricks in each drawer before lifting it again. Still easy. I kept adding bricks until each drawer was full. Twenty-four bricks in total. About three kilograms per brick. Seventy-two kilograms plus the weight of the filing cabinet itself - call it about eighty kilograms. Or twelve and a half stone. Which I could perform thirty overhead presses with before feeling the burn.

And I was still getting stronger.

After the first few days, I made a mistake. A stupid one. I'd skipped breakfast, grabbing a banana and some crisps on the way out. At Tilkley, halfway through the weightlifting session, I ran out of steam and felt dizzy. I put the cabinet down and sat on the stairs, breathing hard, feeling sick. I was hungry. Really hungry. I wolfed down the banana and crisps and stood up to try again. This time, I lifted the cabinet halfway over my head before the dizziness came back. I dropped it with a crash that echoed for half a minute. I sat down again.

I waited for about an hour, but I was still feeling shaky. Literally. When I held up my hand, I couldn't keep it still. My mouth was dry. I'd finished the bottle of squash I'd brought.

It might seem obvious that I wouldn't be able to expend crazy amounts of energy without putting crazy amounts of calories into my body, but it was only at that moment, head swimming, that I made the connection. Stupid boy.

I decided to go home. That was when my problems really started.

When I got to the fence, I knew I couldn't summon enough energy to jump it. For a few minutes, I stared dumbly at the trees beyond, thinking I would be trapped there until someone rescued me. Then I remembered the pallets in the office block. I turned back.

It took me over an hour, slowly walking between the fence and the building, dragging pallets through the window and stacking them by the fence. All my limbs were heavy, and my brain's functions seemed slower. I could only focus on the next thing I had to do. Walk to the office. Get a pallet. Drag it to the window. Push it through. Drag it to the fence. Put it on top of the other pallets. Walk back to the office. The hunger I felt was like nothing I've ever experienced. It was as if I hadn't eaten for a week. Combined with the lethargy and the light-headedness, I doubted if I could even climb the pallets I'd stacked.

After a rest of a few minutes, it was clear that my physical condition wouldn't improve until I'd eaten. The hunger was all-consuming, a need so powerful it was pushing everything else out of my mind. I couldn't wait. I had to get over the fence before the last of my strength went. I knew I had one shot. If the first attempt failed, I would have to drag myself over to the front gate and start yelling, which would lead to lots of questions I didn't want to answer.

I'd better make the first attempt count.

Without stopping to think about it, I climbed the pallets, hauling myself forward and up with all the strength I had left in my arms and legs. When I reached the penultimate pallet, I shoved the top one forward so it pushed up against the fence, resting against the razor wire.

I stood, my whole body trembling. I think I knew there was no way I would make it. But I took one, deep breath. And I ran.

My trainers pounded up the pallet. Too slowly. I would make the top, but I wouldn't clear the wire.

One shot.

I jumped. Well, it was more of a stumble.

I fell forwards and landed squarely on the razor wire. My weight shifted and I heard my clothes ripping.

I passed out.

6

Cressida

June 11th, 1978

I admit it, I normally resent the fact that our quarterly meetings always take place on a Saturday. It's the one day I normally have entirely to myself. Shopping, lunch with a couple of the girls, maybe a hot date later. Ha! In one of those parallel universes Father was speculating about, perhaps, but, sad to say, not this one of course. If I'm not home to cook for him, he won't eat. He'll still drink though, and at least when I'm around, I can water down the whiskies.

That sounds bitter. I'm not - I'm really not. It's just that I have this ridiculous feeling that I've missed all the opportunities life may have thrown my way. I missed an education, Abos turned out not to be the world-changing scientific discovery we all hoped for, and romantically, I feel like I've been left on the shelf. I'm only twenty-seven, but I feel older. The few relationships I've had have been with older men, two of whom turned out to be married. Is this going to be the pattern of my life?

Today, I even caught myself looking at Roger and wondering, "what if?" After what he did. I know, I'm furious with myself, but I promised to be honest in this diary. For the past six years, I've only seen him four times a year, and he's always been on his best behaviour. He's married now, two kids. His hair is receding. I wouldn't be surprised if he's bald by the time he's forty. But he still has a twinkle in his eye when he looks at me, and I still get butterflies. Hopeless.

Luckily, he made such a scene today that I think he might even be asked to leave the team. That might be best for everyone.

It all started as usual, Father delivering a report on the last quarter. It's a bit of a joke, really, as nothing has ever changed, but we all nod along and make notes. Then Roger stood up and said he had a suggestion.

"We have been sitting on this for the best part of a decade without any progress. Who knows what secrets lie inside that container? The fact that the best scientific minds have been unable to find a way to penetrate this unknown material suggests that a treasure trove of new science might be our reward once we find a way in. No, I've been speaking to Hopkins—,"

—That's Lieutenant Colonel Hopkins these days, of course. He hates it when I still call him Captain. Naturally, I try to do it as often as possible. He really is an awful man—

"—and he is willing to sign off on some new attempts to penetrate the container."

"New attempts?" McKean's head shot up like a Scottish terrier spotting a rabbit. "What the hell is that supposed to mean? We've tried everything."

"Not quite."

I could see McKean's complexion darkening. He stood up, too, jabbing his finger towards Roger.

"If you mean what I think you mean, you stupid Yank, you'd better bloody think again."

Roger smiled as if McKean amused him, which was guaranteed to wind him up. It worked, of course. McKean has a short temper at the best of times. I could see him grit his teeth.

Roger walked over to Abos and looked down at the cylinder.

"Hopkins agrees that our best chance is a controlled explosion. He can provide the expertise necessary, and we will oversee the attempt. I suggest starting with twenty-five grams of PE-4, increasing in ten-gram increments until we have a result."

McKean had followed him over to the cylinder and was now jabbing his finger towards Abos.

"What part of my initial assessment of this substance confused you?"

"Is there a problem, Pete?"

McKean dislikes being called Pete. He will allow Peter, occasionally, but has always made it clear that he wants to be addressed as McKean. When he ignored this jibe, I realised just how angry he was. He spat out his next words, glaring at Roger.

"Let me make this nice and simple for you, without any long words. This substance - Abos, if you like, is alive. Alive, Sullivan. Living. Changing. Possibly conscious."

"Don't be ridiculous." Roger laughed in his face. McKean clenched a fist.

"How dare you have the gall to call yourself a scientist? Abos doesn't conform to your expectations, doesn't resemble anything remotely familiar to us. It is new, it is unknown. We cannot apply our paradigms to a being utterly unlike anything ever classified in the history of our planet. This could be a new species of plant or animal, or...who knows?" McKean's vocabulary often fails him when he's angry.

"Who knows?" Roger was mocking him. "And you're lecturing me on how to be a scientist?"

"Yes, I am!" McKean was spluttering now. "The scientific mind should be curious and humble. Always curious so we can advance our knowledge, but humble enough to know we know nothing."

That was so eloquent considering the rage he had worked himself into that I suspected he was reciting something he'd written in one of his books. I did try reading one once. A bit too dry for me.

Roger was angry too, I could tell, but he's the sort of man who hides it and seems to get more and more calm. On balance, I think I prefer McKean's red-faced rants. At least we know how he feels.

The two men were on either side of the cylinder now. Roger leaned across and patted the container as if it was a family pet.

"No point being uptight about it, Petey. It's a done deal. I discussed it with Hopkins this morning."

I was aware of Father bristling beside me. Roger saw it too.

"I'm sorry, Professor Lofthouse, I really am. But we're getting nowhere. This is the last chance saloon. We don't get a look at this baby soon, we can kiss this whole project goodbye. Hopkins pretty much told me as much. He thinks the military should take over completely, and now he's in charge, that's exactly what he's going to suggest to our paymasters."

We were all quiet then. Roger saw the silence as acquies-
cence. He patted the container again.

"Next week, we're moving Abos to a reinforced chamber
designed for bomb tests. Then we're going to slap some
explosives on it and, finally, we'll get to meet our friend here,
up close and pers—,"

He stopped talking because McKean punched him in
the nose. It's the first time I've ever seen anyone get
punched, and it's actually pretty disgusting. There was a
sickening sort of crunching sound, and Roger's face
suddenly changed shape, quite horribly. His nose was
broken, and blood spurted out all over his chin, through his
fingers as he brought his hands up to his face, and all over
the container.

There was a shocked pause, then Roger started
screaming obscenities at McKean. He shut up again just as
quickly as the act of speaking was obviously causing a lot of
pain. Father, Mike, and I were standing now, and, wouldn't
you know, it naturally seemed to fall to me to do the nurs-
ing, as it would seem that men are incapable of going near
an injured colleague. Woman's work, apparently.

As it didn't really seem the right time to take a stand for
the feminist cause, I led Roger out of the room to the first
aid cupboard and cleaned him up. Thankfully, he had very
little to say for himself, other than, "ow," which he said quite
a lot. I may have been slightly less gentle than he would
have liked. Oh, well.

The meeting was pretty much over, then, but Father
made an appointment to see Hopkins on Monday. He hadn't
actually said whose side of the argument he was on, and I
was worried enough that he might have some sympathy for
Roger's suggestion, that I didn't dare ask.

One very strange thing. As I was getting my coat, Mike

caught up with me. He'd been cleaning up the mess in the lab. He looked confused.

"You saw what happened, right, Cress? The blood went everywhere, yeah?"

I nodded. It seemed like at least half a pint had gone down Roger's shirt.

"Well, I mopped plenty up from the floor, but, well..."

Mike flicked a strand of hair from in front of his glasses. He still loves that late-sixties Lennon look. He took a breath.

"Cress, there was no blood on the container."

I frowned at him. "Yes, there was." I clearly remembered the spray of blood spattering the cylinder.

"I know, I know. There was. But not now." He grabbed my hand and led me back to the lab.

I stood next to Abos and peered down through the transparent container at the familiar green-blue slime.

Mike was right. There was no blood at all. It had disappeared.

June 13th, 1978

Everything's changed. Everything. McKean was right.

Abos is alive.

7

Daniel

WHEN I CAME ROUND, it was getting dark. I could hear a rustling noise underneath me. Something had woken me. Then it came again. A high-pitched shriek.

I blinked a few times. The hunger was, if possible, even worse. I had passed out on a bed of razor wire, suspended twelve feet from the ground, and all I could think about was food.

The rustling noise again.

Underneath my uncomfortable perch, a fox was ripping a rabbit apart, shaking its head from side to side as it tore at the smaller creature's throat. Part of me recoiled in disgust, while the rest of me silently screamed, "dinner!"

It was the motivation I needed. With every bit of willpower I possessed, I rolled my aching body sideways, towards the forest. The fence creaked alarmingly as my clothes tore still further. The fox sprinted back to the trees a second before I dropped like a stone. An extremely heavy stone in a shredded tracksuit.

I hit the ground hard, making a small crater.

When I turned my head, I could see the twitching body of the rabbit. With no conscious thought, my hand shot out and pulled the dying creature to my mouth, my teeth closing on its throat just as the fox's had moments earlier.

I ate it, fur, bones and all. Almost immediately, the light-headedness receded and some energy returned. I sat up.

Looking down at my tracksuit, I winced. The top was sliced into ribbons in places, and there were deep tears in the bottoms. I dreaded to think what I would find when I looked at my skin.

Gingerly, hardly daring to look, I unzipped the top. The T-shirt beneath was similarly lacerated. I lifted it and looked at my skin.

Nothing. Well, a red mark here and there as if my shirt was too tight. No blood, no wounds, no cuts. It wasn't just speed and strength, then. My skin was impervious to razor wire. I prodded my belly. It was hard, muscled, but it felt like regular skin: elastic, warm, hairy.

I stood up. I needed to get home. Eating the rabbit had helped, but I could still feel dizziness hovering at the edges of my consciousness. I would need a lot more sustenance, and soon.

I walked towards the road. My stacked pallets would only be seen if someone walked the perimeter of the site. I could catch an earlier bus the next morning and clear away the evidence. I wanted to keep my training ground secret.

Half a dozen people were waiting at the bus stop. An old man caught sight of me as I walked out of the shadows, yelped a little, and moved to the far end of the shelter. When I saw my reflection in the glass, I understood why.

The ripped tracksuit, combined with rabbit blood around my mouth and on my hands, made me look like an escaped murderer.

Still. I had no choice. I had to catch this bus if I was going to get home. I stayed at the edge of the shelter and wiped my mouth on what was left of my sleeve. My fellow travellers huddled as far away from me as possible.

There was a puddle just beside me. I knelt and washed my hands. When I straightened, at least four people were staring.

"Um, fell off my bike," I said. They kept staring. "It's, er, being repaired. Buckled the wheel."

Someone nodded. It sounded plausible. The body language of the other passengers relaxed a little. I glanced at my watch. Five more minutes before the bus was due.

That was when I saw the kebab. It was sitting at the top of the bin. Half-eaten, bits of lettuce sticking out of the pitta bread. Food.

My brain turned off again, and I staggered over to the bin. The other passengers flinched—I'm sure I heard a whimper from one of them—then froze, as they realised they had backed themselves into the corner of the shelter.

Ignoring everyone else, I grabbed the kebab and ate it in three bites. Including the paper it was wrapped in.

It had gone quiet. I turned and looked at some very frightened faces. There was a schoolboy staring at me, a Mars bar halfway to his mouth. He slowly handed it over and scuttled back. I nodded my thanks and threw it in after the kebab.

"Thirsty," I croaked.

An old lady shuffled forwards, reached into a shopping trolley and pulled out a thermos.

"Tea?"

"Please."

She handed it over, and I unscrewed the lid.

"It might be a bit cold by now, sorry about that. Hope you don't mind sugar, I never used to take it myself until the dentist whipped my teeth out and put falsies in, then I thought, 'Well, Ethel, where's the harm? Stick four sugars in if you like.' I said to Bert, I said, 'Stick four sugars in,' didn't I, Bert? Still, if you get to eighty-seven, I reckon you're entitled."

She talked while I tipped my head back and poured about half a litre of glorious lukewarm sweet tea down my throat. It tasted like the elixir of life. I handed back the thermos as the bus pulled up.

"Ethel," I said, "you're a bloody star."

She smiled nervously. I stood back to let everyone on the bus first but, as one, they waved me on ahead of them.

No one else boarded. For some reason, they all waited for the next bus.

8

Cressida

June 19th, 1978

The last seven days have been so surreal it's as if they happened to someone else. This is the first chance I've had to gather my thoughts and write something.

We got the call on Monday morning, just as Father was about to leave for the university. We walk to the Underground together most days, so I was already opening the door when the phone rang.

The morning sun hits the front of our terrace, and as I stood in the open doorway, light streaming in, I couldn't help noticing how old he looks now. I had hoped the Abos project would give him a new passion, a new reason to get up in the mornings, but the way it had ended had sucked the energy out of him still further. I have an awful feeling that the only reason he puts any effort into keeping going is because I'm here, and he doesn't want to let me down.

Which is ironic, because the only reason I'm here is to stop him sinking into a pit of alcohol-fuelled depression from which he'll never emerge. We've trapped each other.

The phone call changed everything.

It was a short call, during which he nodded and said "yes," a number of times. The only other words he said were, "what do you mean, <u>he</u>?"

He put the phone down with shaking hands and looked at me with a spark in his eyes I haven't seen for years.

"That was Ainsleigh. Station is sending a car for us. The project is to resume with immediate effect. There has been a development."

I heard the car draw up in front of the house, but after nine years of looking at that container of blue-green slime without a single visible change, I wasn't going to let Father get away with "there has been a development."

"What do you mean?' What did he say?"

Father guided me out of the hall and down the steps to the waiting car.

"Ainsleigh referred to Abos as 'he.' When I questioned him, he said, 'wait and see'."

As the car pulled into the traffic, I put my hand on Father's arm.

"Have you considered the possibility that, after all these years of sacrificing a promising scientific career, Mike might have lost his mind?"

Yes," said Father, "I have."

No one would have been surprised if Mike Ainsleigh had slipped over the fine line between sanity and insanity. Either out of loyalty to the project, commitment to the advancement of knowledge, or because of the problems he had interacting socially, Mike had spent more time than anyone with Abos. He was paid to go in six mornings a week, record his observations and prepare the report for the quarterly meetings. Up to now, a photocopy of the last meeting's report would have been sufficient, since nothing ever changed. Despite that, Mike once admitted to me that, more often than not, he came in on Sunday mornings, unpaid. He couldn't explain why.

I have a soft spot for Mike, but I would be lying if I didn't admit I feel sorry for him. There's a little of the savant about him. A brilliant brain, but a limited understanding of how to relate to others. And, putting modesty aside for a moment, I would have to be a complete dullard not to notice the way he looks at me.

So my mood, as I took the familiar lift with its industrial beige carpet down to the labyrinthine complex of tunnels, labs, dorms, and who knows what else, was a little ambivalent, to say the least. If this was Mike losing his grip on reality, rather than a bona fide breakthrough with Abos, it might just tip Father over the edge. For three months after Mother died, he was in a place so black that I almost lost hope of his ever coming back. If he were ever to find himself back there, I doubted he would recover.

Mike met us underground as the lift doors opened. His frenetic manner and unkempt appearance did nothing to dispel my worries. He grabbed Father's sleeve and practically dragged him to the lab, such was his excitement. He was gabbling non-stop as we half-walked, half-jogged to keep up with him. I don't think he finished a single sentence before a new thought hit him and he plunged into another. The effect on the listener was very much like that of trying to tune the radio to listen to the news. Words and partial sentences flew out of him as if he were possessed. I stopped trying to understand after the first thirty seconds.

The lab was a five-minute walk away, but that day it felt like an hour. The whole experience was like a dream one might have just before waking, when your mind is hovering around the border of consciousness, telling your sleeping self that this can't be real.

I started to wonder if I was about to wake up and find myself at home. Then Mike opened the door, and I saw what had brought on his manic behaviour.

I grabbed Father's arm to steady myself. He had become rigid, staring straight ahead. I only realised he had stopped breathing when he finally let out one long breath in an explosion of air.

Mike stood back as Father and I approached the metal table.

The cylinder was smaller. That was the first thing I noticed. The top of it had always obscured the clock on the far wall of the lab. Now I could see the time clearly: 8:17. It was so quiet that I could hear the second hand ticking as we reached the table and looked at Abos.

Father slowly and deliberately removed his reading glasses from his jacket pocket before staring at what had, just three days earlier, been a blue-green mass of mushy pea-like slime. What had replaced it was bigger - maybe twice the size of the slime it had replaced. And the transparent interior of the cylinder was now a viscous liquid, surrounding and supporting its occupant.

"Bigger," came a voice from the door. Neither Father or I could look away. Mike repeated it. "Bigger. He's bigger than he was even a few hours ago. He's growing."

What we were looking at was a hairless human body, tucked into a loose foetal position. The foetal comparison was further justified by the softness of the shape, the unfinished nature of hands, feet and skull, the lack of definition. The body we were looking at was still forming, veins visible just beneath the translucent skin, stretching thin red threads of blood out from the hub in its chest. A gently hypnotic rhythmic pulse emanated from a still-developing heart.

Father and I stood in mute awe for a few minutes, then we both bent down to look more closely. The body was roughly the size of a twelve-year-old.

As if reading my mind, Mike spoke again.

"He was about the size of a toddler when I came in. I think he's feeding on the container."

Then I saw the umbilical cord. Instead of connecting the foetus to a host, it floated alongside the body. But the cylinder was smaller than it had been three days earlier, and the body was growing, so Mike's guess was probably a good one.

Father was near the head. He looked long and hard at the face floating just a few inches from his own, his eyes misted with tears.

I knelt and pressed my face close to the edge of the container. Abos shuddered, and I gasped at the unexpected movement. The change of position caused something to loosen and shift before it drifted into my field of vision.

"Oh, my," I whispered. At least one mystery had been cleared up beyond any doubt. I knew now why Mike was insisting on referring to Abos as *he*.

THE REST of the day was a bit of a blur, as were the two that followed. Abos continued to grow, and we watched his development with fascination, hour after hour. Observation is still the limit of our involvement, as the surface of the cylinder is as impenetrable as ever. There has been a twelve-degree rise in temperature, but that's all we know.

The heightened atmosphere around Station has infected everyone. McKean and Roger are behaving as if they never exchanged a single harsh word. Mike can't stop grinning. Father has taken charge and assigned tasks, leading the team with calm, firm assurance. Only I can tell he's as excited as a four-year-old on Christmas Eve.

Hopkins came and barked questions at Father that first morning before disappearing for a few hours. Father couldn't answer many of them. When Hopkins asserted that the scientific team had failed in their duty, since they couldn't explain what had happened, Father calmly reminded him that Hopkins himself had supported the budget slashes leading to this situation. If the budget had been maintained, video footage would be available of the transformation, the moment the familiar blue-green slime began changing into a human shape. Since the cuts, a still photograph taken by Mike each morning is all we have. An argument ensued. Father has the flexible, curious, passionate, intellectually rigorous mind of a true scientist. He argues beautifully. There's no other word for it. Unfortunately, when arguing with someone who operates within certain limits, someone who delegates much of his thinking upwards within a military hierarchy, a well-presented, logical argument is next to useless. It always meets the same response: "because I said so." And, as Hopkins is in charge, the conversation is over.

Hopkins posted four guards in the lab and two more outside the door. We all feel uncomfortable around men with loaded guns. An uncomfortable reminder of who pays our wages.

Tonight—Wednesday—is the first time we've been back in the house since Monday. We slept in the dormitories, after sending home for clothes and toiletries. Abos's development had been so rapid that we didn't dare risk missing the next stage.

McKean's theory has become the model the team is adopting at the moment. He thinks the cylinder acts just as an egg does to a baby bird. Whatever the thick liquid is inside the cylinder, it must provide energy for the growth of the body. Measurements taken every fifteen minutes confirm that the container is shrinking as the body grows. At the rate this was happening, McKean predicted the cylinder would disappear by six pm yesterday.

For much of Tuesday, it looked like he would be right. We all watched as the body grew. We've been filming since Monday as our budget has not only been reinstated but increased. The team has been gathering video footage. This led to another argument with Hopkins, this time with Roger on the losing side. To be honest, 'argument' is too strong a word. Roger suggested we send copies of the footage to his colleague in New York, a brilliant biologist. Hopkins flatly refused. Roger pushed, making demands, insisting Hopkins was standing in the way of the progress of science. Since Monday, I've noticed Roger sometimes acts as though he's auditioning to play the role of Roger Sullivan in Abos: The Movie. It's quite disconcerting, and more than a little childish. Anyway, Hopkins slapped him down so hard, he barely said another word until this morning.

"Mr Sullivan, I want you to listen to what I'm about to say as if your life depends on it. Because it does."

Roger paled.

"When you joined Station, you signed several documents. One of those was the Official Secrets Act, which forbids you communicating any aspect of your work here to anyone, ever, without written permission from the commanding officer. Which is me. Should you break those terms, you will be committing an act of treason. Outside these walls, a conviction of treason might lead to a significant period of imprisonment. But, since you also signed a document accepting secondment to Station, which is part of the British army, any transgression will be dealt with by a military court, convened by me."

Roger had, impressively, paled still further. We were all silent by then. Each of us had signed the same documents.

"Let me assure you, that I will deal robustly with any treasonous act that takes place under my command. And, just in case you're confused about what that means, allow me to clarify. Step out of line and you will never see the sun again, Sullivan. We have cells right here. Station has certain discretionary powers granted by Her Majesty's government, and I will use them without hesitation if security is compromised. Is that clear?"

Roger nodded. I was terrified, so goodness knows how he must have felt.

The atmosphere was more than a little muted after that. Towards late afternoon, we watched Abos and the cylinder, wondering what would happen next.

The word cylinder was inaccurate now, as, minute by minute, it had moulded itself to the shape of the body it contained. By teatime on Tuesday, the container around Abos looked like an aura surrounding him, a crude outline about four inches away from his skin. It was very similar to what happens when I first remove my glasses. Anyone more than a few feet distant has a blurred outline for a few seconds, until my eyes adjust.

What made Abos more unnerving now was his movements. It was like watching some kind of slow-motion modern dance, graceful at times, at others awkward and almost painful-looking. He would stretch out his limbs, raising his arms over his head, fingertips reaching towards the edge of the table. When he did this for the first time, we realised how tall he was. The table is eight feet long, and Abos nearly covers the length of it. I'm ashamed to admit I let out a little scream when I witnessed it. I pretended to sneeze afterwards so I may have got away with it. Not that I was the only one to react. Roger took a step back, McKean's massive eyebrows went so high they looked like they were trying to catch up with his receding hairline, and Mike actually giggled. Father was outwardly calm, although his hand was shaking a little when he checked his wristwatch.

The movements that followed that initial stretch turned out to be a sequence, repeated twice every hour. There were more stretches, contracting and extending muscle groups in the legs, arms, chest, and back. There were sudden jerks of the arms and legs. The muscles in the neck flexed. The whole body turned onto its front, before rolling onto one side, then the other.

Throughout each performance, Abos's eyes remained closed. The face itself was eerily unformed. All the expected features were present and intact - eyes, nose, mouth, ears, and so on. He was bald, but there were early signs of hair growth - a dark stubble shadowing his scalp. It was an anonymous face, impossible to describe due to the lack of prominent features. It didn't help that we hadn't yet seen his eyes.

As McKean's predicted deadline approached, the

process of change and growth slowed. Measurements confirmed that the cylinder was now shrinking at a far slower rate; a few millimetres per hour.

We pulled chairs around the metal table and watched. It was oddly like a hospital bed vigil, the main difference being that the body we were watching went through a series of contortions every so often.

It was Father, after watching for a few hours, who came up with an explanation for the slowing down of whatever process is underway.

"The brain of a human foetus develops most rapidly late in pregnancy. If Abos is developing in a similar way, the growth that is taking place may not have slowed at all. It may even have accelerated. The difference is that we cannot directly observe this period of development. Gentlemen, Cressida, I believe we may be witnesses to the final developmental stage before birth. What birth might mean for Abos, none of us can say, but I suggest we prepare ourselves. Cressida?"

I blinked. Father rarely addressed me directly when working. It was as if I were an invisible team member. I knew this wasn't meant as a slight, and I never took it personally. For my observations to remain objective and pure, it was best that I should be almost unnoticed. So when he said my name, I barely reacted at first. Then I blinked again and looked at him.

"Professor Lofthouse?" Never Father when we were working.

"You did some pedagogical training after A-levels, did you not?"

He knew that I had volunteered at the local primary school, although pedagogical training was far too grand a term for it. Mostly, I had cleared up paint and glue and handed out milk and biscuits.

"If my theory is correct, Abos will need a teacher."

My mouth went dry.

"But I have no experience...you need an expert, not..."

He waved his hand in a characteristic gesture of dismissal.

"Hopkins has tightened security. We have no access to any outside agencies. Until that restriction is lifted, we are limited to the skills we have available in this team."

I am to be Abos's teacher.

WEDNESDAY, Thursday, Friday, and the weekend suggested Father's hypothesis was correct. Abos's visible development continued, but far more slowly. His musculature has taken on definition, and the evidence confirms puberty has occurred. He looks like an athlete in his twenties. A seven-foot athlete with a chest like a bodybuilder. There's something about his face that I find unnerving. A kind of familiarity. I almost said something about it, but it sounded so silly in my head. "Is it just me, or does he remind you of someone...?"

I didn't dare say it out loud.

We're all spending an unhealthy amount of time down there. I finally cracked this afternoon and demanded we go home and rest properly. Father looks drawn, and I barely know what day it is anymore. Besides, I wanted the chance to write this week up.

Father and I have a perfectly good house a few miles away, and Roger's wife and children are only just across the river. We can be back at Station within thirty minutes of a phone call. Mike and McKean are both happy to stay in Station's dormitories, so Abos will still be under constant observation.

It's now midnight on Sunday, 19th June, 1978. I've unearthed my old box of teaching books and prepared alphabet cards, picture books, and learning games. Impossible to know what to expect, and I feel woefully unprepared. Scared, and excited too, of course. Who wouldn't be? Whatever Abos is, we will be the first people on Earth to find out. And when he wakes up, we'll be the first people he sees. It will be an encounter unlike any other in history.

And he might wake up tomorrow, the next day, next week, or next month. Maybe next year, even, although that seems unlikely given the speed of his early development.

All we can do is wait.

9

Daniel

EVERY DAY, I learned something new about my increased strength and resilience. After the incident with the razor wire, I experimented with various sharp objects on my skin. It was just as difficult as it sounds.

I started small, with a stapler. Positioning it on my forearm I tried to push down but was too much of a wimp. Despite my experience at Tilkley, I still imagined stapling myself might sting. It's hard to convince the human brain to allow you to do something painful or dangerous. I even worried about biting off my tongue in pain. In the end, I stuck a copy of 2000 AD between my teeth, turned away, and went for it. I felt the pressure, heard the *clack* of the stapler, but there was no pain. The bent and flattened staple slid onto the carpet. I tried again, watching this time. The stapler made no impression at all on my arm.

Time to up the ante.

I went downstairs and fetched skewers, a vegetable knife and the automatic carving knife.

When I got back to my room, I turned my music up a little. It was only ten in the morning, so it was unlikely Mum would surface, but if she did wander into the bathroom to throw up, I didn't want to have to explain why I was attacking myself with an electric carving knife.

The skewer was fun. I was tentative at first, just as I had been with the stapler. I put the point on my stomach and pushed. Nothing. I pushed harder. Still nothing. I stabbed myself harakiri style. The skewer bent double. My skin was fine.

Wedging a second skewer between two books on my shelf, I ran at it, jumping when I got close. The skewer snapped.

I turned to the vegetable knife. It was a sharp blade. Mum had cut her thumb on it slicing lemons a few days earlier.

I tried my leg first. Sitting at my desk, I stabbed myself about three inches above the knee. The knife bounced off. I got the giggles. Thirty seconds later, I was stabbing myself all over my body, like a frenzied lunatic. One particularly savage attempt produced a tiny pink mark on my neck, which faded almost immediately.

I reached for the carving knife, plugged it in and went to work.

I started with a finger, then my upper arm, thigh and buttocks. Finally, I went for my wrist. I pushed harder and harder. The only result was that the blades moved more slowly, and the motor made a peculiar whining sound. There was a small bang, and the electric carving knife expired in a puff of blue smoke. I unplugged it and hid it at the bottom of my sock drawer.

Then I remembered the electric drill.

I crawled into the cupboard under the stairs, a torch between my teeth. Actually, my days of being able to crawl into the cupboard were over. I could fit my head and one shoulder inside, but that was it. I shone the torch around the small space. Shoes, the iron, some carpet cleaner, and a hoover. The toolbox was in the far corner, in front of a pile of women's magazines. I pulled it towards me, but the magazines shifted ominously. I stopped. They didn't fall. Gingerly, I opened the nearest side of the tool box nearest and gently extracted the yellow and black drill.

Back upstairs, I eyed my prize appreciatively. I had been allowed to use it just once when I wanted to hang a cork board on my wall. A combination of inexperience and plain ineptitude had led to me choosing the wrong length bit, a higher speed than I needed, and an inadvisable section of wall to drill into. I went all the way through the wall into the spare room, taking out an electrical cable on the way. The electrician wasn't cheap, although Mum did have sex with him, so maybe she got a discount, I don't know.

The upshot for me was a lifetime ban from power tools until, in Mum's words, there was, "a shithole of your own to destroy."

I fitted the heaviest duty drill bit in the chuck and plugged in, then stuck an old Kraftwerk tape in the ghetto blaster and whacked the volume up. I thought Mum, if she heard anything, might assume it was part of the music, particularly if I made my attempt rhythmical.

I wasn't a hundred percent confident, so I started with a toe. A girl at school only had three toes on one foot, and she seemed to get by fine. If my foot turned out to be less than indestructible, I would, at worst, be down a toe. I could live with that.

Pulsing the drill in time to The Robots, I attacked my toe with a kind of mad glee. Nothing. No pain at all. I pushed harder and harder, stopping only when tiny flakes of metal flew off the drill.

I thought I heard something and turned the music down. Mum's voice.

"Keep it down, you selfish bastard."

Good morning to you, too.

I turned off the tape. After a few minutes, I heard her snoring.

I took the drill downstairs, eased as much of myself as I could into the cupboard and reached over to the open tool-box. I dropped the drill inside. Even as it slid out of my fingers, I knew what would happen. The tower of Woman's Own, House Beautiful, Hello, OK, and Cosmopolitan toppled forwards.

"Shit." I tried to stop them, but it was too late. They fell everywhere, about a hundred of the bloody things.

I had just resigned myself to the uncomfortable and annoying task of re-stacking them when I saw it. Flat against the wall, concealed by the magazines piled in front, was a large, brown envelope. Stretching as far as I could, I got my fingertips onto one corner and, by a series of tiny move-ments, teased it out.

I went back to my bedroom and quietly closed the door, listening. She was still snoring.

The envelope wasn't sealed. Before I tipped the contents onto my bed, I had a sudden premonition. Mum had always said I was the product of a one-night stand, a man she met at a party and never saw again. The few times I had brought up the subject, wanting to find out more, maybe even meet him, she had laughed.

"Go ahead, if you like, if you can find him. He was a

salesman. Dave. Possibly Steve. Or was it Phil? Whatever. You're nothing like him if that's what you're wondering. He was quite a looker, for a start. Fit. Not a fat waste of space like you."

She tried hard to keep that tone of casual cruelty in her voice when she dismissed my questions, but I knew her too well. She was hiding something. And the way she looked sometimes, when I caught her crying for no reason, looking out of the window. She was thinking about him. My father.

I spread the documents out on the bed. There were a few letters in there, some pages ripped out of a magazine. But the newspapers caught my eye first. Because Mum's face was on the front of them. National newspapers. I looked at the headline and wondered why I had never even considered the possibility before, knowing immediately it was the truth. Reality can be funny like that sometimes. It can be right in front of you for years, waving its arms, letting off party poppers and shouting, "Over here! Over here!" and you don't notice a thing until you trip over and land in its lap.

I walked around my tiny bedroom on the verge of hyperventilating. I opened my window and stuck my head out for a few minutes, then went back to the bed. The newspaper was still there, Mum's face staring up at me. Alongside her was a photograph of the most famous man in history. I read the headline again.

SUPERSTUD KNOCKED ME UP!

Mum and I needed to have a little chat.

BY THE TIME SHE SURFACED, I had spread the newspapers on

the kitchen table. The magazine articles told the same story and featured colour photos of Mum. Often in her underwear.

I felt tired. I would never meet my father. He had died the year after I was born. I knew some people said he'd survived, but they were kidding themselves. How could a seven-foot tall man hide from the entire world? No. He was dead.

The letters were sad and desperate. The first few were replies from the Ministry Of Defence, who, politely at first, then more bluntly, asked her to desist making ludicrous claims about a national hero. Letters from three legal firms regretted they would be unable to take her case. One firm advised her to get back in touch if her baby started flying around the nursery. They were laughing at her.

When Mum finally made it downstairs and saw what I was reading, she stood in the doorway for a few seconds, then bypassed her usual cup of tea in favour of an earlier than usual raid on the drinks cabinet.

"Well, you were going to find out sooner or later, I suppose," she said as she filled a tumbler with vodka, reached for the tonic water, then changed her mind and took a gulp.

"Why didn't you tell me, Mum?"

She sat down and looked at the photographs in the newspaper. One of them showed her lying on the bed wearing a black negligee, pouting at the camera.

"I had quite the body, didn't I?"

I didn't respond. She smiled.

"It was good enough to get the attention of The Deterrent, so it doesn't matter what you think, does it?"

I kept my silence. She took another long swig. Neither of us spoke for ten minutes. I've read about 'companionable silences.' I've never experienced that, but I can confirm the existence of uncompanionable silences. The atmosphere in the kitchen was thick with nearly eighteen years of bitterness, negligence, regret, and failure. I looked at my mother. The only thing we had ever shared was self-hatred. Now we didn't even have that. The past weeks had seen me change in ways well beyond the physical. I could feel a new feeling of self-assurance every time I got out of bed. I had found myself looking forward to the possibility of a life where I could make things happen, rather than work on ways to prevent life happening to me in its usual, painful fashion. It was possible that I might even, one day, not be unhappy.

Finally, she spoke.

"Look, I know this is a lot to take in. I couldn't bring myself to tell you, Danny."

Danny? No one called me Danny. I couldn't even remember the last time Mum had used my name.

"I had post-natal depression. Could barely bring myself to look at you. Then your nan died, and I had to deal with everything on my own. I know I've been a terrible mother. I know it."

I looked up at her. She was actually crying. I felt nothing.

"But you have to understand, Danny. Those newspapers twisted everything. I only called the army people because he...he didn't answer my letters. They said hundreds of women had claimed the same thing. Didn't stop them sending some bloke round when you were born though. I saw him at the hospital, looking at you, shining a torch into your eyes, trying to take a blood sample. When I shouted, he left. Bastards."

She waved at the photos. "The papers offered me a lot of money to take my clothes off, Danny. A lot of money. And I needed it, we had nothing. Nothing. But I was a virgin before...him. I want you to know that."

I snorted. Whatever goodwill she was hoping for had been crushed by years of bullying and neglect. I think she knew it, too.

"Danny, look, give me another chance, will you? I'll work on the drinking, cut down. In my own way, I've tried to love you. I kept you, didn't I? And we've got a roof over our heads. I could've had you put into care. That's what my mates all told me to do. Back when I had mates."

I looked at her, haggard, ill-looking, her face streaked with mascara tears, eyes puffy and red. She was trembling. I felt myself thaw just a tiny bit. Despite myself, I reached over and took her hand. She was a terrible mother. An awful, appalling, selfish, bitter woman. But, somewhere in there was the lost girl who'd found herself alone and pregnant in her teens. And she was all the family I had. Perhaps I owed her one more chance.

"Okay," I said. "Let's talk about it. About what we do next."

She looked up at the word "we," the naked, desperate hope clear in her face. She squeezed my hand.

"Do you mean it, Danny? Do you really mean it?"

"No promises, Mum. We'll see how the next few days go, see if you can sober up. We'll talk more."

She squeezed more tightly, nodding, not daring to speak.

"But I mean it, Mum. No promises."

She looked at me strangely. It took me a few seconds to work out what she was doing. Even as a baby, I imagine I'd never seen that particular arrangement of her facial features.

She was smiling.

She stood up and made me a cup of tea. Another first.

But the day wasn't quite finished with us yet. As she sat back down, the phone rang. She half stood up, but I waved her down again.

"Let the machine get it, Mum."

When the caller left his message, she got up again, in a hurry this time, but I reached across and grabbed her arm. As the voice spoke the words that ended our relationship, she went pale, then all the strength seemed to leave her body, and she slumped at the table.

"Miss Harbin, this is Barry Grogan from the Mail. I've been thinking about what you told me earlier and, if it's all the same with you, I think I'll come over a wee bit sooner than we arranged. I'm going to drive up tomorrow evening, have a chat with your young superhero, get photos of both of you. I should be at yours by six. See you then."

Mum said nothing as I climbed the stairs and packed some clothes into a rucksack. I took a rolled-up sleeping bag, some candles, matches and a map. I lobbed my house keys into the kitchen as I passed on my way out of the front door.

I was a few days shy of turning eighteen. I was alone. I had superpowers. And I had the rest of my life in front of me.

10

Cressida

June 23rd, 1978

One mystery was cleared up today, much to my relief. I'm not going mad after all. For days now, I've been looking at Abos's face as he sleeps, wondering if anyone else was seeing what I was seeing. The resemblance was fleeting at first, but as the days went on and the facial features defined themselves, losing their generic nature, it became harder and harder to ignore what was happening.

Finally, I broke my silence when I was sharing a shift with McKean. It was something in his expression that prompted me to do it. McKean had just leaned in closer to Abos, making notes. He studied the face, and I saw his brief look of distaste. I sighed with relief. His reaction confirmed my own observations.

"You see it too, don't you?" I asked.

McKean looked up at me in surprise.

"His face," I prompted. "You recognise it."

McKean grunted dismissively, then looked at me again and shook his head slowly, reconsidering. "I admit there is a strong resemblance," he said, "but it's not a hundred percent. The symmetry is stronger, for example. The cheekbones are more pronounced and the jawline stronger. This is the face of a much younger man - a much bigger one, too. Also,"— He grunted again, and I realised he was amused—"his nose isn't broken."

We both agreed, as did the rest of the team later that day. Abos looks very, very like Roger.

August 27th, 1978

Father and the team have come up with a theory about why Abos looks the way he does. Father presented their findings to Hopkins and some high-level military types in the briefing room opposite the lab yesterday. He's always been a good lecturer, and I could see he was holding the attention of his audience, all older men, sharp-eyed and serious. They made me nervous, but it didn't seem to affect Father.

"During the years since the item was discovered in Marsham Street, we have been trying to amass as much data as possible about it. We have run every conceivable test, and we have exhausted all known methods in our efforts to get a sample. As our reports have shown, nothing has worked. The cylinder's construction is beyond anything of which we are capable. Well beyond."

"Russian? Chinese?" The questioner was a tall, lean man in his seventies. He wore a suit. All six of them other than

Hopkins were wearing suits, but their bearing gave them away as military.

"No."

"You're sure of this?"

"Completely." Father's tone was confident. "Whatever material was used in the cylinder's construction, it is far beyond our current understanding. Imagine a stone age man confronted with a solid steel door. Not only do we not know what this material is, we lack the technology even to begin to analyse it."

Another man spoke up. I won't describe all of them as they seemed interchangeable.

"What are you saying, then? It's from another planet? It's from the future? What?"

Father sighed. I knew why. He has never been a fan of what he calls fruitless speculation.

"Your guess is as good as mine. I'm a scientist. I deal with facts."

Before he could go on, the same man spoke up again. Father hated being interrupted.

"On the contrary, Professor Lofthouse, my guess is not as good as yours. My expertise regarding the security of this country surpasses your own. I also deal with facts. But, when necessary, I am prepared to use guesswork in the field. On some occasions, my guesses are good enough to save lives. Put aside your professional modesty, or pride, for the moment, and indulge me. Guess. Where did the item come from?"

I couldn't prevent myself leaning forwards. Even in private, Father had never speculated along these lines. He put down his notes and paced in front of the blackboard.

"Time travel is a meaningless theory, as there is no logical basis for it." He scanned the room, but no one pushed him on the statement. "I could spend the rest of the day explaining why, but you asked me to guess. Likewise, the idea that this came from another planet. More feasible, but still unlikely. We saw no evidence of a craft, and the cylinder has no means of propulsion."

"Might it not be the final component of a rocket-based ship? Like the moon lander?"

Father nodded, dubiously. "It's possible, yes, but there is one huge flaw in that theory. Yes, the cylinder may be constructed from material that could withstand the heat generated when entering Earth's atmosphere, but let me remind you once again that it has no means of propulsion. It would have fallen at a velocity between two and four hundred miles per hour before striking the ground in the middle of one of the most densely populated cities in the world."

The university lecturer in him was fully present now, and he had picked up a piece of chalk, quickly sketching the imaginary trajectory of the cylinder as it headed for London.

"How many reports did the authorities receive that day from witnesses to this event? Thousands? Hundreds?"

No one spoke. We all know a rhetorical question when we hear one.

"None. And when the cylinder was discovered, there was no physical evidence of an impact. No evidence at all. Gentlemen,"—he does that sometimes, forgets I'm there—"I do not believe that the item came from beyond this planet."

He picked up the board rubber and erased his diagram before drawing a horizontal line halfway up the blackboard. He drew an x about three inches below the line.

"No. The only hypothesis that makes sense is that the cylinder was already there. The new building in Marsham

Street is to be a tower block, which means much deeper foundations than the building it is due to replace. The construction company uncovered the cylinder when they reached a depth of just over five metres. Material found at that depth in other parts of the city has been dated around the end of the Roman occupation of Britain."

The original questioner spoke up again almost immediately.

"You're suggesting the item has been in that location since about 400 AD just waiting to be discovered. And it's been dormant during that whole period?"

Father frowned. "I'm suggesting nothing. You asked for a guess. Now you have it."

"It doesn't help us much," said another man. "We're no further forward."

"Hence my reluctance to guess. Can we move on to something vaguely empirical?"

I'm not sure if his audience realised that this was also rhetorical, but if anyone had intended to ask another question, Father gave them no time to do so.

"We do have a theory about Abos's recent development which fits the currently known facts."

"Abos?"

Father grimaced. He had taken to using the name along with everyone else, but he couldn't hide his embarrassment when he explained it.

"Amorphous Blob Of Slime." He waved a hand in the air as if to distance himself from the name, then quickly moved on.

"One of our team developed a nosebleed on the eleventh of June. Some of the blood touched the cylinder and was absorbed by it."

I smiled a little at Father's slight obfuscation. It wouldn't do to admit that a pair of top scientists had resorted to fisticuffs.

"Absorbed how?"

"Good question, and another which we lack the knowledge to answer. However,"—Father raised his hand to deflect an objection—"we can speculate in this instance, based on observation."

He started to pace again. This was a sign of great excitement although anyone who didn't know Father well would never have known it.

"Whatever the composition of the cylinder, we now know it has an organic element. We believe the blood started a process which led to the rapid changes we have recorded in the weeks since then. The cylinder is acting very much as a bird or reptile egg does, providing sustenance to Abos as he grows. In a sense, the blood fertilised the egg, but the process is asexual. The blood contains genetic information, which has been used to create an organism almost identical to a human."

"A clone?"

"No. A clone would be an exact copy of the original. Abos's physiology is based on Doctor Roger Sullivan, but there are noticeable differences between them. The main difference is scale. Doctor Sullivan is Five feet, eleven inches. Abos is seven feet, one inch."

There were a few sharp intakes of breath around the table.

"Doctor Sullivan is in average physical condition for a man in his late thirties. Abos has the physique of a man at least fifteen years younger. He looks like a trained athlete. It seems that the cylinder, in this egg-form, has provided energy to enable Abos to grow a body based on Doctor Sullivan, but without imperfections, and on a larger scale. The body itself stopped growing over a month ago, but if the foetal analogy still holds up, we believe brain development continues."

"This is all very well, Professor Lofthouse, but what's next? What happens when...Abos wakes up?"

"Ah." Father stopped pacing. "We're back in the realm of guesswork."

"What I'm asking, Professor,"—it was the original questioner—"is whether this thing is a threat? What does it want? Is it friend or foe?"

Hopkins stood up.

"Gentlemen." (With Hopkins the sexism is deliberate. He doesn't like me. Then again, I don't think he likes anyone. He just reserves a special store of contempt for females.) "We don't yet know whether the item is an opportunity or a danger. But it is contained within the most secure facility in the country, deep underground, guarded by the most highly trained soldiers in the British army. If the item is hostile, I can shut down this wing within seconds. If necessary, I can shut down the entire facility. And, as you are aware, Station itself can be destroyed if the Prime Minister orders it."

Father looked up sharply at that. Hopkins nodded.

"Security is my concern, Professor, there was no need for you to know. If Station is compromised, our last line of defence is to detonate the charges planted in the office block above our location. The entire complex would be buried under tonnes of rubble."

I coughed. Several heads swivelled my way in surprise as if to see me there. Men.

"And how do we get out, if that happens?"

"We don't, Miss Lofthouse. Thank you both for your time today."

And with that, we were dismissed. Both of us were quiet

for the rest of the day. It's a sobering thought. If Abos is deemed to be a threat to national security, we might all die down in those charmless catacombs by Liverpool Street Underground Station.

August 29th, 1978

Oh. OH. It happened. He's awake.

Take a deep breath, Cress.

I'm still shaking. I can't stop myself.

I've been sitting at that table, day after day, waiting for a change. Watching Abos stretching his impressive physique, his Roger-like face an impassive mask. Although I'm present at a scientific miracle, I've had to remind myself of that fact now and then, because, honestly, I've been bored. I could only admit it in these pages, but it's the truth.

I've taken to bringing paperbacks into work with me. Lurid, cheap, and corny romances, but they are easy to put down and pick up again without losing the thread. We watch Abos in shifts, and when it's my turn, I dig out my book and read. I wish they'd do something about the covers. It's bad enough that I'm enjoying stories about strong, arrogant, dominant men proving impossible to resist. The heroines may seem feisty, intelligent, and strong on the outside, but introduce a muscular builder called Tom, who's rebuilding his life after a spell in prison, and suddenly, it's all furtive glances, breathless exchanges, and heaving bosoms. Not that I'm in any position to criticise - I can't get enough of it, I'm ashamed to say. Emily Pankhurst owes me a big slap.

I sit on the far side of the table, so the guards at the door can't see the book cover. This morning, after checking Abos for any changes, I allowed myself to get immersed in a scene where Clara, the kitchen girl, was rudely asked by her employer to clean his shoes while he was wearing them because he was late for a meeting. She's secretly studying to be a doctor and suspects her boss has early rheumatoid arthritis, but she doesn't know how to broach the subject while kneeling in front of him as he stares down her blouse. Okay, it's trash, I admit it, but there's something about it I like. Don't judge!

I was enjoying this passage and wondering why it was getting warmer in the lab when I was struck with the feeling that someone was watching me. Growing up with a scientist father, I'd asked him about this sensation before, as it seemed to defy logic. He had been dismissive - not unkindly, but firmly.

"You probably imagine you're being watched a dozen times every day, Cress. One time in fifty, you look up sharply, and someone is staring right at you, so you give credence to the theory that, somehow, you felt the weight of their attention without the use of your normal senses. You conveniently forget the forty-nine previous occasions where no such coincidence occurred. You also fail to take into consideration the possibility that your sudden movement, when you raised your head to look up, may have caused someone to glance your way."

Which is all very well, but when the feeling came over me this morning, it was so powerful that I deliberately didn't look up right away. I stopped reading, gently removed my glasses, then slowly raised my eyes to watch the soldiers on either side of the door. Neither of them was looking at me, just talking quietly to each other. As I looked across the table at the far end of the room, I abruptly became aware of the only other possible candidate that might have provoked my intuition. I believe I stopped breathing for a few moments, then allowed my eyes to drop and refocus on the table right in front of me.

Abos's eyes were open. His eyes were as golden as an autumn sunset. And he was looking right at me.

There was a protocol for this moment. We had all discussed it. On the desk behind me was a button which, when pressed, would cause a red light to flash outside the lab door. An alarm would also begin to sound, although the subtle sound that had been chosen for it was designed to attract attention, rather than cause concern or panic in either us or Abos himself.

I didn't press it. I ignored the protocol. I couldn't stop looking into those eyes.

I started breathing again, albeit in shallow gasps, wet my lips and prepared myself to speak. This, after all, was the moment when humanity would first communicate with a being outside of all known species. This could be an alien visitor, a theory which still had some traction among the Station hierarchy, despite Father's scepticism. I had a flash of panic remembering Neil Armstrong's slight fluffing of his own line when stepping onto the moon's surface. I thought of the way I had felt when I heard Doctor King's "I have a dream" speech. I made a huge effort to compose myself. I was determined to make this good. I smiled at his beautiful face and prepared to make history.

"Hi, Abos," I said, "are how you?"

Oh, God.

Abos swung his legs around and raised himself up to a seated position facing me. I was dimly aware of the soldiers reacting, one of them hitting the button by the door. The low-key alarm began to sound.

Abos smiled at me. He smiled. At me. I felt the blood drain from my head, pinpricks of light appearing at the edges of my vision.

Then he spoke.

"Hi, Cress. I'm fine, thanks. How are you?"

He had a wonderful voice, and his accent was British, which I only thought about later. I suppose I had expected him to sound American, like Roger.

As I fainted (I know, I know, how embarrassing and nineteenth century of me), the last thing I saw was his beautiful naked form springing from the table and catching me as I fell sideways from my chair.

11

September 3rd, 1978

Today, I was told I'd be allowed to spend time with Abos again. After my initial reaction and subsequent debrief, Hopkins was against letting me "engage with The Asset," at all. He never referred to Abos as anything other than "the item" before now. I'm not sure I like this new term any better.

According to Hopkins, I am too much of an unknown in this situation. I am no scientist, I am only here to record events as they unfold. It's a good job I've been thorough in my duties. At least Hopkins couldn't claim I was incompetent. Still, for a few days, I thought I would be sacked. Hopkins considered my response to Abos to be a demonstration of civilian female frailty, and he suggested my immediate transfer. Father, McKean, Mike, and Roger argued against this, but, ultimately, they have no power in Station.

I was sent home. I moped. Even the kitchen girl and her arrogant but irresistible employer couldn't hold my attention. All I could think about were those incredible golden eyes.

Don't get the wrong idea, dear diary. Just because Abos looks like a perfected version of a man I once found attractive, and he has beautiful eyes, does not mean that I am experiencing some kind of silly romantic delusion. I do not know precisely what Abos is, but I can be sure of one thing he is not: human. I have watched him change from a large bowl of unappetising mushy peas to a strong, handsome man with the body of a Greek god. But I still remember the mushy peas. I must never forget the mushy peas.

Last night, Father told me the good news. He was pleased but also a little wary. I found out why when he broke with tradition and, after pouring his own J&B, took out another glass and poured one for me. We sat in front of the fire. Today was the first day I've lit it since Easter.

"I'd like you to come back, Cress," he said. "Let's start the educational programme you suggested. Primary school level."

"Don't tell me Hopkins has had a change of heart? I didn't even know he had a heart."

"I don't believe that man is capable of changing his mind. I've never known anyone less flexible. No, Cress, he doesn't want you back."

I stared at him, confused. He took a long swallow of his whisky.

"Abos wants you back. He asked for you."

I took an even longer swallow of whisky. J&B whisky is very close to the colour of his eyes. Oh, dear, I'm still doing it.

"How? When?"

"It started yesterday. We have all tried speaking to Abos, but other than saying hello and exchanging basic pleasantries, he has very little to say. He shows no real curiosity, allows himself to be prodded and poked around, but is strangely passive, makes no demands."

Father told me how they had managed to get a blood sample. At first, needles would snap when they tried to do it, but when Abos showed signs of understanding what they needed, he took the needle himself and slowly pushed it into a vein. It was all for nothing, though, because the blood was type O, and showed no abnormalities.

"He let us run basic physical tests but showed no interest in them. Then, this afternoon, he turned to me and said, 'Where's Cress?'"

All my whisky had gone. Father topped me up.

"He stopped cooperating on the remaining tests, but he continued to ask where you were. I asked if he would like you to come in tomorrow, and he said yes. Hopkins has agreed, although all teaching materials will have to be cleared by his staff before use."

I grinned. The smile I was trying for was meant to look calm, professional, and controlled. It was supposed to reassure Father that I would be fine. I really don't think the grin helped at all.

He stood up and paced a little. He scratched his earlobe every few seconds. This meant he was excited and worried. I could tell there was something he hadn't yet told me, and he was looking for the right words. It was very unusual for Father to struggle this way. The last clear memory I have of him in a similar fix was when he told me about Mother's illness.

"Just tell me," I said, and he stopped pacing. "I'm twenty-nine years old, Father. I'm not a little girl anymore."

He smiled at that and managed to stop pacing although his hand went to his earlobe again.

"Abos was shown around certain areas of Station today. Hopkins took personal charge of the tour. He showed no curiosity and didn't question anything. When we got back to the lab, I pushed at the door, but it didn't open immediately."

I nodded. The lab door was steel. Solid, heavy and, often, tricky to open without putting your shoulder into the job.

"Abos was right behind me. He gave the door a push. It came off its hinges, buckled slightly where he had pushed it, and ended up halfway across the lab. The two soldiers on duty lifted their weapons, but Hopkins shouted at them to stand down. Abos just walked in as if nothing untoward had happened."

My grin seemed even less appropriate now.

"Cressida, we know virtually nothing about this creature. You're my only daughter. You're all I have left of Mary. No one can force you to do this. I'm not at all convinced that you should. But you're right, you're not a little girl. It's your decision."

I remembered the smile on his face when he looked at me. Father was right, we don't know what Abos is. But I can't believe he would hurt me.

"I'll do it," I said.

12

Daniel

TILKLEY PARK LOOKED different at night. The security lights were triggered by a motion detector, but, since only three small lights still worked, the intended effect was lost. Once inside my favourite office building, the lights clicked off again. I waited for almost an hour before concluding no one was coming to check.

I looked out of the window. It was a dark night, but even the shadows seemed to have deeper, more suspicious, shadows. I could have sworn I saw figures moving on at least five separate occasions, and I held my breath, staring into the blackness without blinking.

For someone who, it seemed likely, couldn't be harmed, I was bloody scared.

At about two in the morning, I curled up on the floor in a foetal position and cried like a giant baby. Eventually, exhausted and unable to think straight, I fell asleep.

BY THE TIME I was old enough to understand it, the joke that went, "Just because I'm paranoid doesn't mean they're not out to get me," was already so clichéd, it was practically meaningless. It popped into my mind a couple of hours later when I opened my eyes, my head resting on a solid cement bag.

I had heard a noise. Nothing loud, nothing obvious. Something so subtle, it might have gone unnoticed. But it had woken me. I knew every sound in Tilkley Park by then. The scurrying of rats, the creak of door frames expanding and contracting, the almost musical note of the wind finding gaps in boarded-up windows.

This sound was new. I waited to hear it again, keeping perfectly still, my breathing as calm as I could make it.

Finally, as I was beginning to suspect I had been dreaming, it came again. It was the sound of footsteps, but there was something unusual about it, something that made me doubt I'd heard it at all.

It was as if dozens of people moved at once, in a kind of light-footed run lasting about four or five seconds. Then it stopped for half a minute before being repeated. It was getting closer.

I got up slowly, first rolling away from the cement bag, then rising to my feet. My knees cracked and I froze for a second. I stretched my arms and legs, feeling like I'd aged twenty years while sleeping on the hard floor. My bladder was killing me. I tried to think about something else. I thought about the footsteps and imagined a platoon of highly trained armed soldiers convening on my position, surrounding me. That didn't help my bladder at all.

I moved as slowly as I could towards a window with a

knothole in its wooden board, all the while berating myself for imagining something as ridiculous as a platoon of soldiers surrounding me.

I looked out of the knothole, blinking against the sudden daylight. There was no sign of anything different at first, then the noise came again, and I saw them. A platoon of highly trained armed soldiers was convening on my position, surrounding me.

"Oh, bollocks," I whispered.

I looked around. There was a door at the front. A second door behind me, padlocked like the first, led to a small courtyard. There were windows on either side. I crept to one of them and found a gap to peer through.

I saw no soldiers at first. Then a weak burst of early morning sun broke through the clouds, and something flashed on the roof of the building opposite. I looked up and saw the top of a green helmet, visible over the barrel and sights of a long, lethal-looking rifle.

I backed away. The mind of an experienced fighter automatically clicks into a rarified state of high alert in a crisis. It processes strategies, assesses three or four escape options, chooses one that might work, then takes action.

My mind, on the other hand, doesn't work that way at all. I've improved since, but I still remember precisely how I reacted at that moment. Two distinct mental events occurred simultaneously. The first was me wondering why the manufacturers of rifles hadn't yet come up with a way to stop sunlight glinting off the scope, giving away the sniper's position. I'd seen it happen in a few films over the years, and here it was in real life. It was a basic design flaw. Embarrassing.

The second mental event was the onset of an ear worm. *Don't Worry, Be Happy*, by Bobby McFerrin started playing in my head. Before I could stop myself, I was whistling along. And I couldn't stop.

All in all, my response to a life-threatening situation was less than optimal.

I had no idea who these people were, *don't worry*, but, given the otherwise shoddy security arrangements at Tilkley Park, I was sure they weren't the twenty-four-hour security firm mentioned on the rusting signs, *be happy*.

When I'm anxious, I eat. To be fair, when I'm unhappy, tense, excited, nervous, happy, tired or bored, I eat. I had left a bunch of bananas to ripen in the office as I had read that they were an excellent source of slow-releasing carbohydrates. I started un-peeling and eating them as I paced, opening a couple of packets of malt loaf and adding them to my unconventional breakfast. I might need all the energy I could get.

The truth of what was happening, obvious as it was in hindsight, hit me as I chewed. If Mum had kept demanding The Deterrent admit he was my father, perhaps the government or the army would have kept tabs on her. Maybe even gone as far as tapping her phone. In which case, they would have known about the reporter coming to interview her. They would have heard whatever she'd told him that made him so keen. They might have been watching the house ever since. In which case, I'd led them to a secluded spot miles from any witnesses. And I'd gone to sleep there, giving them plenty of time to call in as many soldiers as they thought it might take to capture someone with enhanced physical abilities.

No one could know what I was capable of. I didn't even know that myself yet. But they would be crazy not to err on the side of caution. They now suspected Mum's claim was true, which meant they were dealing with the son of a bona fide superhero. For all they knew, I might be able to fly.

I heard the distant sound of rotor blades.

They obviously wanted me pretty badly. Whoever they were. I knew what happened when government departments got hold of people with strange powers. I'd read the comics and books. I'd seen the films. They experimented on them. And, given that whoever was out there had turned up en masse, heavily armed and with helicopters, I had no reason to believe their intentions were benign.

I came up with a plan. It was a completely crap plan. I looked at the boarded-up window I used as my entrance. Two nails held it in place. If I hit it at speed, the board would give easily, and I'd be outside. I'd have the element of surprise. I picked up two cement bags. I could lob them at the first soldiers to show themselves. Then I could sprint for the fence, jump it and run like hell.

Like I said, it was a crap plan. It also relied on the fact that I hoped they wanted to take me alive. A superpowered corpse wouldn't be much good to them.

There was the possibility that I was wrong, and they were willing to shoot me. Skewers, electric carving knives and drills were one thing, but bullets were another. I didn't know if my skin could repel bullets, and—since the only way of finding out was to have someone shoot me—I was in no hurry to put it to the test.

I stuffed the last banana in my mouth and paced back from the window until my back was against the wall. I started whistling the Bobby McFerrin tune again, which sounded even worse around the banana. I gave myself a countdown.

"Three."

I braced one leg on the wall behind me.

"Two."

I stopped whistling and tensed my body.

"One."

I stared at the spot on the board I was aiming to smash through. My heart was beating so hard I could feel it in my teeth.

There was a knock on the door. A brisk tap tap tap. Businesslike, no nonsense. I stayed where I was, my eyes flicking to the door, then back to the window.

"Good morning, Daniel."

The voice was upper-class, clipped. Military sounding. I imagined a moustache.

"My name is Colonel Hopkins. I was your father's commanding officer. May I come in?"

13

Cressida

September 4th, 1978

What an afternoon. I'm still struggling to take it in.

I attended the meeting of the scientific team, convened to discuss and compare their reports from the past few days. Father wasn't at the meeting. One member of the team stays close to Abos at all times.

They are finding out more and more about Abos's capabilities day by day. The evidence suggests these abilities are still developing as was demonstrated by video footage Mike showed at the beginning of the meeting.

The footage was filmed in the lab. Abos was sitting in front of the metal table. That was my first shock - he was wearing clothes. Not just any clothes, but a British army uniform. I asked about it, but Roger cut me off.

"It's tailor-made. Hopkins gave us no choice about his outfit, and Abos showed no particular interest. Now watch."

On the projector screen, Abos was picking up objects as they were placed on the table. A two by four plank of wood was first. I heard McKean's voice off camera.

"This is pine, Abos. Can you try to break it? We'd like to test your strength today."

So they'd decided to keep calling him Abos. I suppose the habit was too hard to break. I wonder what we'll say if Abos ever asks what his name means?

He picked up the plank, studied it, then snapped it between his hands, seemingly with no effort.

The next item was also a plank, thicker this time, made of oak. It gave Abos no more trouble than the pine.

A selection of progressively stronger materials was brought in by the soldiers on duty and, one at a time, placed on the table before Abos bent, or snapped, them. Plastics, composites, glass, metal, alloys, steel. He showed no signs of physical strain.

The final item was so small, I had trouble making it out. As I fumbled for my glasses, the camera zoomed in to show a diamond on a black mat. Abos picked it up between finger and thumb, looked at it with little curiosity, then squeezed. I saw his thumb and finger meet. A trickle of fine dust fell back to the table as he rubbed what remained of the diamond from his skin.

"Oh my goodness," I said, looking at Roger. I couldn't help comparing the original Roger with the man on screen who had, somehow, become a close copy. Roger did not fare well in the comparison.

I fancy he had an inkling about what I was thinking because he scowled and pointed at the screen.

"Pay attention. This is what we wanted you to see. We filmed this two days ago. It was the first time he did it."

"Did what?" I said as I turned back to the screen. One

soldier was bending over the table to remove the diamond dust. As he brushed the dust into his hand, Abos made a small gesture towards him. There was a loud crack. The soldier yelped in surprise and jumped back from the table. Instinctively, he went to lift his weapon. It fell apart in his hands.

I stared at the screen in disbelief. Without turning, I said. "Can you wind that—"

Roger was already doing it. I watched the same few moments over and over again until there could be no doubt about what had happened. When the soldier stepped forwards, his gun looked normal. The loud crack occurred at the precise moment Abos made his gesture, which—once I had watched it a few times—looked like he had taken hold of an invisible key and was turning it in a lock. When the soldier grabbed his weapon, it fell away into its individual parts. I started to ask a question, but Roger again anticipated my thoughts.

"They took it away and screwed it all together again. It worked. It's as if it were stripped back to its pre-assembly state. But he's done it three times since when someone with a weapon has been close to him. Hopkins has ordered his men to maintain a distance of at least six feet from Abos at all times."

I gaped at him, considering the implications.

"So Abos can...influence matter without touching it?"

In answer, Mike loaded another film and let it play.

"We filmed this yesterday."

I recognised the dining hall. It's called the mess hall, but as I have joined none of my country's armed forces, I refuse to adopt all of their silly jargon. Father was there this time, as was Roger and Hopkins. There were two soldiers at the door, four more in the room, all armed. It didn't seem to worry Abos, who, as usual, appeared oblivious to his surroundings. There's a placid, passive quality about him which intrigues me. Physically, he is, literally, head and shoulders above anyone else, and he has a powerful impact on anyone who sees him. But he doesn't seem to notice this. Or much else, for that matter.

"This was his first meal outside of the lab," said Roger. "We wanted to know how he would react to a change of scene."

On the screen, Abos, Father, Roger, and Hopkins had taken a seat at one of the tables and were eating. It looked like Irish stew. It had been filmed yesterday - Saturday. Definitely Irish stew, then. Poor Abos. Station's culinary offerings were poor at the best of times, but their attempt at Irish stew was an insult to the palate. Again, it didn't appear to affect Abos, who ate it without enthusiasm or disgust.

Another thought crossed my mind and wouldn't go away.

"Um," I began, "does Abos ever, er, what I mean to say is, does he need to, ah, well,"

"Take a crap?" Americans do have a way of cutting to the heart of things, don't they, although Roger can be a little crude.

"Well, yes. Does he?"

"He does. Once a day. He sleeps from two till six, then uses the john. Takes a pee that lasts the best part of a minute, then follows it with a crap. We showed him how to use the bathroom after the first time when he did it in his clothes."

"Oh." I'm rather glad I wasn't around to see that. Might have tarnished the Adonis-like image somewhat.

"We've tested his stools and his urine. All normal. Like

his blood. Which is impossible, of course, as we know he's not human. Oh, here we go. Watch this."

On screen, Hopkins was saying something to Abos, who was looking at him with that same inscrutable expression. For an inappropriate moment, he reminded me of Lucky, the Labrador I'd had as a child. Sometimes I'd look at Lucky, and he'd look back at me, and—as much as I adored him—I could feel a gulf between us, an untraversable distance hinted at by the expression in those eyes. I was a girl, and he was a dog. Now I was a woman. What was Abos?

Hopkins was waving a hand towards the adjoining tables. The solid oak tables could seat eight people on the benches each side. Abos turned his head towards the table. Almost immediately, the whole thing rose into the air as if it had been a plastic toy tied to a bunch of helium balloons. About six feet up, it stopped, hovering.

Hopkins glanced at the table before returning his focus to Abos, his expression intense. Abos was taking another mouthful of gristly stew. I couldn't hear what Hopkins was saying as the film had no sound, but as Abos stuck a fork into a dumpling (which, if you'd ever tried Station's dumplings, you'd accept as another demonstration of his inhuman strength), every other table apart from their own flew upwards to the same level as the first.

The soldiers positioned around the room reacted by moving forwards, taking their rifles from their shoulders and holding them in a ready position.

Abos looked up from his stew. He stood up. Hopkins said something to the soldiers, and they lowered their weapons. I saw Father and Roger watching Abos intently as he approached the nearest soldier, who was doing his best not to be terrified. Abos held his hand out as if to take the gun.

The soldier took half a step backwards, then—at a command from Hopkins—handed the rifle to Abos.

The next few moments were fascinating but must have been incredibly tense. Abos studied the weapon in his hands, turning it first this way, then that. He examined the trigger mechanism before doing something I couldn't see as he had turned away from the camera.

"He checked the chamber." Roger's voice had a slight tremor. I felt a flicker of trepidation. What was I about to watch?

Abos turned back and was holding the gun by the barrel, looking into it. There was a sick look on the young soldier's face. No doubt it had been drummed into him by years of training that it was a bad idea to stare down the barrel of a loaded weapon. Then Abos placed his other hand on the trigger.

The horror of that moment was so palpable that I felt like I was in the dining hall with them. A huge figure, the rifle looking small in his hands, surrounded by shocked and helpless men as nineteen solid oak tables floated above them.

When the small puff of smoke emerged from the barrel, and Abos's head jerked back, I clapped a hand over my mouth to stop myself from screaming. Then every table fell out of the sky, hitting the floor at the same moment. One of them hit a soldier, and I saw him spin away as the camera fell, knocked by the impact.

I realised I had looked away from the screen. I forced myself to look back. There was little to see as the camera had ended up on its side. Broken tables, feet rushing backwards and forwards. One pair of feet moved more slowly, with no indication of panic. No shoes. I realised it could only be Abos, as his feet were probably too big to fit into the largest army boot. (I found out later that they are having some made for him.)

I looked away from the screen. Roger was shaking his head slowly.

"I've watched it a dozen times, but I can still hardly believe it, although I was there."

"Is he okay?" My voice was probably a little shrill, but I had just seen Abos shoot himself in the throat, and, despite the film of his feet, I could only assume he was horribly injured. "How badly was he hurt?"

Roger shrugged in an unconvincing display of nonchalance. "Oh, he's fine. Keep watching, you will want to see the last part. By the way, the soldier who was hit by the table? Broke his arm in two places, but he'll be okay. Just in case you were worried at all."

I barely heard him. On screen, the camera moved again as someone picked it up and steadied the tripod. I was looking at Roger's face, sweaty and scared. He stared into the lens for a second, then held his hand up. On his palm, there was a small metal disc, about the size of a halfpenny.

The film stopped, and Roger flicked on the lights.

"Well?"

"Well what?" I said. "Am I supposed to know what that means? Just tell me if he's okay. What was that in your hand? A coin?"

He laughed. He actually sounded a little scared.

"That was the bullet. It hit him in the neck at point-blank range, and that was the result. Abos doesn't even have a bruise."

14

Daniel

COLONEL HOPKINS HAD A MOUSTACHE, just as I'd suspected.

I waited while one of his men used bolt cutters to on the padlock on the door, then Hopkins walked calmly in, his cap under his arm, a briefcase in his hand. He indicated an empty holster at his side.

"I'm unarmed, Mr Harbin. I am not here to hurt you." He looked up at me, at the cement bags in my hands. "Not that I imagine I could."

He waited and, after a few seconds, I dropped the bags. There was a loud bang as they hit the floor, and Hopkins barked an order over his shoulder.

"Stand down."

I hadn't heard anyone move outside, but, in my mind's eye, I saw dozens of guns trained on the doorway, soldiers ready to rush me if Hopkins gave the word.

He walked across the room and sat on the stairs. I sat on the pile of cement bags.

"I won't lie to you, Daniel." I suspected he was about to do just that, but he was more subtle. He gave me an edited version of the truth. It would be decades before I found out all of Station's dirty secrets.

"Your father was not quite as pure as his press office wanted the country to believe, I'm afraid. We became aware, well after the events in question, of some of his, er, extracurricular visits to women. We did not appreciate the scale of the problem until news of the first pregnancy appeared in a national newspaper."

He nodded at me. "Your mother's pregnancy, Daniel. As far as we know, she was the first. I admit we were gravely disappointed when she shared her news with the press, but you must remember that we thought, at the time, that she was lying."

"You had your chance to do the right thing," I said. "She called, she wrote, I've seen the letters. You did nothing."

Hopkins was impassive. "Daniel, we received dozens of letters every day for years suggesting all sorts of nonsense about The Deterrent. Your mother's claim seemed no different. When we discovered that The Deterrent had, indeed, been promiscuous, we began to monitor all the women who had contacted us."

"You spied on them?"

"Not all of them. Even if we had wanted to, we do not have unlimited resources. In the interests of national security, we tapped your mother's telephone, and we checked on you regularly after your birth. Once a month, at first, then annually. When you started school, we stopped visiting, as you had shown no hint of the abilities you now possess."

I said nothing. I thought there was an element of

bluffing going on. How could this man know anything about my powers? Mum didn't know about my abilities, just that I'd grown over half a foot over the summer and become a lump of solid muscle. No one had seen what I was doing at Tilkley Park. I was pretty sure of that.

When he saw I wasn't going to comment, he continued.

"The intelligence we received suggested that your abilities became apparent during adolescence. I understand you experienced puberty recently, Daniel?"

I went red.

"Since making that link, we have traced other women in our files. We can only find those who previously contacted us. There may be many others who told no one that they were visited by The Deterrent. Daniel?"

I looked at him. He held my gaze.

"Of the twelve children we've found, nine of them have gone through puberty. They all died. In the cases where we were able to perform post-mortems, the bodies displayed dangerous internal changes, rapid-growing tumours that shut down vital organs."

I didn't think he was bluffing now. Somehow, I knew he was telling the truth. I don't mean that in a kind of woolly, new-agey *I just, like, you know, got a feeling* kind of way. I thought it might be another ability linked to my physical changes. My mind felt sharper, somehow, more engaged with reality, and I found I could tell a great deal about people from their facial expressions, their posture. I had seen an interview on the news a couple of nights ago and had known that the politician being questioned was lying.

Hopkins was telling the truth. Or, at least, he believed he was, which isn't always the same thing.

If he was right, I wasn't an only child anymore. There were half-brothers and half-sisters out there somewhere. Or, at least, there had been. They had hit puberty, and it had killed them.

"Daniel, we don't believe you're in any immediate danger, although I'd like you to check in with our medical staff as soon as possible. And I want you to know that the soldiers outside are only here as a precaution. I'm here to make you an offer. A chance to find out who you really are, and to serve your country, if that's what you choose."

He kept talking, but I was tuning him out and thinking fast. The last thing he had said had been a lie. There would be no choice. I knew he intended to bring me in, and he was telling the truth about serving my country, although I didn't much like the sound of that. I never wanted to be a soldier. I had a feeling I wouldn't be very good at taking orders. Especially from a mustachioed prat like Hopkins. No, when he talked about serving my country, everything in his voice, face, and body told me I would do so with, or without, my consent. I didn't know how he could be so confident they could force me to do anything. I didn't intend hanging around long enough to find out.

The rotor blades were louder. If I was going to do something, it would have to be soon. If I left it any longer, I'd be up against whatever the helicopters were bringing, and the soldiers I'd already seen. And if they managed to take me in, they'd lock me somewhere so secure I'd never get out. Then they'd have all the time in the world to experiment on me, which was surely what they intended to do. And who would ever find out? I mean, after the way I left, Mum wouldn't be expecting a call or a postcard.

"What do you say?"

Hopkins had reached the end of his pitch.

"Come outside, Daniel. We have transport on the way.

Ever been in a helicopter? I can answer any questions you might have while we're in the air."

He motioned towards the door. He was used to being obeyed. Everything about him radiated the arrogant assurance of a man well versed in wielding power. Often, when someone exhibits that much confidence, it becomes difficult to resist. Hopkins showed no doubt. He *knew* I would walk through that door with him.

I made up my mind, grabbed him by the throat and squeezed as gently as I could, making sure I closed his windpipe but didn't snap his neck. His eyes bulged in outraged disbelief, he went an interesting colour, then sagged in my hand. I lowered him to the floor.

I hoped that my plan's simplicity might compensate for what it lacked in other areas. I reviewed it.

The plan: run like hell.

Yep. Good to go.

Ignoring the door and the window, I ran headlong at the wall, putting my shoulder to it and crashing through in a cloud of brick dust and debris.

Then I ran like hell.

MY PLAN RELIED HEAVILY on the element of surprise. The doors and windows were being watched, but I doubted the soldiers were keeping their eyes on the walls.

I had failed to factor in the reaction times and expertise of trained soldiers. My unusual choice of exit gained me about a three-tenths of a second head start.

I sprinted for the fence. It was about a fifty-yard dash, which I could make in six seconds in optimal conditions. The conditions weren't optimal.

The first tranquilliser dart hit my shoulder after I'd covered just a few yards. Then a second hit my right buttock. They both bounced off. So far, so good, although I stumbled a little. On my right, I saw two men set off at speed, carrying something between them, aiming to intercept me before I reached the fence. I could see they wouldn't get there in time, so I discounted them.

Other figures burst out from concealed positions and braced rifles against their shoulders.

"Hold your fire!"

Hopkin's second-in-command must have been ordered not to shoot me. That was good. Not being shot was good.

I corrected my stumble and picked up my pace. A soldier on my left started swinging something. I ignored him and sighted my launch point about four strides away. There was no way they could anticipate how far and high I could jump, so all I had to do was—

My legs abruptly snapped together, something smacked into my shins hard, and I went face-first into the gravel. I took a couple of seconds to roll over and react, which gave the snipers plenty of time to hit me with more darts. They stung a bit, didn't penetrate my skin, but delayed me enough for the first two soldiers to reach me. They threw something. A weighted net came down on top of me.

I heard the sound of running footsteps. They were going to rush me. I was extremely glad I had eaten the bananas and malt loaf. Breakfast. The most important meal of the day.

I felt the buzz start as I fought back.

When I had been training, I had focussed on one task at a time and used whatever strength I needed to accomplish it. I hadn't forgotten how it had felt waking up in a field after destroying Piss Creature's car. Giving in to the temptation of using all my strength was fun—there was no other word for it— but, in retrospect, it was dangerous. Trying to satisfy an insatiable appetite for destruction by thumping inanimate objects was one thing, but how much control would I be able to maintain against flesh and blood?

The rotors were louder now.

I flexed the muscles in my legs and felt the rope tying them break. They had used a bola to bring me down: multiple weights at each end of a rope which, when thrown, would wrap itself around the target. Illegal in the UK. A covert military outfit using illegal weapons? Shocking.

The net was next. It wasn't normal rope, it was made of some kind of flexible metal, strands of the stuff wound together forming a tight webbing. I tore it like paper, even as the two soldiers reached me and clubbed me in the face with their rifle butts.

Ignoring my assailants, I stood up and faced the fence. Just a few paces more and I'd be clear to jump.

I registered the fact that the rotors were now very loud as two ropes dropped from the air and soldiers swarmed down from the belly of the helicopter like hyperactive spiders. Spiders with guns.

I looked up. The side of the helicopter was open, and I could see a burly man crouching behind an enormous machine gun. He was pointing the painful end at me.

"Daniel!"

I looked over my shoulder. Hopkins was made of stern stuff. He was holding a megaphone and walking towards me.

"Please stop running. We don't want to hurt you."

One of the men with the net saw his chance at that moment and clubbed me from behind with his rifle. I flinched, turned and punched him in his chest. I heard ribs break as he left the ground, flew through the air, hit the fence and bounced back half the distance before coming to rest on his front. He didn't move.

"Back away!" barked Hopkins, and the remaining soldiers retreated, their fingers still on the triggers of their weapons.

"Hold your fire. You have your orders. Daniel, don't move."

It was too late. That last blow to my head was one too many. Even though I could see I was outnumbered and out-gunned, my brain was way beyond making rational decisions.

I ran. Straight towards the helicopter. And jumped.

The face of the guy behind the machine gun was a picture. I didn't know what orders he had been given, but I imagine they didn't cover dealing with a superstrong assailant who could leap twenty feet straight up (using the top of the fence as a springboard) and join him in his aircraft. He took the most sensible course of action possible under the circumstances. He looked at me as I hauled myself in, and jumped, grabbing a rope and rapidly lowering himself to the ground.

I tore the machine gun free of its rivets and, grabbing the barrel, smashed it over and over into the metal floor. Bits flew off, a few rounds exploded, then the barrel snapped off. I threw it out.

By then, the pilots had realised something wasn't right. They had to choose between flying off with me on board or landing as quickly as possible.

We hit the ground hard, straddling the fence, and I realised I was back where I started. I was past caring by then, and I ran towards the armed men.

"Fire!" Hopkin's voice. It seemed that the orders had

changed. As I reached the first two men and swung my arm, sweeping them to one side and knocking over three more, I felt sharp pains in my legs a fraction of a second before hearing the rapid fire from my left.

I looked down at my legs. Shredded cloth flapped over my skin, which was red, but unbroken. That answered my question about bullets. They couldn't penetrate my skin. But they bloody hurt. A lot.

I turned and faced my attackers, reaching behind me and grabbing one of the soldiers I had just knocked over. I got a good hold on the front of his combat jacket, then hurled him like a javelin. It was a decent shot, taking three more down.

I felt more pain, in my back this time. What had happened to aiming at my legs, then?

I turned and saw Hopkins pointing a handgun at me. So much for his fine talk about not wanting to hurt me. When he saw he had my attention, he fired straight into my stomach. I howled with rage and went for him.

He sprinted back to the office, darting through the door. I was there three seconds later, just in time to see him jump through the window, screaming, "now!"

The grenade came in through the door behind me.

I didn't even have time to acknowledge my stupidity before it burst apart with a loud crack, filling the enclosed space with smoke.

The smoke smelled like French cheese. And that was the last thing I remembered.

15

Cressida

September 5th, 1978

My first session with Abos took place this morning. As Station's lift has no visible cues to help me gauge how fast it's descending, I still have no idea how far underground we are. There are other levels below us, accessible only by stairs behind doors which require codes to open. I've never asked what's down there. Station is built on secrets, and too much curiosity might, I suspect, be rather a dangerous indulgence.

Abos has been assigned living quarters on the first level, the only level the lift stops at. The same level as the lab, just a two-minute walk along the orange line corridor. To navigate the Station labyrinth, we all follow the thin coloured lines painted at waist height on the drab walls. They seem to use the same colour system as the Underground - or perhaps it's coincidental. Following the red Central line leads you to the office of the Colonel and his staff. The black

Northern line reputedly leads to a weapons testing area. I was very firmly discouraged from following it when I looked for the nearest toilet during my first week. If you are hungry, the purple Bakerloo leads to food, which makes me wonder if the architect or designer had a sense of humour.

So today, I followed the navy blue Piccadilly away from the lab to an area about a three-minute walk away. I had never been inside those rooms before - they had always been locked. Whatever they had contained before had been cleared away, and the space, as one of Hopkins' men put it, "re-purposed". What an ugly expression.

The rooms themselves still smelled of fresh paint. The soldiers tasked with decorating showed no imagination, using the same drab olive green that covers almost every wall in Station. Occasionally, perhaps as an attempt to stop us going mad with the sheer monotony of the colour scheme, a grey wall makes an appearance. A more likely explanation is that they only use grey when they've run out of olive.

Hopkins has allocated three rooms for Abos. One is a small bedroom, another a functional washroom with sink, toilet and shower. The biggest room, which was probably used as a storeroom judging by the shelves, contains a metal desk and two chairs. Light comes from a single, bare bulb overhead. Not a picture on the wall. I rolled my eyes when I walked in. The whole place has all the charm of a police cell.

Abos was waiting for me, sitting at the desk. It wasn't a small chair, but his bulk made him look like a grownup squeezing onto a child's chair at primary school.

He smiled when he saw me.

"Cress."

He didn't stand up, but his face was still nearly level with mine. I looked at his throat, but couldn't see any sign of where the bullet had hit his skin.

"Hello, Abos. It's good to see you again."

He didn't reply. I put out my hand, and he looked at it, blankly.

"This is one way that we greet each other. Hold out your right hand."

Abos mirrored my action and lifted his left hand.

"That's your left hand, Abos."

He dropped his hand and lifted the other.

"Right hand," he said.

"Yes." I put my hand in his, used my left hand to move his fingers into place. Then I gently moved both of our hands up and down the traditional British two and a half times.

"We call this 'shaking hands'."

He nodded. I took the other chair and sat at the end of the desk. There was a small pile of books waiting for me. I had to submit them to Hopkins' office for approval before being allowed to use them, although I questioned how much dangerous sedition might be found in the pages of the Ladybird ABC, or Read and Write with Peter and Jane.

I smiled up at him in what I hoped was a brisk, professional way.

"Before we start, I have a question."

Abos didn't respond at all to this. I'm still struggling with the idiosyncratic ways he interacts with me. Questions and answers are a case in point. In response to a question, he rarely reacts at all. Father mentioned this in the pep talk he gave me before I started this first lesson. Father is unsure about how much, if anything, can be read into Abos's facial expressions, or his choice of words. Because he looks very much like us (I didn't interrupt, but I wanted to add, "yes, just taller, more handsome, bulletproof, able to move objects with his mind and with beautiful eyes like the colour of treacle") and he speaks the English language doesn't mean he <u>is</u> like us. I reassured Father, mentioning mushy peas. He looked confused.

"What is your question?" I haven't described his speaking voice, have I? It's as if an aristocratic European had been taught the English language from a young age, but had never used it. Now, years after mastering it, he is called on to speak English constantly. He does it perfectly, but there are strange pauses, the odd hesitation, sometimes an odd use of a familiar word.

"Why did you ask for me, Abos?"

"For what did I ask for you, Cress?"

I took a few moments to unpick what he meant, then gave up, and rephrased my question.

"You told Professor Lofthouse and Colonel Hopkins that you wanted to see me."

He nodded at this, a very human gesture.

"Yes. To see you, and to hear you. To speak and listen."

"Why?"

Again, it looked as if I would not get an answer at all. Abos looked blankly at me for a few seconds. Then he smiled. That smile has quite an impact. I don't want to keep mentioning it, but, and I'm trying to be scientific about this, it produces a physical response in me every time. I feel foolish even writing that, but there we are. When he finally spoke, I became aware that I was smiling back at him like a smitten teenager. With an effort, I forced my face to adopt a more neutral expression.

I've just had a thought. Babies learn to smile within a few weeks because they mirror their parents. Abos smiled at me almost immediately. Was it because I was smiling at him? He's no baby, obviously. Obviously. But there is something unformed about him that reminds me of a tiny infant.

I digress. Abos smiled at me. Then he said, "I learned more about how to speak from you than I did from your colleagues. You choose different words. Your vocabulary is wider."

I looked down at the ABC book and wondered how useful it would be for a man who could already use the word 'vocabulary' correctly in a sentence.

"Well, thank you, Abos."

"And, I..." He seemed to search for a word for a moment - something I haven't seen him do before now. "I...like you, Cress."

I've always, much to my embarrassment, been someone who readily blushes. It annoys me that my body can so easily betray me. After his admission, combined with that smile, I'm afraid I blushed from the roots of my hair to my fingertips. I fought a short, fierce internal battle to regain that neutrality.

"Thank you, Abos, I like you too. Father said you want to learn how to read."

"Very much. I am learning the two primary methods of communication through daily interactions with Professors Lofthouse, McKean and Sullivan, Mr Ainsleigh, Colonel Hopkins and personnel one to seventeen, but reading requires guidance if I am to master it quickly and precisely."

I took a moment to review the sentence I had just heard. Two things stood out. I tackled the latter first.

"What do you mean by 'personnel one to seventeen?'"

A long pause, then, "I attribute no meaning to them."

"Let me rephrase. To whom are you referring?"

I'll stop mentioning the long silences. Every time I asked a question, everything ground to a halt for at least a minute.

Sometimes longer. When it happened, Abos never appeared to be thinking, he looked at me, or around the room, blinked, scratched his nose. All normal-looking behaviour, apart from the fact that any other person would have answered the question. I soon learned that he would get there in the end if I gave him enough time. As the days went on, the pauses became much shorter, but they never stopped entirely.

"I am referring to the personnel. Hopkins said that personnel would be allocated to guard my quarters, and I have met other personnel in the mess hall. Seventeen discrete personnels so far."

He could use 'discrete' correctly but didn't know the plural of personnel. I was fascinated that he had accepted Hopkins' description of the soldiers and had not ascribed them the same status as individuals as he had with those he had named. I asked about the other thing bothering me.

"You spoke about two different primary methods of communication. What methods do you mean?"

Silence, then, "Unconscious and conscious. Body and speech."

I wondered if the order he'd placed them in was deliberate. I asked him to elaborate.

"Most information comes from body communication. Speech adds detail, clarification."

"But, surely, speech is more important than that. We use it in almost all communication."

"No. Body communication is primary. You are unaware of the extent to which you communicate through your skins. The limbs, the hands, but mainly the face. Most words confirm what has already been communicated by your body."

Father tells me Hopkins is expecting the military's top

psychologist to join the team. He is not going to be short of material.

Abos continued. "Sometimes, body communication and speech contradict. This is very interesting. I cannot learn this behaviour. I do not understand its value."

I wasn't sure I did, either. But this was turning into a rabbit hole I don't have the expertise to explore. I reached for the books and opened the first one, moving my chair to sit alongside him.

"A is for apple," I said, pointing to the letter then the picture.

"A. Apple," he replied, dutifully. I turned the page.

"B is for ball."

"What is ball?"

I was pleased that the book had prompted him to ask a question, but I began to see the challenge of using tradi-tional picture books to teach reading to a creature who had never seen a ball. Or a car. Or a dog. Or an elephant.

We raced through the books in a few hours despite this challenge. Abos is unlike any other student. He only needs to be told something once, so the repetition built into the books we were using was unnecessary. After I'd closed the last book in the pile, Abos made his request. Well, more of a demand, really. The tone wasn't demanding, but his intent was unambiguous.

"I understand reading, but only language, only concepts. Now I must go outside."

He stood up as if we were leaving immediately.

I couldn't quite suppress a smile. I was already imag-ining Hopkins' reaction.

But who was going to say 'no' to a seven-foot bulletproof god?

I meant man. Freudian slip, dear diary, Freudian slip.

16

September 8th, 1978

I didn't get to witness Hopkin's reaction. I was told to stay home Wednesday and Thursday and was only called back in early this morning. And when I say early, I mean to say the driver knocked on our door at 4:45 am.

I was taken directly to the Colonel's office. Hopkins was furious. Furious. If this is what he's like after a couple of days to get used to the news, perhaps it's better that I didn't see him immediately afterwards.

He didn't shout and bluster. That's not his style. Hopkins is the sort of man who never threatens. I've had plenty of time to observe him, and he displays no outward signs of anger. Inexpressive man at the best of times, the only indication that he is enraged is a state of physical immobility even more pronounced than usual.

He didn't ask me to sit. He was standing when I entered, and—judging by the fact that he was ramrod-straight with his arms glued to his sides—I knew he was irate. He didn't even move his head as I entered the room and stood across the desk from him; his eyes swivelled in their sockets like a lizard's.

"You are here at The Asset's request. Against my better judgement, Miss Lofthouse."

No time for 'hello,' then.

"The Asset is under the protection and supervision of Her Majesty's armed forces. Specifically, he falls under my command, as head of Station."

Oh. "Under my command." There was so much I wanted to say, but I'm not that empty-headed.

"As do you, Miss Lofthouse, so rather than waste more of my time, here are your orders for this morning."

I bristled at that word but, strictly speaking, he was right. I have been seconded to the military, and Hopkins is in command. I am supposed to follow orders. His moustache moved as he spoke, every hair trimmed at precisely the same length as its neighbour.

"You will accompany The Asset on his trip outside this facility. The exercise will last one hour. You will be driven to Finsbury Circus, then on to your residence, after which, you will return here for a debrief."

I stood there like a lemon for a moment, then realised what he'd said.

"He's coming to my house?"

"Correct. He wants to see how people live. McKean trained as a medical doctor. He will accompany you. Major Harris will be in command. Dismissed."

He pulled a cardboard file towards him, opened it and started to read. I was so flummoxed by what he'd said, that it was all I could do not to salute. Instead, I turned on my heel and walked out of his office.

A short woman in army uniform was waiting for me outside.

"Ms Lofthouse? I'm Major Harris. Good to meet you. Are you ready?"

She put out her hand, and I shook it, dazed.

"But...you're a woman," I said. Station was so patriarchal that the presence of a female senior officer had, apparently, rendered me temporarily witless.

"No, Ms Lofthouse, I'm a soldier."

She led me to the lift where McKean and Abos were waiting for us.

THE CAR JOURNEY was short but memorable.

I had been watching Harris in the lift, and I have to say, I was impressed by her self-control. She may have already spent a little time with Abos. I've been away for a few days, so I don't know when she arrived. She showed no overt signs of interest in him at all. She's about five foot five, a little shorter than me, and Abos towers over her, but she maintained her composure as if she sees physical specimens like him every day.

Perhaps her insistence on pretending he was nothing out of the ordinary led to the problem with the car.

I'm not interested in cars so I couldn't say what make it was, but it was very big, shiny, dark grey and luxurious. The driver held open the back door for Abos and waited until he was seated before closing it. At that point, it got farcical for a few minutes, and I had to stifle an inappropriate bout of giggling.

Major Harris directed McKean to get into the back first,

then indicated that I was next. But no one had allowed for the fact that Abos was so much bigger than most people. When McKean got in, he found that Abos had only fitted in at all by turning sideways and putting one foot on the seat and the other in the footwell. With a great deal of effort, McKean managed to squeeze himself into the space remaining, but there was no way I could follow. Harris stuck her head through the open door and asked Abos and McKean to move various limbs this way and that in an attempt to make it work. It was when McKean's foot appeared out of the passenger window that I had to turn away to stop myself laughing.

Fortunately, Harris is a practical woman. She'd obviously been given orders about the seating arrangements - the glass in the rear windows was dark and would conceal the car's occupants. When she realised it would not work, she sighed and made a decision.

"Okay, McKean, stay where you are. Ms Lofthouse and I will join you in the back. Mr—"

She stopped abruptly. If she had been briefed by Hopkins, she had probably been about to call him 'Mister Asset'. There was an awkward silence until Abos spoke.

"Abos."

"Mr Abos, please come and sit in the front."

Even then, the front seat had to be pushed so far back that Harris was pinioned in place. The driver started the car, two soldiers lifted the barrier to the car park, and we drove out as the sun began to rise.

Abos spent the first minute or so watching the movements the driver made to control the vehicle. After he had seen enough, he looked away and out of the window. The early morning sun was painting the dirty buildings with that magical light that makes everything it touches temporarily beautiful.

There was barely another car on the streets. No one spoke as we drove. I watched this newborn man greet his first dawn, his perfect face expressionless as he drank in the sight.

In a few minutes, we reached Finsbury Circus. A circular green area on the site of one of London's first parks. I've often sat on the benches there or listened to a concert in the bandstand on a sunny afternoon.

Abos unfolded himself from the car and stood at the edge of the park. When the driver shut the door, there was a sudden explosion of sound as a dozen pigeons, woken by the noise, took flight from the nearest tree. Abos watched as they circled the park before returning to the same branches and settling again. He turned to me.

"Peter and Jane are feeding the pigeons."

I nodded, wondering if it was just luck that he'd picked the right species of bird.

"Yes. Excellent."

He walked into the park, squatting on the grass and running the backs of his hands along it, before looking at the dew on his fingers. Then he stood and went to the nearest tree.

"Squirrel," he said as the curious creature he was walking towards sprang for the trunk and disappeared into the upper branches.

Abos put his hand on the bark, feeling its contours and examining it. I watched him for a moment, then caught something out of the corner of my eye. I turned to see Harris speaking into a radio handset. She had an earpiece, the wire curling down to her collar. She was speaking softly and glancing up at the roof of one of the surrounding buildings.

I moved closer.

"Understood," she said. "Stand ready."

Her body language had changed. She was tense, her eyes flicking across to the far side of the park, then back to Abos, who was now peeling the bark away from the trunk and examining the insects he had found there.

I looked at the far entrance to the park. There was a flashing orange light as a bin lorry made its way along the huge Edwardian terrace opposite, the muffled thump of each refuse bag hitting the inside of the lorry carrying clearly across the space. I couldn't see anything amiss. I looked back at Harris, who was listening intently to her earpiece.

"Dammit," she said. Then I heard the sirens. Far off. Difficult to tell which direction they were coming from as the sound bounced off the city's buildings. A few seconds later and it was obvious that they were heading our way.

Harris was speaking into her handset again.

"Understood. Is there any way we can divert—no, just monitor the situation. I will protect The Asset."

She moved then, joining Abos, who was looking up at the rapidly lightening sky, watching clouds scud across the skyline.

"Sir, er, Abos?"

He turned towards her.

"We have a situation. A police pursuit is underway and is likely to pass nearby. There is nothing to be concerned about, please remain calm."

Abos, as always, looked calm. We hadn't really covered high-speed pursuits in Peter and Jane Go Shopping.

The sirens were loud now, and I could hear the screech of tyres on the dawn-wet tarmac. Seconds later, on the far side of the park, headlights appeared, and a large car came round the corner so fast that its rear end swiped a lamppost, smashing the vehicle's indicator. There was something about the eerie dawn calm which made this noisy intrusion even more shocking.

Then I saw him. A binman, halfway across the road, frozen in a moment of indecision, a cigarette dangling from his lips. He dropped the sack he was carrying, but as he looked up towards the oncoming car, it was obvious that he wasn't going to be able to avoid it.

At the last second, the poor man threw his arms in front of his face as if to avoid seeing his own death.

I turned away, and heard the sound of a brief skid, followed by two distinct noises. The first— like a sudden gust of wind—quiet compared to the smash that followed. Then all I could hear was sirens. After a few more seconds, they fell silent, and everything was still.

I realised I had closed my eyes. I opened them to the lazy blue flashes of the police car's lights strobing on the path at my feet. I didn't want to see the inevitable result of the crash, so I looked towards the tree where Harris had been standing with Abos.

Harris was there, looking stunned, all composure lost, her eyes fixed on the scene of the accident.

Abos had gone.

I turned my head and followed Harris's gaze.

The source of the second, louder crash was immediately apparent. The car fleeing the police had driven straight into the back of the bin lorry. The skid I had heard may have slowed their speed a little, but not enough to prevent the front half of the car folding up, the bonnet crumpling like cardboard. One wheel had, somehow, been dislodged, and was bouncing down the road like a child's toy.

I was squinting at the occupants of the car, checking that they were moving (they were) when I saw him. Abos was standing on the far side of the square, holding the arm of the bin man I had seen a split second before the car hit him. The car that, even given the rudimentary knowledge I possess about the laws of physics, must have hit him. The car that was now bent around a lorry, its engine smoking as the first drops of a rain shower began to fall.

Abos had covered the distance, which was at least fifty yards, in the time it took me to turn my head about four inches to the side. I watched numbly as he said something to the man whose life he had just saved, nodded at the police officers who were exiting the two pursuit cars, then turned and walked back towards us.

Without turning her head away from the scene, Harris whispered, "What do you think he is, Ms Lofthouse?"

I thought for a moment before replying, as Abos get closer, his physique dwarfing anyone nearby. Behind him, the man who'd avoided death jabbered something at a police officer, pointing at the man who saved him.

"And do you think he's on our side?"

I turned to look at Harris, but she continued to watch Abos approaching.

"I don't think he'd have the faintest idea what that question means."

Harris's eyes flicked to the left, and she swore under her breath.

"What? What is it?"

In answer she grabbed my arm and headed for the car, waving Abos over as we walked.

"Press," she hissed. I looked back and saw a figure slide off the seat of a scooter, one hand reaching into a jacket pocket and pulling out a notebook.

Uh-oh.

WE WERE HUSTLED AWAY QUICKLY, Harris trying to shield Abos's body with her own so that the reporter wouldn't see him. A good idea in theory, I suppose, but as he's the best part of two feet taller than her, not very effective in practice.

In the car, McKean, who is the least talkative man I've ever known, couldn't shut up. He fired question after question at Abos, none of which seemed to be answered to his satisfaction. Next, he speculated about possible answers to his own questions in a slightly manic monologue which, although annoying, did at least give me time to get my breathing back to normal. Harris's first question had reminded me of that which I still, somehow, keep conveniently forgetting.

"What do you think he is?"

I couldn't answer that.

McKean, meanwhile, seemed to have come up with a theory that, at last, stopped him jabbering away like a four-year-old.

"The most telling piece of evidence is, surely, that the clothes would have been ripped from your body if you had run across the park. At that speed, it's simple physics."

That little piece of speculation distracted me momentarily, I confess, as an image of Abos shedding his clothes as he ran came into my mind. I must get myself a boyfriend. This is getting ridiculous.

"Your skin is different to ours, Abos, but when we checked your blood, it was as human as mine. I wonder...I wonder. Might it be that your skin is also human, that, in fact, other than your size—which is unusual but not unheard of—you are, actually, completely human in your physical makeup? If so, then either the material which made up the cylinder still surrounds your body in some way, like an invisible outer layer of skin, or..."

His voice trailed off, and he stared up at the roof of the car, his mouth opening and shutting soundlessly.

Harris looked like she was about to speak. I put a warning hand on her arm and shook my head. I'd seen McKean like this before. He was thinking, not having a seizure, but if you'd never seen him deep in thought, you could be forgiven if you assumed the latter. Eventually, his mouth stopped moving. He smiled.

"No. No, that might not be right. Another possibility is brain function. We know you're using more of your brain than the rest of us."

During the few days I had been away, Abos had been submitted to a battery of medical tests. Father told me that one of these involved a revolutionary new piece of equipment that can photograph the brain. The scan of Abos showed activity in parts of the brain which are almost dormant in humans. Although, as Father reminded me, our understanding of human brain function is still at a primitive level. He believes this is an area of scientific research which will undergo a revolution in the next hundred years. Meanwhile, Abos may be accessing parts of the brain that the rest of us can't. McKean was warming to this idea in the car.

"If it's brain function that enables you to do what you do —control your body and, to an extent, your surroundings— then you may represent the future of our species, Abos. You could be a few more steps along the evolutionary path."

He carried on speaking like this until the car came to a stop. He was only thinking out loud, but it was as if the possibilities had so excited him that he had to vocalise his thoughts or risk forgetting them. When the driver turned off the engine, he lapsed into his more customary silence, much to our relief. I've tried to convey some of what he said here, but he used terminology which was beyond me and, at times, babbled so quickly that I couldn't keep up.

I looked out of the window. We were outside my house.

Father appeared at the door. He walked down the steps and waited. When Abos got out, he smiled and shook his hand. Abos responded naturally. He was a fast learner.

"Welcome to our home, Abos."

Harris and McKean waited in the kitchen while Father and I gave him the tour. I said little. It was an odd experience, following them around my house, hearing it described room by room, Abos ducking as even the high Victorian lintels were too low for him.

Father sounded like an estate agent showing a house to a ten-year-old foreign dignitary.

"And this is the larder. In here, we keep various food-stuffs and, I believe, some cleaning equipment, is that right, Cress? Yes, yes. Good. Ah. Some food is tinned, which seals the food in an airless environment, keeping it fresh until required. We also have dry food in here, and staples such as sugar and flour. Flour can be used for the baking of bread and, er, suchlike."

Suchlike. I believe this may have been the first time Father had seen the inside of the larder.

Abos seemed particularly interested in the stairs, stopping at the bottom and looking at them, following their progress upwards. I realised he had only seen one floor of Station. This was the first staircase he had ever seen. After a few moments hesitation, he followed Father up, and I trailed along behind.

Father started this part of the tour in the bathroom, so I took a moment to check my bedroom. I don't know what made me do it, really, and I know I will find it hard to explain what happened next. I looked in and saw my dressing table, the jar of cream, the brush and makeup, a couple of scarves hanging on the back of the chair. The bed was made, my nightgown on the pillow. The nightgown suddenly seemed absurdly unfashionable and frumpy. In the middle of the bed was Mr Tedkins, a stalwart of my childhood and still much loved. I felt a warm flush on my neck. My room looked like the room of a spinster, an old maid, not a woman just shy of thirty.

I backed out and shut the door behind me. When Father and Abos emerged from the bathroom and looked as if they might head my way, I gave a brief but firm shake of my head to Father. He looked a little confused but steered Abos away to his own bedroom. I stayed on the landing, picking up snatches of their conversation. Abos must have asked a question.

"Well, yes, indeed, it is wider than yours. This is called a double bed. You're quite right, it is designed for two people. I was married for many years and—"

"Peter and Jane's mother and father are married. They love each other and have children. What is love?"

Although I listened carefully, as it's not just Abos who would like the answer to that one, Father did little more than stammer and cough, mention the human drive to reproduce and something about societal norms, then attempt to move on to a different subject. As much as I adore him, Father seems as emotionally stunted as the rest of his generation much of the time. Not that I'm one to talk.

"Where is your Mrs Lofthouse?"

"She died, Abos. Many years ago."

"What is died?"

Sometimes it's easy to forget that Abos only knows what he has been told, what he has read, or what he has worked out for himself. The books I had left with him were all aimed at children under ten. None of them covered death.

I heard Father begin to pace, then stop. I walked quietly to the doorway and saw Father standing at the window, looking out. Abos was behind him, reading the titles of the scientific journals on the bookshelf.

"Death is the inevitable end to life," began Father without turning. "Taking humans as an example, we live approximately seventy to eighty years. Our bodies grow in childhood, then, very gradually, begin to decline. From our late thirties onward, there may be thinning of the hair, some wrinkling or flaccidity of the skin, and decreasing muscular strength. In most animals, once the ability to reproduce has gone, death follows shortly afterwards. Humans are unusual in this regard although much of our increased longevity can be attributed to our advances in medicine and increased knowledge about the benefits of balanced nutrition and regular exercise. However, although the average lifespan of humans continues to rise, it is still limited. Death is inevitable. The body shuts down, the respiratory systems fail, the heart no longer beats. Our brains cease functioning. The body, once death has occurred, is no longer able to sustain its form and will begin to rot. We bury our dead."

After a pause which must have lasted a few minutes, Abos spoke.

"The body dies, yes. What happens to the person? The person is not the body, perhaps?"

Father turned. His eyes were bright with tears. He didn't see me. I wondered, not for the first time, about the sadness he hides behind his formality. He's kind, patient, and loving towards me, but I've always felt locked out from the man that Mother must have fallen in love with. And yet, here he was, opening up to someone not even human. Perhaps it's easier to be vulnerable in front of someone who can't understand your pain? I don't know. I stood in the dark hallway, out of sight, watching and listening.

"Perhaps. It's hardly my province, Abos. Science is my speciality. I study facts and only draw conclusions when the facts support them. Thus, I believe that the person is the body, and dies with it. There is no evidence to suggest otherwise."

Abos turned his head and looked at the double bed again, but said nothing.

The last bit of drama occurred as we were leaving. We were about to get into the car when we realised Abos was missing. One moment he was walking down the steps towards the car, the next he was gone. He had moved so fast in Finsbury Circus that he had seemed to vanish. If he had pulled the same trick, he could be anywhere.

Harris looked sick. He was her responsibility.

Next door's dog saved the day. Not normally one for barking, he erupted in a burst of frenzied yapping. Mrs Cole, our elderly neighbour, let her terrier have the run of the garden during the day, and that's where the noise was coming from.

I ran up the steps and let myself in through the side gate, Harris and the others following. Our garden, like many others in this part of London, isn't large, so when I rounded the corner of the house, it only took me a couple of seconds to see that it was empty. I looked over the fence at Tupper, the terrier. He was jumping up and down with excitement, his eyes fixed on a spot above my head.

I looked up.

The first thing I saw was the soles of a pair of army boots, about six feet above me. They looked brand new.

Abos had finally picked up the promised handmade pair a few days earlier.

He was standing on thin air, looking into my bedroom. He glanced down at me.

"You forgot to show me your bedroom, Cress. It's very nice."

Nice. Another Peter and Jane word. For some reason, it made me angry. In fact, I felt frustrated and upset, although I can't explain why.

"Get down this minute."

Abos obediently floated down and joined me. By that time, the others had arrived, and their expressions as he sank to the ground were full of wonder, awe, disbelief, suspicion, and fear. Harris, if possible, looked even more ill than she had when he'd vanished. She may have been considering the report she would have to deliver to Hopkins.

I, meanwhile, was pointing my finger at Abos as if he was a disobedient child.

"You should not have done that, Abos. It was wrong. You should have asked me."

I spun on my heels and walked off.

I've thought about it all day. I still don't know what I was so upset about.

17

Daniel

OFTEN, you don't get to decide when one chapter of your life comes to an end, or when a new one begins. Sometimes, those decisions are made for you. That's been the case for most of my life. I was an overweight, shy kid. One day, that was over. I became a young man with superpowers, trying to work out my place in the world. After that day at Tilkley Park, that was over too.

I ended up working for the same secret government department that my father had worked for. Willingly. Or so I thought.

My memories from the moment I passed out at Tilkley Park to when I started working for Station are confused, hazy and full of gaps. I know I spent a long period in what I thought was a hospital. After that, I moved to my own windowless room.

I have no memory at all of changing my mind, trusting

Hopkins and agreeing to work for Station, but it happened.

The first clear recollection I have from that time is of walking into the mess hall with Hopkins and sitting with other soldiers. I was dressed like they were. I felt that this was where I belonged.

That sense of belonging lasted for four years. Then, one terrible night in Shoreditch, that was over too. And the chapter that followed was the worst of my life.

I was the only member of the crew with enhanced abilities. That made me an outsider. The other soldiers had lives beyond Station's concrete walls. Husbands or wives, partners, children. Friends. Hobbies. Not me. I wanted their friendship, their approval. They were my unit. And yet I can't remember a single name.

Station was my life. I ate there, worked there, slept there.

Station looked after me, treated me well. And they helped me manage my "condition". Another early memory: they explained why it had been necessary to capture me by showing me photographs of other children of The Deterrent who hadn't been as lucky. I saw ribcages torn apart by rapid, uncontrolled tissue growth. I saw the broken bodies of those who had, one day, suddenly risen into the air, able to fly but unable to stop themselves, until their power was exhausted and they fell to their deaths. I saw one girl whose brain had expanded inside her skull, pushing cartilage out of her nostrils and forcing her eyeballs from their sockets.

There was a morgue one level under my quarters in Station. Hopkins showed me some of the bodies. He talked about scouring the country, searching for The Deterrent's children, only to find disease and death.

There had only been one other exception. A girl they had brought in just as the symptoms of her power started to show. Hopkins opened a folder containing a photograph of a girl in her teens, propped up in a hospital bed, smiling.

"We had hoped to help her survive puberty, maybe learn more about the power she had inherited. Unfortunately, she lapsed into a coma shortly after her first menstrual cycle. We kept her alive for nearly three months, but she never regained consciousness. It was hugely disappointing."

I was still looking at the photograph. So full of life.

"That's terrible," I said, then I registered the word he'd used. It broke through the customary fog of confusion I lived with at that time. "Disappointing? You were disappointed?"

"Devastated." He arranged his features into an approximation of sadness. Then he took the photo and slid it back into its folder.

"What was her name?"

I watched him struggle to remember.

"Kate." I had a feeling he'd just made that up.

The visit to the morgue is one of the memories I was allowed to keep.

There are flashes of memory from that time. Sometimes, when I'm drifting off to sleep, I remember a humming sound, a kind of buzz in my head and a woman's voice, a kind voice, telling me that Station would take care of me, Station was good, Station was right, I would feel good if I worked for Station.

According to George, Station is a world leader in the use of chemically assisted suggestion programmes. Brainwashing, to you and me.

My brain, during my four years working for Station, was thoroughly washed. Washed, rinsed, spun, dried, and washed again. I was one of Pavlov's dogs, salivating whenever they rang my bell, doing whatever they wanted me to do.

After six months, I was put to work. I remember the build-up to a mission, the briefings, the preparation. But as hard as I try, I draw a blank if I try to follow a memory past the point at which Station has blocked it. The few moments I can picture are tantalising or scary. I remember sitting in the back of a lorry with a platoon of soldiers. Once, I was in the belly of a huge plane, in the dark, clipping my parachute's release mechanism to a line as the cold wind roared in my ears.

I remember nothing of the missions themselves. I've trawled the internet since, read speculation about the assassination of certain of our country's enemies, deep in hostile territory, under seemingly impossible conditions. Was it me? Possibly. I've also seen the reports of the disappearance, or deaths, of suspected halfheroes. Me again? I wish I could be sure it wasn't.

George said perhaps memory loss was a blessing in some circumstances.

The only mission I remember in every terrible detail is the last one. When someone reached into my mind and pushed away all the structures Station had so carefully built. When I suddenly saw what I was doing, and what I had become.

18

I t was 4 am. I was in the passenger seat of a police van. Dawn was still hours away and, despite the fact that I was keyed up, my knees bobbing up and down against the dashboard, some 4 am magic still managed to seep through the tension. It's a dark, disquieting hour. It doesn't matter who you are, or where you are. At 4 am, nothing feels entirely real, which is a good thing as this is when the human capacity for regret and remorse is strongest.

Luckily, there wasn't much time for navel-gazing. At two minutes past the hour, the radio on the dash crackled into life, and the visibly intimidated police officer crammed in beside me picked it up.

Police officers speak to each other in code. I never did bother to learn what meant what. He said a couple of things along the lines of a "ten eight-three," and a "DX7," then turned to me. "Time to go."

My handler was sitting in the next van along. Every mission had a handler whose job was to babysit me and, when ready, switch on my power button.

The power button was another Station trademark, along

with brainwashing and moustaches. It contained a mixture of drugs—I know adrenaline was one of them—kept in a tiny canister inside my upper arm, ready to release its contents when triggered remotely. Hopkins told me it would help me to control my strength and aggression. This was a perfect example of Station doublespeak as it actually did the opposite. The moment my handler pushed the power button and my body experienced its effects, my inhibitions went out of the window along with my instinct for self-preservation and personal moral code.

Whatever instructions I'd been given dropped into the front of my mind and nothing else mattered. I knew what I was going to destroy, or who I was going to kill.

I had dreamed of becoming superhuman. Station made me sub-human.

My handler that night was an older man, with cold eyes and an expression that suggested he knew someone had just farted and I was top of his list of suspects. I'd never seen him before. I rarely saw the same handler twice. It was Station policy.

He wound down the window.

"Ready?"

"Yes. Wait until I reach the wall and make sure you give me the full five minutes before you let anyone follow."

He waited.

"Sir," I added.

"You know your route?" He was excited or anxious, I couldn't tell which. I had an intuition that he was pretty high up in Station's pecking order. Which meant tonight's mission was a big deal.

"Yes, sir."

Once I was in, speed would be important. The police vans faced the side of a warehouse. It was a single floor brick building divided into four units. The target wasn't in the first building, she was in the third. My briefing had warned that she and her companions were not only armed, but had explosives they wouldn't hesitate to use.

My briefings were always just that: brief. The official reason was that, as an undercover operative protecting my country, it was in my own interest, as well as my nation's, that I knew the minimum needed to do the job. If I fell into enemy hands, I would have very little to tell them. Of course, the unspoken reason was that they didn't trust me. Not even pumped full of their drugs. I was a son of The Deterrent, the superbeing supposed to usher in a new golden age of prosperity and security for Great Britain. When he'd first donned the cape (figuratively speaking), the word *empire* had even been bandied about in certain wood-panelled private London clubs. And look how that had worked out.

Unusually, I had been given more detail on this occasion. The briefing had painted an appalling picture of the group I was about to encounter. The targets were home-grown jihadists, intent on committing a terrorist atrocity. If successful, they would kill thousands of innocents.

Hopkins himself had attended my briefing, saying nothing until the end. Then he'd put a hand on my arm and looked me in the eye.

"Daniel, these traitors won't look like soldiers. They have to blend in with society unnoticed. They've been lying to their families, friends, neighbours, and co-workers for years while they prepare for this attack. These people will do or say anything in pursuit of their deluded ideals. Do not give them that chance. Hit them fast, hit them hard, and send a message to others of their ilk that their cowardly acts will only get them killed."

He'd turned to go, then changed his mind, facing me once more. I'd found something to look at on the ceiling. I may be able to crush a house brick between my finger and thumb, but something about Hopkins has always given me the willies. His moustache twitched.

"The good, decent folk of Great Britain can sleep easy, safe in their beds while you're around to defend them. I'm proud of you, my boy."

It was the longest speech I'd ever heard him give. He put out his hand and shook mine gravely and with absolute sincerity. If I hadn't spotted him using half a bottle of hand sanitizer thirty seconds later, I might even have been moved by it.

As I walked towards the warehouse, its dark brick exterior lit by a single lamppost, I wondered again why he'd decided to add his personal authority to the briefing.

I was three yards away from the wall. I slowed, watching and listening. The bricks looked to be the usual grimy, soot-stained variety, their layers of dirt probably dating back to the reign of Victoria. The floor was littered with sweet wrappers, dog shit, newspapers, and cheaply printed leaflets for prostitutes. The only sound was the usual London hum of traffic and a fox screaming a few streets away.

I reached the wall and put one hand on it. Then I waited.

Back in the van, my handler pressed the button that triggered the drug's release into my veins.

My pupils shrank to pinpricks before dilating again.

My awareness of my surroundings dimmed for a few seconds, then everything hummed into raw, vibrant life around me. I saw tiny insects crawling across the wall, I felt the bricks themselves vibrating under my fingers as I took three or four quick, deep breaths.

The power started its inexorable build-up to unstoppable violence and temporary madness.

I wonder if my handlers felt like bomber crews in military planes, the ones who pressed the button and released the payloads. Was there an emotional reaction as that grim piece of death-dealing machinery dropped away from the aircraft? What went through their minds as they dispatched a machine whose only purpose was to destroy everything it encountered?

There were four walls between me and the terrorists in the third room.

I took two steps back, turned my shoulder towards the first wall and ran straight into it.

19

I felt the wall crumble as my body followed my shoulder into the warehouse. The first unit was an empty shell. Rats scurried in panic as I thundered through, picking up speed.

Twelve seconds after breaching the outer wall, I hit the next. The interior walls weren't as thick as the exterior, and I barely slowed as I crashed through.

The second unit was half-full of cars. Stolen cars, I later concluded. There were number plates stacked on a low table at the back, and one corner was set aside for respraying vehicles.

There were three rows of cars between me and the targets - the last row parked against the far wall.

A gap had been left between the cars as a walkway. If I had been capable of making logical decisions at that point, I might have swerved onto the walkway and hit the wall there. As it was, my mind was empty of anything other than the desire to run, to punch and kick, to tear apart, to crush, to pulverise.

Mindfulness gurus might do well to consider what was

going on in my brain, as I was a model disciple. When you are washing up, just be washing up. When you are eating your breakfast, just be eating your breakfast. When you are violently maiming and killing people, just be violently maiming and killing people. I don't imagine they'll be featuring me in any commercials.

I jumped as I got close to the first row of cars, then three metal-crunching big paces took me to the wall. It was a freakishly destructive hop, skip, and jump.

After landing on the bonnet of a bright red Mazda, I hopped onto a Ford Focus, then skipped to a Range Rover, in all three cases denting the cars beneath my feet. From the Range Rover, I leaped at the wall.

The element of surprise had been slightly lost by the amount of noise I'd made.

In an explosion of brickwork and plasterboard, I hurtled into the room and landed on the floor, rolling and standing up in a movement Station had made me practise so often it had a kind of balletic grace. Even when I did it.

I scanned the room. It looked like a terrorist cell should look, according to my briefing. Camp beds along the wall, four of them. Rudimentary washing facilities in the near right hand corner. A screened-off area, possibly a shower. A big table in the far right corner with the remains of a meal on it. Two people sitting there, looking up in shock.

To my left, a man rolled off another bed. He was scrabbling around at his feet, reaching for a shotgun. I ran at him before he could lift and aim.

I was almost close enough to swing my first punch when something hit my left shoulder and spun me to one side. I skidded on the concrete floor and looked behind me. Another man had appeared from the screened area. He raised a hand and slapped the air in front of him as if swatting a fly. Ten yards away, I felt a blow to the side of my face that rocked me. I paused for half a second, confused, then roared with fury.

At that stage, I was still in there somewhere, still able to direct my behaviour. I can't—I won't—pretend otherwise.

"Christ, Carrie," said the one who'd slapped the air, "he's strong. How can he be that strong?"

He raised both hands this time and swivelled as if he were an Olympic hopeful swinging an invisible hammer. As his clenched fists came around, I felt a blow on the side of my head that made me take a correcting step to the side.

And that was when the balance shifted past the point of no return. The firework display began inside my head. All I could do was watch the show. I was no longer in control.

I turned to the nearest hostile. He pumped the shotgun and fired into my chest. I was pushed backwards by the impact. I almost fell and screamed with pain. Shotguns hurt.

My other attacker used this distraction to hit me again with...whatever it was he was hitting me with. I think the blow might have done more damage if I hadn't been pushed out of position by the shotgun. It felt like someone had slapped my ear and something skimmed the side of my head.

I grabbed the smoking shotgun by the barrels. It was still hot. I jabbed at him with the stock and heard his skull crack before he fell. If his brain had survived the force of the blow, it wouldn't be good for much from now on.

I heard a woman's voice screaming something over and over. The other figure at the table with her was standing now, keeping his body between the screaming woman and me.

I turned and ran for the second attacker, picking up

anything I could find and throwing it at him as I approached. A mattress, a saucepan, a suitcase, a pile of books, they all flew towards him.

Nothing hit him, despite the speed and accuracy behind my throws. He held his hands in front of his face and seemed to brush them aside before they reached him. Not that it made much difference, because by the time he had deflected the last book, I was on him.

I didn't waste time on niceties. I was here to kill terrorists. Somehow, this man had hurt me. I punched his ribcage through his lungs and heart. His expression as he died was one of shock and frustration.

Now it was two against one. Not good odds for them. I ran towards the table and met the final man halfway.

My fist was raised when my power-fuelled brain decoded what it was the woman was screaming, over and over.

"Daniel! Daniel!"

For a split second, my brain re-engaged and allowed a coherent thought to materialise. How? How did she know my name?

My hesitation was tiny, but enough to allow my assailant to throw the first punch, which wouldn't normally bother me.

This punch bothered me.

My head snapped back, and I tasted blood. Enraged, and incredulous, I flung myself onto him.

I can't describe the fight that followed. It's not that I don't want, or can't bring myself to detail the struggle between us, it's just that I was on such a power-high that I had no idea what I was doing. I was a raging, screaming, superstrong killing machine with no way of stopping.

He was about my age, broad, incredibly strong. Just not as strong as me.

After a few minutes filled with the savage, grim sounds of a fight to the death I pulled myself up from the floor, my hands wet with blood.

The final target was still sitting at the table, looking at me. She had stopped screaming during the fight. Her expression was numb, but her voice, when she spoke, was surprisingly calm.

"Daniel, I know it's hard for you to hear me, but I need you to try. Daniel, please."

By then, I was at the stage where language had little meaning. As the power surged, my rational mind retreated, until little capacity for thought remained. The power was everything, my self-awareness virtually gone. The final stage was unconsciousness, my strength burned out like a tissue thrown into a roaring fire. I felt a moment of confusion at the fact that I could understand her words.

As I walked towards her, I could sense my power reaching the end of its surge, the heavy, irresistible weariness pulling at the edges of my awareness. I would have to be quick.

"Daniel, I know what Station is doing to you. This is not who you are."

I stopped. A sudden flash of anger, confusion, fear, and shame shot through me. I looked at her properly. She was short, had long red hair pulled back into a ponytail. Green eyes. She looked tired, scared, and desperately sad.

I took another step towards her.

"I know how you felt when your power first kicked in. I know how scared you were that morning when your bed collapsed. When you looked in the mirror and saw a new face appearing. The day you asked your mum to tell you the truth about your father."

I stopped again and shook my head. How was this possible? How could this crazy jihadist know about me? How was I able to think at all? Every other mission had ended with me unconscious after the power had run its course. This was different. Something in her voice had reached through the fog and found me.

I felt the exhaustion tug at me, more insistent now. There was no time. I stepped forward and put my hand around her neck. I could make it quick, at least.

"You're not the only one, Daniel. Think about it. You're being used." She seemed unafraid as I prepared to squeeze. Once again I hesitated.

"You must fight what they're doing to you. They drug you to keep you compliant. Wait."

My hand was still at her throat, but I didn't tighten my grip. Waves of exhaustion were coming faster now. Soon, I wouldn't be able to stand. She looked as exhausted as I felt. She was finding it difficult to speak, sweat breaking out on her brow, her breath shortening. She put her hands on mine.

"Daniel. Look around you."

I looked back at the carnage I had left in my wake. Followed the direction of her gaze. She was staring at the body of the final terrorist. The strong one. His face was swollen and bloody. I felt cold shock numb my senses. When he had attacked me, I had seen a stranger, bearded and wild-eyed. The face of a crazed terrorist, a fanatic. Now I saw him as he was. Underneath the damage I had inflicted, it wasn't the face of a stranger. He looked so much like me, he could have been my brother.

What had I done?

The woman's voice reached me as if she was speaking from the end of a long tunnel. With a huge effort, I wrenched my attention back to her.

"Your masters at Station are not your friends, Daniel. You are not helping your country. Look around you. What did Station tell you? Who do you think we are? We're—"

She stopped, then took two quick, horrible rasping breaths, before her head fell backwards. That was when I saw the bullet hole in her neck and the hot red blood arcing away from the wound, spattering the table and the pages of the book she had been reading as she slumped sideways, her life ebbing away.

I sank to my knees, the unstoppable debilitation finally claiming me. I fell sideways to the floor and, through a curtain of red rain, watched my handler walk towards the table, his cold eyes focussed somewhere beyond me, his right hand holding a pistol.

20

Cressida

September 9th, 1978

The news broke this morning. No photographs, so much of the piece comes across as conjecture, but still. It's unhelpful. Whatever Abos is, or may become, he's not ready for the intense attention that would ensue if his existence were to become common knowledge. I just wrote 'if', but it's 'when.' A secret this big is too big for even the most secret of the British secret agencies. One day soon, everyone will know him.

And I will have lost him.

The piece, by Justin Needham, may make his name when the rest of the world catches on, as the first documented public sighting of Abos. Although, if Mr Needham is serious about his career as a journalist, he will have to go easier on the wild speculation. It's almost laughable. Almost.

I have the newspaper clipping.

The Daily Herald. Saturday, September 9th, 1978
A REAL SUPERHERO...AND HE'S BRITISH!
By Justin Needham, Crime Reporter.

A DAWN RAID on Hoxton's, one of Old Broad Street's most exclusive jewellers, ended in dramatic fashion yesterday when a mysterious superhuman figure intervened. A police chase had closed in on the two thieves' getaway vehicle in Finsbury Circus when they crashed into a refuse lorry on its morning round.

The two suspects in the robbery, Barry Gregory, forty-two, and Kevin Innes, twenty-eight, were taken to nearby Royal London Hospital, where they were treated for whiplash and minor injuries, before being remanded in custody.

This is the third raid on a London jewellers in the last four months, and a police source confirmed they were 'confident' the pair were behind the earlier crimes.

However, the crash that ended the criminals' spree has an incredible twist, which would be almost impossible to believe if it were not for the presence of witnesses.

Council worker Fred Ward, fifty-one, was standing directly in the path of the getaway car when it drove around the south-west side of Finsbury Circus at speeds approaching sixty-five miles per hour.

"I left it too late to run," Mr Ward told me, minutes after the incident. "I knew my number was up. I closed my eyes and waited for the car to hit me."

What happened next was seen by two independent witnesses.

Before the car hit Mr Ward, a man ran from the park,

lifted him off his feet and brought him across the road to safety. An amazing act of heroism but there's more to this story. No one saw the man anywhere near the road before the crash - in fact, all three witnesses insist he wasn't there. The speed at which he ran was so fast that no one actually saw the moment he saved Mr Ward. And, although there is some confusion about what this mysterious stranger looks like, on one point all accounts agree: he is the tallest, biggest man they've ever seen.

Mrs Sylvia Lewis, sixty-three, watched from her bedroom window as the car approached. She described what happened.

"I can still hardly believe it, to tell you the truth. If it had been night time, I bet you'd have thought I'd been drinking, but at that time in the morning, well, sober as a judge, I was. As a judge. I saw the car hit the bin lorry, and I thought to myself, 'well, that's it, Syl, he's a goner, isn't he? He'll be all squashed and suchlike.' Awful. So I had a good look, but I couldn't see him at all, just the car all smashed up. Then, stone me, but I look down, and he's on the pavement under-neath my window. Chatting to this big bloke, he was, thanking him, like. And I'm telling you, as God is my witness, the big fellow wasn't there when I first looked out of my window. I swear it. I reckon that binman had a guardian angel, and I saw him."

Terry Gannon, thirty-one, is a colleague of Mr Ward's, and had just collected the bin from number thirty, Finsbury Circus. He was on the other side of the lorry when the thieves' car crashed into it.

"I didn't see nothing cause the lorry was in the way, right, not until Fred appeared on the pavement with that massive bloke. I mean, you got to understand, this bloke is huge, right? You ain't ever seen nothing like the size of him. That

Giant Haystacks on the telly would look like a midget against this bloke. About ten-foot high, I'm telling you. Almost as wide, too. Built like a brick, well, you know, like a brick...like a brick. He talked to Fred for a minute, then he walked off. I reckon he's a science experiment by the army or something. He was wearing green, like a soldier, Maybe he's, you know, one of them test tube babies or something. Have to be a bloody big test tube, mind you."

Mr Ward got the closest to his mysterious benefactor, but admitted he was so shaken up that he 'couldn't take it all in.'

"He was big, I remember that. Looked a bit like James Bond, only really, really tall. And he hardly spoke. I know he must have been running like a blinkin' Olympic sprinter to get me out of the way of that car, and he had to pick me up, but he wasn't even out of breath. I kept thanking him and thanking him. Couldn't believe I was alive, could I? I managed to ask him his name, though, just before he went. He didn't answer, just said, 'hey, boss,' and walked off."

The police present at the scene confirm that a passerby, seen by Mr Ward, was being sought as a witness to the crash, and anyone with any information should get in touch with the Metropolitan Police.

If any of our readers happen to see a ten-foot tall soldier who can run faster than a car, please call us. Particularly if you have a photo!

I SUPPOSE it could have been worse. Mr Needham's sign-off suggests he's not really taking the story seriously, but page four coverage means it will be seen by tens of thousands.

Hopkins will have something to say about this.

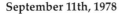

September 11th, 1978

An awful day.

The grapevine has it that Major Harris was summoned to Hopkins' office at eleven am Saturday morning, and was out again at eleven-eighteen, after a bout of shouting that even the supposedly soundproofed doors couldn't quite contain. Apparently, she's been shipped to somewhere miserable. Poor Harris. It was good to have another woman around, however briefly.

The big change is the addition of a new team member. Captain Harold Carstairs is a military psychologist. Father now answers to him.

The first I knew of that development was when Father got home last night, later than usual, looking haggard and old. When I gave him his second J&B, he told me to leave the bottle with him. I was relieved it was only a third full when I saw the size of the measure he poured for himself.

He told me about Captain Carstairs, but only gave me the vaguest of details. I tried to draw him out, but, for the most part, failed. It's clear that Father is wrestling with some dilemma that he will not share with me. I remember all too well the awful few weeks when he had been given Mother's diagnosis and shocking prognosis, but had not yet told me about it. I saw the same haunted look in his eyes last night as I had seen then.

He's hiding something from me. Whatever it is, it's not good.

The only hint was something he let slip as I helped him out of his chair before bed. He was muttering to himself. I guided him to the bottom of the stairs, and as he put out a hand to steady himself on the bannister, I heard him say something incomprehensible that sounded like 'psycho farm.' Then he turned and grabbed my hand.

"I have no choice, Cress, no choice. You have to understand. I can't let someone else take over my role. I can't. I had to agree to go along with it."

Then he stumbled upstairs to sleep it off.

This morning, he was pale and grim. At breakfast, I tried to steer him round to Captain Carstairs, but he cut me off and said he wouldn't discuss it further. Deeply frustrating, but I know him well enough not to force the issue.

I met Carstairs myself today, at lunch. The rest of the team had already made up their minds about him, it seems, as they were sitting at a table on the other side of the dining hall. They all looked subdued, there's no other word for it. Mike is the easiest to read - he seems to have no concept of disguising the way he feels. He looked down at his plate throughout the meal, his shoulders slumped. McKean, Roger, and Father were speaking in low voices, occasionally darting a glance in Carstairs' direction.

When I took my tray over to Carstairs' table, Father stiffened in disapproval, McKean and Roger looked away, and Mike stared, his mouth open.

Carstairs was writing in a small notebook with one hand while spooning pasta into his mouth with the other. He's in his early fifties, I'd guess. Salt and pepper hair cropped short, grey eyes, a long, thin face. He nodded as I approached, and I took that as an invitation to join him.

"You must be Miss Lofthouse."

He didn't have to be an expert in deduction to reach that conclusion as I was the only woman left in Station since Harris's departure.

"Cressida," I said. He closed the notebook and looked at me.

"You've spent more time with Abos than anyone else, I believe? Talking to him, teaching him. How would you describe his mental state?"

Right. This wasn't going to be a get-to-know-you chat, then. Carstairs, as became apparent during our conversation, is all business. He is entirely focussed on Abos. He asked a series of quick questions, paused to clarify a couple of times, then stopped talking once he had what he needed.

I made one or two attempts to make small talk, but he ignored them. Finally, he held up a hand.

"Miss Lofthouse."

"Cressida."

"Miss Lofthouse, I'm here to do a job. I don't need to tell you how important the discovery of Abos is to this country."

"To the whole world."

He ignored that.

"Colonel Hopkins advised me of your role. I must inform you that, as of today, your interaction with Abos will be limited, and conducted only when I am present. We are in unchartered territory, and I cannot risk an amateur hindering healthy mental development. Your reports will be required on a weekly basis from now on. I expect them to be short, and factual."

I bristled at the implication that they had ever been otherwise, but mainly I recoiled in shock at what he had said about Abos. Never to be allowed to see him without Carstairs present?

"What does Abos have to say about that? He's not a science experiment. What gives you the right to—"

Carstairs was giving me the stare again. With some difficulty, I stopped talking and glared at him.

"An outburst like this confirms my reservations about you. The Asset is not your friend. He, or rather it, is an unknown life-form. A life-form with considerable power. It is a dangerous individual, Miss Lofthouse. Giving it a cute name changes nothing. You could try keeping a tiger as a pet and call it Tiddles, but that wouldn't stop it ripping your throat out."

I got up to leave. He had a parting shot for me.

"Consider yourself on probation, Miss Lofthouse. I will review your position in six weeks' time. If you wish to continue with this job, you will do as I say. If I feel you are hindering my work in any way, you will be dismissed."

I would have loved to be able to report that I responded with something pithy, but I'm afraid I simply bit my lip to stop myself crying until I was out of sight.

Father handed me a schedule this afternoon. I will spend an hour with Abos on Friday morning. I will hand in my report on Monday morning. Tuesdays, Wednesdays and Thursdays I have been assigned to Hopkins' secretarial staff. I'm so angry I could break something.

21

Daniel

THE LIGHTS WERE off when I opened my eyes. There was the distant rumble of a train. I was back at Station. The sound of waves lapping up against the shore came from tiny speakers high in the corners of my room.

I ran my fingers along the inside of my arm until I found the plaster. Super-toughened skin was all very well, but as long as they put the needle in slowly, I was just as easy to inject as anyone else.

I felt groggy but rational. For a few seconds, I was just a man lying awake in the middle of the night. Then I remembered. I remembered the woman falling sideways as she bled out, the awful noise she had made. And I remembered what she had told me.

Station had lied. I was being drugged. The people I had been sent to kill weren't jihadists. They were...

What was it she had said?

"Who do you think we are?"

It was a good question. Although my mind was clearer than usual, I struggled to recall every detail. But what I could remember was enough to make me recoil in horror.

They weren't terrorists. Only one of them had been armed and there had been no evidence of bomb-making. They had hurt me, but only in self-defence. One of them was able to attack from a distance without a weapon. Another had been almost as strong as me.

I reached out and clicked on my bedside light, but nothing happened. There was a switch on the wall for the overhead light. It wasn't working either. As I had never tried to turn on a light during the night, I had no idea if this was Station policy in all sleeping quarters, or only my room. The speakers were working, and I could hear the hum of the air conditioning, so it was no power cut.

She had known my name.

Even after I had murdered her friends, the red-haired woman had looked at me with understanding. And she had cut through the killing haze and reached me, spoken to me, brought me back.

Whatever she had done, it was still working. I'd never woken up during the night before.

I listened as a voice spoke over the soothing sound of the waves.

"When you think back to tonight, you will remember only that the mission was a success. You will feel pride in serving the British people. You are keeping your country safe."

There was a gap of about fifteen seconds, then the voice resumed.

"Station is safe. Station is good. Station protects this

country. Work for Station. Obey Station's orders. Protect your country."

Another pause, then the voice was back.

"When you think back to tonight, you will remember only that the mission was a success. You will feel pride in..."

I ignored it and sat up. I was thinking clearly for the first time in years. The recorded voice seemed almost laughable now that the drug wasn't affecting me, but I knew this was no joke. If every mission Station had sent me on had been like tonight, they were using me as an assassin. I didn't believe the people in Shoreditch had posed any threat to the country, but they might well have posed a threat to Station.

I felt a wave of nausea as I remembered again what I had done, the blood on my hands as I put them around the woman's throat. I found the bathroom in the dark before vomiting. I turned on a tap and splashed water on my face, forcing myself to think.

Pushing the bloody images out of my mind, I focussed on what I needed to do next. Station thought I was safely tucked up for the night, having my memories expunged ready for the next mission. My clearness of mind was either temporary or permanent. If permanent, I could afford to take my time, play along and pick my moment to escape. If temporary, I had tonight, and only tonight, to get away from Station.

Logically, there was no choice. I could confirm that the effect was permanent by waiting. But if I waited, and the effect was temporary, I would be trapped.

I had to escape now.

And so began my first attempt to break out of one of the most secure facilities in Britain.

⁓

I DRESSED IN THE DARK, then walked up to the door and stopped. I rarely bothered locking my door on the inside, and there was no point in anyone locking it from outside, as I could rip it from its hinges with one finger. But another possibility had occurred to me.

Slowly, I pressed my ear against the door. My room is near the end of one of Station's dozens of long corridor. It's hardly a thoroughfare, so it was unlikely anyone was around.

Unless they had posted guards on my room.

I breathed as slowly and quietly as possible, listening intently. Silence. I was about to move when I heard a male voice just a few feet away. The door was too thick for me to make out any words, but the tone was easy to discern. He was asking a question. A second later, there was an answer from a second voice. Then they both laughed.

I pictured their positions. One on the right, one on the left. They sounded relaxed. They weren't expecting any trouble during babysitting duty.

I was going to have to disappoint them.

My fingers slid down to the door handle. I counted down from three to one and pulled, hard.

It wasn't locked. The door flew open, and I stepped through smartly, flinging my arms open and back as if I was about to address a huge crowd. This gesture was powerful enough to lift the guards off their feet and slam them into the wall. They dropped to the floor.

I waited. No alarm went off. All was quiet. Dragging the guards into the room, I tore up my sheets and tied the two men together. Then I ducked back out into the corridor.

Station is a twenty-four-hour operation, but certain areas are quiet at night, and the lighting was dim. I walked through a monochrome world.

I passed the lab where Hopkins had said The Deterrent had spent much of his time. It was a gleaming, state-of-the-art room now, full of instruments, test tubes, massive fridges, computers and devices whose function I couldn't guess. A few people were in there, monitoring, making notes. I knew they had blood and skin samples they took from me once a week. Hopkins had intimated that my cooperation with the lab was as important as my help on the missions.

"If we can find out why you survived when so many others died, we can help those whose power might damage them."

It had seemed a noble aim. Now I questioned if that was really why they were studying my DNA.

That question was answered a few minutes later.

I continued towards the lift. My best chance was the stairs, which were operated by a code combined with a thumbprint scan. I intended operating it with my shoulder after taking a decent run-up. They were strong-looking doors. Probably *too* strong, but I had no other option.

I never got close enough to test my theory. As the corridor reached an intersection, I slowed and listened. Hearing nothing, I walked briskly out, doing my best to look slightly irritated, as if I had been summoned to an unnecessary meeting in the middle of the night.

A door opened and a man and woman I didn't recognise came out. I forced a weary smile onto my face. They barely looked up from the notes they were discussing, the man giving me a cursory nod as we passed.

I felt my confidence grow a little. This might work.

Even as that thought entered my mind, the speaker in the corridor crackled into life, and Hopkin's familiar voice spoke.

"Daniel, please return to your quarters. You are not well."

I quickened my pace, shooting a glance up at the security cameras. After trussing up the guards, I had crushed their coms and ripped the phone out of the wall. There was no way they had alerted anyone. I wondered if opening the door had triggered a silent alarm.

Too late to speculate now. I broke into a jog.

"Daniel, you are having a reaction to the medication we use to help you control your condition."

I ran faster.

"Stop immediately. That's an order."

"Screw you, you lying, murderous bastard."

At intervals along Station's endless system of corridors, there are gaps in the floor, ceiling, and walls about four inches wide. If you stood near them, you could feel a breath of cold wind. They were almost like the spaces between carriages on the underground.

I was just approaching one of those gaps when the lights brightened, and a huge steel door dropped from the ceiling, filling the space with a deafening boom.

I stopped running. I had few illusions about the likelihood of my breaking through a four-inch steel door, but I gave it my best shot. After backing up, I ran at it full pelt, my shoulder hitting it with all the power I could muster.

There was a dull thud that rattled the fillings in my teeth. The steel buckled, but not much. Not enough. Given enough time, I thought I could break through. But only by using all my power, resting and eating, then starting again. All Hopkins would have to do was wait until I was exhausted and send in a crew to pick me up.

No. I was beaten. Unless I could override the system somehow, find some explosives, or hunt for another exit. Station must surely have a back door.

I remembered the lab. Plenty of material there. Some scientists, too. Maybe I could take hostages, negotiate my way out.

I turned to run the way I came. As I started down the corridor, I heard another thud ahead. Around the corner, another steel door blocked my path. I was boxed in. I felt myself getting angry.

When I found the nearest camera, I spoke into the lens.

"You lied, Hopkins. About everything. Who were those people tonight? They weren't terrorists. Does anyone know what you're really doing down here? Does the government know you're murdering civilians?"

"Don't be naive, Daniel. Of course the government knows."

"Well, I'm out. Next person to try and stick a needle in me gets his arm ripped off. Go ahead, keep brainwashing me. I know you're doing it now, so from now on I'll fight it. If it wears off one day, I hope I'm standing next to you, Hopkins, I really do."

That was kind of a stupid speech, I admit. I should have kept my mouth shut. But I was in shock, not thinking. And I was angrier than I'd ever been in my life. Understandable, maybe, but stupid all the same. Tell the bad guy what you're going to do. Duh.

Hopkins' voice sounded as businesslike as ever. Nothing seemed to rile the man.

"Yes, thank you for your thoughts, Daniel, but you work for us. I could release gas to make you unconscious, then send a team to get you. There are still many ways in which you can be useful."

"I don't think so."

"I wasn't asking for your opinion. Anyway, you've

handed me an opportunity to run a little test. Do you remember me mentioning hybrids?"

I did. He said it might be possible, by analysing my DNA, to create medicine that imitated my fast-healing ability. It could revolutionise patient recovery after trauma. He referred to the technology as a hybrid. I couldn't see what that had to do with anything. I said nothing.

Then, out of sight, I heard the first steel door move, opening, grating where I had dented it. There was an echoing crash as the door closed again.

Hopkins spoke.

"You are a treasure trove of genetic material, Daniel. Come and meet the result. Let's see how well you fight against a hybrid."

I turned the corner and stopped dead. Thirty yards away, two figures were facing me. They were short and squat, wearing army issue tracksuits. They looked like twins, their broad upper bodies and huge arms supported by trunk-like legs.

Their heads...their heads were a mess. They regarded me without curiosity as I got closer. Mouth breathers, the pair of them. They had been given an army buzz-cut, so it was easy to see the lumps and protrusions on their skulls. Their eyes were dull and glazed. One of them had a line of snot running from one nostril. The other one was sucking his thumb.

They were built like me. Just shorter. And I couldn't see much sign of intelligence.

Hybrids. If that's what they were, I wasn't impressed. If Hopkins had been trying to scare me, he'd failed.

"Looks like they fell out of the ugly tree and hit every branch on the way down," I said, with more bravado than I felt. "Tweedledumb and Tweedledumber."

"Very droll. Trigger them."

"Do what?" Then I realised that last remark wasn't meant for me. I swung back towards the hybrids. Their expressions changed, their pupils shrinking then expanding, their bodies shaking. I knew that feeling. Tweedledumber made a strange cracking noise with his mouth and spat something onto the floor in a spray of blood.

It was his thumb.

I looked back up. They were both staring at me now. Still without any obvious intelligence, but with purpose. Hey, a great white shark may not be able to solve a crossword, but he can take off your leg with one bite.

They ran at me.

Oh, shit.

22

I ran for it.

I had to buy myself some time to think. I didn't know how strong the hybrids were, but if they were as powerful as they looked, I might be in trouble if they caught me. Especially as I had only managed half a night's sleep since the last use of my power. It wasn't as if Station would trigger me in turn, give me an adrenaline boost to match theirs. I wondered if I could outrun them. I could.

They lumbered after me at a fast trot, but I easily outpaced them. The problem was, we were sealed in a small, L-shaped section of corridor. Each side of the L was about twenty yards long.

I reached the second door and turned. The terrible twins were already round the corner. They were making a horrible, growling noise, more animal than human. The blood on Tweedledumber's face and the blood-gushing stump where his thumb had been made him look like a monster in a Hammer horror film.

Their attention was focussed on me.

"Can we talk about this?"

Well, it was worth a try. But they weren't up for a chat. These boys were more basic. Kill or die. Binary logic.

Like me a few hours previously.

I timed my move well. As they narrowed the gap between us, I ran straight at them and jumped. I never thought I'd have cause to be grateful to Station's architects, but right then, I could have kissed them. Nice high ceilings, about twelve feet. Victorian, perhaps. I didn't have time to check for ceiling roses.

I cleared their heads by about three feet, hit the floor and ran back the way I'd come. At the corner, I looked over my shoulder. They were slow to react, running until they reached the second steel barrier, before turning, snarling and spitting.

My brain would have to get me out of this. I couldn't keep avoiding them indefinitely. I guessed I might be stronger one on one, but there were two of them, and I was tired.

I scanned the first corridor. One door led off it. There had been two doors in the other side of the L. If the layout of the parts of Station I was familiar with was any guide, they would be dead ends. One or two rooms behind each door, but with lower ceilings. It would be much harder to avoid the hybrids inside.

I kicked open the first door, hoping for weapons. I found a caretaker's cupboard, full of mops, brushes and cleaning equipment.

A glance was all I had time for before I had to run for the steel door again.

The twins stuck to their strategy, which consisted of running towards me while making horrible noises. I knew they intended to rip me limb from limb if they caught me, but I hoped they would hit their wall at some point, just as I always did. I didn't know when it might happen, and I couldn't afford to rely on it occurring before they got hold of me.

I repeated the same trick, leaping over their heads. Tweedledumb made a grab for me, but his arms were so massive it made it hard for him to reach directly above his head. Luckily for me.

I sprinted harder this time, giving myself time to kick open both doors in the other corridor. The first opened into a classroom, complete with whiteboard, TV, and a few rows of chairs. Nothing useful.

I had read a terrible book back when I was overweight and working on my self-esteem. The author claimed I could have anything I wanted. All I had to do was ask the universe for it, and it would be mine. I wondered why the author hadn't asked the universe to make her rich rather than rely on millions of desperate people with anxiety or depression to stump up fifteen quid each. I knew the book was bilge, but at that moment, I admit, I asked the universe to send me an armoury packed with big, easy to use, weapons.

The universe said no. The next room was an office. Unless the psychotic twins had a fear of staplers or were dangerously allergic to A4 paper, I was out of luck.

I barely made it over them the next time.

My brain chose that moment to put a useless image into my head. I'd had a retro-style arcade game at home, and by far my favourite game had been Donkey Kong. It had just occurred to me that all those hours perfecting the art of jumping over barrels rolled at me by a giant gorilla had been excellent practice for timing my leaps over the heads of the Tweedles. And to think Mum had said I was wasting my time like the lazy, fat little shit I was. Just goes to show.

As if the Donkey Kong comparison had given my

subconscious time to work up a little magic, a useful fact chose that moment to surface. Drain cleaner contains hydrochloric acid. Or was it sulphuric? I hadn't been paying *that* much attention in science class. I just knew drain cleaner was bad. Which, in my current situation, meant good.

As I ran, I looked into the cleaning cupboard. There were four shelves, and I only had time to check one as I shot past, my pursuers thundering after me. I started with the bottom shelf and checked the next shelf up on each subsequent pass. Naturally, the drain cleaner was on the top shelf.

I was planning what I needed to do as I jumped over the twins' heads one more time. My timing was off. Tweedledumb got a meaty hand on my ankle and slammed me to the floor, coming down with me.

I managed to get my arm up and take some of the force out of my fall. If I had been concussed, I'd be dead. As it was, I was able to kick out with my other foot. I felt it make satisfying contact in the middle of Tweedledumb's head, spreading his nose across his face. If anything, it actually improved his looks.

I felt his grip loosen but still couldn't pull my left foot away. I put my right boot on the edge of the left and pushed hard. The boot came off, Tweedledumb still hanging on to it. I scuttled backwards, but Tweedledumber was quicker. He fell onto my leg and, without a second's hesitation, sank his teeth into my foot.

The pain was immediate and unprecedented. I had once had anaesthetic wear off during a root canal, but that was an absolute pleasure compared to the messages my nerve-endings were currently sending to my brain. I screamed, then looked on in disbelief as the misshapen creature bit through skin, muscle, sinew, and bone. I remembered the day I'd taken a drill to my toe with no result other than a ruined drill bit. What kind of power could push teeth through my flesh?

I saw his lips meet, and I was abruptly released. He had three of my toes and part of my foot in his mouth. He spat, then fought his twin over the grisly tidbit.

I skidded backwards on my arse, then stood and hobbled as fast as I could back to the cleaning cupboard. I knew I wouldn't be doing any more leaping today. No more jumping any barrels. It was nearly game over.

I grabbed the drain cleaner as the twins grew bored with their prize (or ate it, I don't really want to think about it) and resumed their pursuit.

Childproof caps. Why? I mean, I know why, I understand the logic, but wouldn't it make more sense to lock the sodding cupboard if you've got a toddler?

I had run out of coordination, patience, and time. Lucky I'm so bloody strong. I ripped the cap away from the bottle as they came round the corner, held the five-litre container between my palms, and waited, despite every instinct in my body screaming, "DO IT NOW!"

When they were close enough for me to smell their foul breath, (foot and toe carpaccio, anyone?) I tilted the container and squeezed it flat, its contents spraying directly into the Twins' faces, before throwing myself to one side. My bleeding foot sent fresh waves of agony up my leg.

The Tweedles took no evasive action at all, still completely focussed on their crippled prey. The drain cleaner went into their eyes and mouths, and the reaction was instant. They clutched at their faces making guttural sounds of pain, fingers scrabbling at their flesh, leading to their fingertips burning.

Despite being blinded, they weren't done with me.

Tweedledumber was closest to where I had fallen, and he reached out, stumbling towards my position. This was what I had been hoping for, and I swept my leg across his ankles, bringing him down on his front. Immediately, I leaped onto his back and rolled, wrapping my arms around his chest. He was so wide I could only just get my fingers together across his ribs, interlocking them and holding tight.

I rolled him face-to-face with his blinded twin, whose wild punches now found a target.

They fought each other with insane ferocity. I held onto the back of Tweedledumber as he punched, kicked, jabbed, tore and bit, while receiving the same treatment. The air was speckled with droplets of blood, and all I could hear were snarls, panting, and the ripping of flesh. I clung on to my perch as if my life depended on it, which it very much did. It was like riding a bucking bronco designed by HP Lovecraft.

It seemed to take forever, but gradually, the fight lost some of its ferocity, the blows coming less frequently. There was so much blood on the floor I was amazed they were still conscious. Then I remembered how much of it had likely poured out of my foot and wondered how I was still conscious.

The killing blow came from Tweedledumb, who had been pummelling Tweedledumber's neck. With a nasty, permanent-sounding crack, something gave in Tweedledumber's throat, and I loosened my grip as he rolled away. He emitted one last croak that sounded like an outraged frog.

I may have cramped his style somewhat by clinging to his back for the entire fight.

There was still the surviving Tweedle to deal with. He was gasping now, his acid-blinded eyes a reddened, bloody mess, his fists swinging in front of his face. I didn't move. His movements got progressively weaker as he wound down like a clockwork monkey.

About ten seconds after he stopped moving, I leaned over and prodded him. Nothing. He was dead.

I dragged myself over to the wall and leaned against it, my sight blurring. I wondered how much blood I had lost. I also wondered why it was my foot didn't hurt anymore. In fact, I couldn't feel my left leg at all. Was that good? On balance, I thought, probably not.

It was almost a relief when the gas hissed in from the vents in the wall. My head sagged, and the floor smacked me between the eyes.

23

Cressida

November 13th, 1978

It's been a horrible couple of months. I haven't felt like writing at all. Everything is going wrong, but I am powerless to do anything about it. I keep reminding myself that I am working for my country, that national security is at stake, and that my opinion counts for nothing in Station.

But still.

Abos has changed.

I didn't notice much the first few times I was allowed to speak to him. With Carstairs present. It was the fourth Friday meeting that upset me.

The first thing I noticed over the weeks was that Abos was asking even fewer questions. I've got used to leaving gaps after telling him something so that he can digest it then ask a question. He's stopped doing that. He seems much less curious about the outside world than before.

Oh. I have to be honest, don't I? This is my diary, after all. It's the way he looks at me that's the real problem. Or rather, the way he looks at me compared to the way he used to look at me. On the third Friday, he didn't make much eye contact at all. Then, the following Friday, he actually looked me up and down. In a kind of calculating way. Oh, God, Cress, just say it. It was sexual. The look he gave me lingered on my breasts. I was horribly uncomfortable, it just felt inappropriate. Then I glanced at Carstairs and felt worse. He was watching Abos's face with interest and making notes.

Someone else has taken over Abos's education. I had assumed that would happen. It's not as if I'm remotely qualified. But I still felt hurt. I'm struggling to come to terms with my diminished role in Abos's life, and having him look at me like I was a piece of meat really didn't help.

I say 'education,' but I'm not sure that it's the correct word. Abos talked a little about what he had learned recently. He spoke about the British Empire, but as he spoke, it became clear that he considered the Empire to have been a golden age. According to Abos, the world at large had misunderstood Great Britain's colonial incursions, by considering them as hostile and damaging to the countries affected. On the contrary, he told me, the world had missed an opportunity to embrace the values of the greatest nation on the planet. To listen to him, you'd think they should approach us, cap in hand, begging for the opportunity to put the queen on their banknotes and start drinking tea.

During this horribly skewed diatribe, I looked across at Carstairs again. He shook his head. I'm still on probation, was the unspoken warning. I didn't know what to do. I still don't. So they're giving him a white-washed version of our nation's history. It can't hurt, can it? Abos was speaking from the moment he was 'born', so I'm confident he's intelligent enough to draw his own conclusions. He's no pushover.

Except...he's changed. He was looking at Carstairs for approval occasionally. It was so strange. Like a child checking with a parent.

And when Abos wasn't looking at me as if he wanted to see me naked, he wasn't really looking at all. Those golden eyes stared right through me as if I were invisible.

It sounds stupid, I know, but I feel bereaved. Where has Abos gone?

Diary, my immediate impulse was to leave Station. I feel rejected. But I'm old enough to have stopped acting on first impulses a long time ago. I examined my motives for leaving and found them wanting. I was being selfish. Abos is surrounded by scientists and the military, living in an underground bunker. I'm the closest thing to a 'normal' person he has. He may not know it but he needs me. At least, I think he does, and that will have to do. I'm staying.

24

January 1st, 1979.

Happy New Year. I'm still here.

Everything changed for the worst when Carstairs turned up, and it hasn't got any better.

From Station's perspective, Carstairs' work with Abos has been a success. I don't know if I was being naive, or wilfully ignoring the obvious, but Station obviously intends to use Abos as some kind of supersoldier. When I brought this up with Roger last week, he shrugged.

"More of an international ambassador for Britain, I guess."

"An international ambassador who is bulletproof, can fly, and has superpowers?"

"Well. Yes. Why not?" Roger lit his pipe. I can't believe he's taken to smoking a pipe. It's such an affectation. It makes him look older. He's let himself go over the last few years, his pot belly growing as fast as his hair has receded. I can hardly believe I was ever attracted to him. The contrast between him and Abos is so pronounced now that no one would ever guess the source of Abos's DNA.

Mike and McKean have been working on a theory about Abos's use of genetic material. From the blood Abos has allowed them to take, they found nothing other than what they'd expect to find in a human. Mike suggested taking a skin sample - something they have been unable to do up to now, as Abos's skin is so unyielding. Since Abos's conversion to the Great British cause (such cynicism, Cress), he has been more willing to cooperate fully, and he used his own fingernail to provide a skin sample. Mike found two distinct types of cells. One type was human, the other was not. The type which was not human has not yielded any more information, as it is impossible to break it down still further, and the laboratory instruments—which are the best available—are unable to unlock Abos's secrets. The team's report to Hopkins concluded that future technological developments may one day discover how skin can be mostly human, yet bulletproof. They take the long-term view of scientists.

Hopkins does not.

He burst into the lab just after Christmas, holding the report between two fingers as if it were so distasteful he could hardly bring himself to touch it.

"You are supposed to be the best scientists working in the fields of chemistry, biology, genetics, and technology. Correct?"

No one was sure if this was rhetorical or if Hopkins required an answer. Either way, he didn't wait long enough to get one.

"If this is the best you can do, you'd better start considering other careers."

He flicked through the report and quoted it.

"'Although current computer processing speed is not yet sufficiently powerful, we believe that the next decade may bring advances capable of producing machines that can model the cellular complexity of The Asset's skin samples. Even if this proves possible, there is, as yet, no way of reproducing anything close to the biological material we have sampled. We can merely express awe at the subject's capabilities, and hand our findings to those who will come after us.'"

Hopkins paused and gave us the full benefit of his cold sneer. "We can merely express awe?"

He closed the report and made sure he had everyone's attention.

"You will be handing over your findings sooner than you think if you don't start producing results. The military opportunities afforded by The Asset is unprecedented, but he is one individual. Work harder. Find a way to reproduce these abilities. I am halving annual leave until further notice."

No one said a word. I looked around the room and became painfully aware of how much has changed since Abos was first discovered. The excitement back then was palpable, the sense of being present at such a historic moment. Now, the excitement has been replaced with a kind of resignation. When Hopkins dropped the report on the floor and walked out, no one protested. I looked at each face and saw defeat. Then we all went back to work.

Something is going on here. Hopkins has a hold over Father that I don't understand and Abos is, well, he's just *wrong*.

My suspicions became deepened over the next few days when I didn't see Abos at all. Carstairs cancelled our Friday session, claiming Abos was "too busy."

Diary, I will find out what's happening. Why Abos has changed, and why Father meekly goes along with Carstairs.

It may take some time, but I'm determined to get a look inside the room where I once taught Abos. The room where he seems to spend most of his time now.

I'll report back.

25

May 14th, 1979

Now I know. I wish I didn't because of what it means.

Father is away until tomorrow. I will confront him then. I've thought about it all day, and I imagine I'll be lying awake most of tonight. I can't see any way this could have happened without his involvement, but I must give him the chance to convince me otherwise. Although I already know he won't be able to. Oh, Father, how could you?

I had no idea it would take this long, but perhaps I shouldn't have been surprised. After all, I'm working in the most secure facility in the country. The most secretive, too. Everyone who works at Station knows, in the event of a foreign invasion, a nuclear attack, or a direct attack on Station itself, the order would be given to detonate the charges that will bury the entire facility and everyone in it.

When someone cares that much about security, it's difficult to sneak into an off-limits room.

Difficult, but not impossible. And I had to do it. I've become more and more convinced something is terribly wrong. There's nothing new to say about my weekly meeting with Abos. It hasn't got any better. He's changed so much that his personality now bears little resemblance to the shy, strange, curious man I got to know last year.

Carstairs is behind the changes in Abos. Today, I confirmed it. I just wish he was acting alone.

Right. There's no easy way to admit this, so I'll just come right out and say it. I used my feminine wiles to get what I needed. I took the example of Mata Hari and seduced my way into the forbidden room.

I'm not proud of it, but it had to be done. I sometimes suspect I'm the only person in Station who thinks of Abos as anything other than something to be manipulated and used. Maybe letting myself be used in turn is justifiable under the circumstances.

By varying the times of my toilet breaks over the first few months, I built up a picture of who went to Abos's room, and when. The corridor with the blue Piccadilly line on it passes the lab and leads to his room. Father is an intermittent visitor, but he has refused to say anything about what he does there. Now I understand why. Carstairs is in the area every morning between ten and twelve-thirty. He comes back every afternoon between four-thirty and five-thirty. Abos accompanies an army squad for training every day between one-thirty and four. Two or three times a week, they leave the facility by helicopter, training outside in various locations. Abos wasn't allowed to tell me where. Or why. Or what they were doing.

Due to the restrictions enforced by the regular hours I keep at Station, I couldn't find out any more about who visited Abos, and when. Carstairs cuts off questions he considers inappropriate. However, by keeping an eye on the window in the laboratory door, I could work out how many guards are assigned to Abos's room and jot down the pattern of their shifts.

By the time Easter rolled around, I knew that my clearest opportunity to get a look would come at lunchtime. Twelve forty-five looked like the best bet. Abos and Carstairs would both be in the dining room. When Abos was present, two soldiers stood guard on his room. When the room is empty, only one guard is stationed. It's never unguarded.

So my problem was simple: how to get past one guard without being seen or reported. I considered drugging the guard's food, hitting him over the head or setting off an alarm. The risk of subsequent discovery was too high in each case.

I think I always knew what I was going to have to do. When I finally allowed myself consciously to consider using seduction as a tool, I conceded it made perfect sense, however distasteful it might seem. No one would have to get hurt.

I picked my beau carefully. Soldiers assigned to Station serve long stretches. The fewer changes of personnel, the fewer chances of any rumours surfacing about Station and its secrets, I suppose. We all signed the Official Secrets Act, but still. One careless remark off-duty in a pub...why risk it? What this means for me is that I already have a friendly relationship with many of the soldiers. They spend much of their time underground, surrounded by other men, so, over the years, I've noticed I attract more than my fair share of nods, smiles, and even the occasional wink when they're certain Hopkins isn't looking. I have remained professional at all times.

Until the week after Easter, that is.

There's a Private Donovan who's been here for about eighteen months. I know he's got a soft spot for me because he once stopped outside the lab for almost an entire conversation before being barked at by a passing sergeant. Fraternisation is not encouraged.

I wore a little more makeup, and attempted to catch Donovan's eye at meal times, give him the little half-smile I've practised in front of the mirror. How very teenaged of me. But it works. Within a few days, I noticed him making sure he could sit at a table affording him a clear view of me.

As phase one was going so well, I moved to phase two. This involved waiting until Donovan was assigned the guard slot outside Abos's room. It took eight days, but one lunchtime, I caught sight of him heading down the corridor. A few minutes later, Carstairs, Abos, and two guards passed on their way to the dining room.

I waited ten long minutes, my heart thumping. Then I slipped out to the bathroom, applied a fresh coat of lipstick and unbuttoned my blouse enough to draw the eye without making me look like a stripper. It's a fine balance, but I think I achieved it.

Private Donovan certainly agreed. As I turned the corner, he moved his rifle across his chest and prepared to challenge me in exemplary military fashion. Then he recognised me, half-smiled, dropped his gaze to my cleavage, dragged his eyes upwards with a clear effort and stammered at me while his neck flushed.

"M-M-Miss Lofthouse, you are not permitted to come into this area."

I paused before speaking. I had put a lot of effort into this and my greatest risk of failure came there and then. If I pushed Donovan too hard, he would do his duty, send me packing, and, if I was very unlucky, report me to Hopkins.

No. I was going to play this very carefully indeed.

I stopped about six feet away from the door to Abos's room. I assumed what I think of as my *demure but sexually available* pose, something else I'd been practising in front of a mirror. I'm sure women have been using it for centuries. So much for my feminist ideals, eh, diary? Perhaps this makes me a more radical feminist? Or am I trying to make myself feel better about behaving like a tart? Anyway, the demure pose. I didn't smile but put my head ever so slightly on one side, my hands flat on my thighs. The hand position was crucial because it allowed me to use my upper arms to push my breasts together. I could feel my blouse taking the strain.

"I'm sorry, Private Donovan," I said, and turned, making sure that he was looking where I wanted him to look. He was. "It's just, oh this will sound so pathetic...no, forget it. I apologise."

I walked away - I've developed a new kind of walk just for Donovan. You can imagine. Oh dear.

I'd almost made it to the corner when he spoke.

"Miss Lofthouse?"

And I knew I had him.

"Cress. Please call me Cress."

I told him I was lonely, lived with my father and just wanted someone to talk to sometimes, but if that wasn't allowed, I wouldn't bother him again. I turned to leave one more time, and he stopped me again. Said I might talk to him at lunchtimes for a few minutes if it was quiet. If anyone saw me, I could always pretend to be looking for someone. I tilted my chin down and looked up at him through my eyelashes. Men still fall for this rubbish, can you believe it?

It took five more visits, one spell of holding hands, two

hugs (one prolonged), plus one lingering kiss on the lips before I was confident of success. I made sure to always leave him wanting more.

This lunchtime, I waited until it was all clear. It was now or never.

DONOVAN SMILED as I came around the corner. He's a sweet boy, really. I felt awful about using him this way. He put his rifle against the wall and held out his hand. For a few minutes, we held hands and talked, then I let him kiss me again. This time, when we broke apart, I put my hand around the back of his head and drew him back, opening my mouth and moving my body against his. He responded much as any healthy male would, and before I knew it, his lips on my neck and one hand was on my breast. I used the opportunity to start unbuttoning his shirt.

He had a moment of clarity then. "I can't," he hissed, moving my hand away. I gently went back to what I was doing.

"I want to touch your skin."

He hesitated, then let me unbutton his shirt down to his midriff. I slipped my hand inside and ran my fingers through the hair on his chest.

In the interests of candour, diary, I will admit I was getting a little hot under the collar myself at this point.

When he had managed to get a couple of fingers inside my bra—which must have been awfully uncomfortable for the poor man, it's far too tight as it is—and reach a nipple, I judged the time was right to initialise my master plan.

I suddenly went still, my body rigid. Donovan stopped what he was doing half a second later.

"What's the matter?"

"I heard something. I think someone's coming."

He didn't waste any time speaking, just took his hand out of my underclothes (with some difficulty) and tried to re-button his shirt. Meanwhile, I rushed over to the corner and peeked round.

"Hopkins and Carstairs," I said, hurrying back. "They've stopped to talk, but they're coming this way."

Donovan paled. He looked on the brink of passing out when I told him his buttons were in the wrong order.

"They can't find me here," I whispered. "You'll be court-martialled. I'll be fired. Hide me."

Fortunately for both of us, no one locks a guarded door. Unfortunately for me—or so I thought at the time—Donovan opened the door opposite Abos's room and, before I had a chance to protest, bundled me into it. I could hear him frantically trying to rearrange his clothing.

I was in utter darkness. I felt around for a few seconds, then found the light switch. A fluorescent bulb flickered into life, and I took stock of my surroundings.

I was in a cupboard. A fairly big one, full of shelves, but a cupboard nonetheless. My heart sank. My plan had failed because I was stupid enough to imagine Donovan would hide me in the living quarters of the most powerful being in Britain rather than the store cupboard opposite. I swore, then resolved to make the best of it. I had a good look around, knowing my time would be short.

The shelves to the right were of little interest. Towels, bedding, soap, and laundry products. Also, piles of over-sized army clothing adapted for Abos. The shelves to the left contained a first aid kit and some jars of vitamin powder. That was it. Frustrated beyond belief, I looked for anything else I could find. A clipboard with a lined sheet and some handwriting hung next to the light switch. I took it and read the entries. They were in date order, and the last entry had been filled in less than an hour ago.

May 14th, 8am, compound C, 125g with water. Subject stable.

I flicked back quickly through the pages. There were four entries every day, the first at eight in the morning, the last at ten pm. They all said the same thing. I flicked back further and found some different results. There had been a compound A and a compound B. Compound A had been used for five days, compound B had lasted just one day. Against the compound A entries, the word inconclusive had been written. On the day that compound B appeared, the word unstable had been written and underlined. That had been the twenty-sixth of December.

There was something about Boxing Day that nagged at the corner of my mind, but I couldn't place it straight away.

There was a gentle knock on the door.

"Cress?"

I re-hung the clipboard. Donovan looked sheepish when he opened the door. He was still pale, and his forehead had a light sheen of sweat.

"They didn't come this way," he said. Bless him, it didn't occur to him that I might have been lying through my teeth.

He looked down at my chest again, and I remembered the state of my blouse. I buttoned up, blushing the whole time.

"Er, Cress," he began. He was about to start stammering again with embarrassment.

"I understand," I said, patting his arm. "We shouldn't have done it. I'm so sorry, Petey." Yes, his name's Petey. You see why I think of him as Donovan.

We parted with a peck on the cheek and a promise to get back in touch once one of us has left Station.

Not that many people ever seem to leave Station, now that I think about it.

I got back to the lab and diverted to the toilet when I saw Father.

I sat in a locked cubicle, shaking for about five minutes, trying to regain my composure. I remembered why Boxing day had stuck in my mind. That had been the day Hopkins had shouted at everyone, demanded results. I remembered how he had pointed at Father. At the time, I had thought something was wrong. It was the same time that Abos dropped out of sight. No one in the lab saw him for four days.

December 26th, 8am, compound B, unstable.

Whatever was in those jars, whatever it was they were giving Abos four times a day, it wasn't vitamins. And the most experienced chemist in Station is Father.

Worst of all, although I was trying to preserve a glimmer of hope that Father wasn't involved with whatever they were doing to Abos, I couldn't ignore the handwriting. They say your handwriting is as distinctive as your voice. And I know Father's as well as I know my own.

I will confront him when he gets home tomorrow. I'll call in sick and wait for him at home. I'll demand he tells me what they've been doing to Abos. What Father has been doing.

26

May 15th, 1979

Father was back late. He telephoned to ask how I was. I mentioned the word 'menstrual,' and he stopped asking questions. He told me he would eat at Station and be back late.

I was supposed to go to bed early like a good girl.

He expected to come back to a warm house and a glass of whisky. What he got instead was me, sitting at the kitchen table in the darkness. He jumped about a foot when he flicked on the light and saw me there.

I've had nearly thirty-six hours to think about it, and when Father sat down in the chair opposite, I knew exactly what to say.

As I spoke, his expression changed, going through bluster, denial, embarrassment, anger, fear, and—finally—shame. For my part, I felt something tearing inside me as, for the first time, I stopped being proud of my father. His fall was that much greater, I suppose, because of the love and esteem I've had for him all my life. Since Mother died, we have been all the other has to rely on. Now, at the end of my twenties, I find that support slipping away forever. I'm not sure I'll ever be able to trust anyone like that again.

To his credit, I suppose, he did at least answer my questions when he realised the alternative.

"If you to refuse to tell me what you've been doing, I will pack a bag now, walk out of this house tonight, request a transfer in the morning and you will never see me again. Never."

White-faced, grim, and looking old, his eyes didn't leave mine as I spoke.

"If you lie about any aspect of what you are doing, tonight or at any point afterwards—and, remember, Station is a small place—I will leave. Don't do it. I expect the truth from you, and I expect it now."

I let him speak.

"And if you don't like what I'm about to tell you, Cress? What then?"

I had barely thought about anything else since the previous day.

"I can't promise anything until I hear what you have to say."

He said nothing, just nodded.

"It started when Carstairs arrived. Abos had shown abilities so powerful that the top level of military intelligence had become involved. Carstairs outranks everyone in Station, including Hopkins. For the first week, he simply observed, then he called Hopkins and me into his office. He believed that there was one aspect to the way we were dealing with Abos that was dangerous."

"What was it?"

"It was you, Cress."

I stared at him.

"What?"

"Carstairs could see a relationship building between the two of you, a relationship that, although formed around a teacher-student model, was still based on an assumption of equality."

I continued staring for a few moments before finding my voice.

"How, exactly, is that supposed to be dangerous?"

"Abos is not human. His development is, admittedly, proceeding at a far faster rate than even the most gifted child, but his brain is still at the most plastic, malleable stage."

"I still don't see how our relationship is dangerous."

"Carstairs considered it so. You would have been left with no contact at all if it hadn't been for Abos himself. He insisted on seeing you."

I blushed. Betrayed by my body again.

"Carstairs then imposed a new approach to his, and our, relationship with Abos. Parent to child, authority figure to subordinate. He set us to work to help him achieve it."

"Wait. Why is it a good thing to have Abos treating you, or Carstairs, as if you're his superior? It's not true."

"Cress, it's not a case of superiority." He looked at my face. "Well. For now, perhaps, it is, but it's temporary. During this foundational period, it's healthy for Abos to look up to us, to have boundaries, to flourish within the same kind of parent-child model that has worked for humanity."

"But he's not human."

"Quite so. Would you want a toddler with superpowers deciding to go on the rampage? Or would you rather a well-behaved child who obeys his elders?"

I glared at him.

"What gives you the right?"

"National security. The safety of the world. And the fact that we agreed to follow orders when we signed up to work for Station. Come on, Cress, it's for the best."

He was feeling a bit more secure. Perhaps he thought I was wavering. He even smiled, tentatively.

"What, precisely, is in that powder you give him, Father?"

He stopped smiling.

∾

FATHER DISTANCED himself from his behaviour by going into professorial mode, knowing full well I wouldn't be able to follow everything. I stopped him and—despite his protestations—made notes.

"The powder is a mixture. We had to experiment with quantities and dosage. There is some vitamin D in there, the label wasn't completely inaccurate. We found chlorpromazine works to a certain extent if we were very careful with dosage. We considered an injection of sodium piothental might be more effective, but it induced an almost catatonic state, followed by an absolute refusal by the subject to allow future injections."

"Boxing Day," I said, but Father was still talking.

"In the end, it was an experimental American drug that proved to be the best fit. It's at its earliest developmental stage, but Quetiapine proved very efficient for our purposes when mixed with chlorpromazine. We used some more common synaptic inhibitors, of course. Considering our lack of a control group, and the highly experimental nature of the treatment, we managed extraordinarily well, developing, within a short period, a—"

"What does the drug do?"

He stopped in mid-flow, then thought for a moment, choosing his words carefully.

"Cress, it doesn't hurt Abos in any way, I want you to know that."

"What does it do?"

"It slows him down, Cress. It makes him more reliant on us. More compliant. It makes him suggestible. The educational programme Carstairs started enables us to help Abos become a patriotic defender of democracy, freedom, and the British way of life."

With an effort, I un-gritted my teeth.

"You're brainwashing him."

"Now, Cress, that's not true. We want Abos to embrace the right values as he grows. We don't want a superpowered Nazi, or communist, flying around the place, do we?"

"You're brainwashing him," I repeated, all the pent-up anger draining out of me in a wave of tiredness. It was all I could do to hold my head up. "How could you? You, a scientist? A father? How can you help Carstairs abuse Abos?"

"Cress, don't be naive. There are some decisions that are too serious to be taken by individuals like us. Some threats to our country must be dealt with by institutions like Station."

"Is that how you see him?" My tone was flat. "As a threat?"

"No, probably not. But that's my point. I am not qualified to make that kind of assessment. Neither are you. Particularly you, I'm afraid."

"What do you mean by that?"

"Carstairs claims you're in love with Abos. I can't say I agree, but I have concerns about your relationship. I worry about it, as should you, Cress. He's not human."

My face flushed again, and I felt some energy finally

return along with my embarrassment and anger.

"How dare you. How dare you." It was good to raise my voice, to challenge Father, to force him to defend the indefensible."If you continue blindly messing around with his brain chemistry, we may never discover who he is. You can't possibly know what kind of damage you may be doing to him. How could you?"

"There are risks, Cress, I don't deny it. But what choice do I have?"

"You have the choice to say no. To refuse to help. To rally support from your fellow scientists and make Carstairs see that this is wrong."

Father shook his head.

"But I don't believe it is wrong. And if I were to walk away, they would appoint someone else. No one has quite the level of expertise and experience with the subject that I do. It would be irresponsible in the extreme. I can't do it."

I sat and looked at him, then stood up and left the room.

An hour ago, Father knocked on my door. I didn't answer, but I listened.

"I don't know what you're thinking of doing, Cress, but please remember how deeply involved I am at Station. I could never walk away without endangering you. Their methods are brutal. Morally indefensible, perhaps. But effective. If you can't trust yourself not to interfere, you must ask for that transfer. An attempt to thwart Carstairs would be seen as treason. Treason, Cressida. They would lock you away for the rest of your life. We are trapped, both of us."

He's right, of course. Such a logical man. I want to hate him for what he's doing, but I can't. He's still my father.

I can't go back to Station. I'll ask for a transfer tomorrow.

I feel like I've betrayed Abos, and my betrayal is the worst of all.

27

Daniel

I UNDERESTIMATED STATION. Hopkins, and others like him, are the kind of people who say, "the end justifies the means," as if it's true. As if repeating it with absolute belief somehow makes it acceptable. As if the "end" they are pursuing justifies any "means" that they choose. Betrayal, lies, manipulation, brainwashing. Violence, torture, death.

Beware those who are certain of their beliefs. If in doubt...good.

I said sometimes you don't know when a chapter in your life is about to come to an end. The chapter that closed for me in that corridor with Tweedledumb and Tweedledumber was followed by blank, empty, wasted pages. Hard to think about it. Even now.

I was a young man. Still a kid in many ways.

At least, at the end of it all, there was the best chapter of all. I met George. The single most important person in my life, even though our time together was short.

I went to sleep one day at the age of twenty-one. When George woke me up, I was thirty-five.

WHEN I LOOK BACK on those years—which is something I've avoided—it's easier to pretend I was unconscious the whole time. It means I can treat any memories as dreams. Or nightmares.

The truth was that I was conscious for between six and eight hours every day, according to George. During this period, I exercised, ate, and performed essential bodily functions. there were children's books to read, to keep my mind stimulated. Not *too* stimulated. Lots of Enid Blyton, but no Roald Dahl. My captors really were prize bastards.

The children's books were necessary because of a side-effect of the drugs. I could reason to a certain extent. I could make straightforward decisions. Should I eat the banana first, or the sandwich? Will today's story be The Faraway Tree or Noddy? But anything more taxing brought on a headache.

I didn't sleep as such. It was more of a daily medically induced coma. I always had a cannula on one of my hands connected to a drip on a wheeled stand.

I would wake at some point every day. I'm only guessing it was every day. I have no way of knowing conclusively as my room had no windows, clocks, or calendars. The first thing I'd see would be a doctor or nurse checking my chart. They would ask inane questions about how I was feeling, then put a fresh bag in my drip. Whatever they gave me kept me docile, obedient, and hardly present in any meaningful way. I would let myself be fed, then led to the toilet. In the toilet, I would sometimes remember to look at my body. There were often dressings on my chest or side. There was no shower or bath, just a small sink. I don't remember that I smelled bad, so they must have given me sponge baths in bed.

There was a small gym next door. It had a treadmill and an exercise bike, plus resistance machines to maintain muscle tone. While I worked out, anodyne new age music played, with a voiceover murmuring feel-good mantras. I can't remember a single one, but I enjoyed listening to them. Remembering that makes me angry. Even now, if I see a motivational poster, I want to puke.

After exercise, there was more food. Sometimes a doctor would visit and ask questions. They would ask me to remove my cotton pyjamas. They'd use a felt tip pen to draw lines and arrows on my body, before making notes.

I was allowed to read afterwards. There was no television or radio. After what seemed like an hour, the lights would dim. My drip would be changed. Soon afterwards, I would feel tired. My eyelids would droop, and a nurse would help me to bed.

I didn't sleep, I was unconscious.

I had no dreams.

That was the pattern of my life. Without variation. For fourteen years.

THE DAY EVERYTHING changed started the same as any other. A nurse, a new drip, a slow float to the surface where a kind of half-consciousness awaited.

"Good morning, Daniel."

This, at least, served the purpose of reminding me of my name. I'm not sure I would have known it otherwise. Daniel Harbin was in there somewhere, but deep down, inert. Waiting.

Food, toilet, gym.

No doctor visited. I sat at the small desk and looked at the selection of books. Had I already read The Adventures Of The Wishing Chair? The cover looked familiar, but I couldn't remember anything about it. I started reading. Within a page or two, I stopped. It seemed unsatisfying. I wasn't enjoying the story. I pushed it away and opened The Faraway Tree. After a paragraph, I dropped it in frustration and picked up Look Out, Secret Seven. My head felt strange. Things were moving inside my skull, the tectonic plates of personality shifting. I felt adrift, confused.

The door opened, and someone came in. It took me a while to respond. I read the same line a few times, then lifted my head.

A visitor. Not a doctor, or a nurse. This was new. I stared at her.

She was in a wheelchair and was the first person I'd seen in more than a decade who wasn't wearing a medical uniform.

She was about my age, mixed-race, wiry black hair pulled back with a red headband. She wore a shapeless brown and black dress that gave little indication as to the shape of her body. Her face was thin, her skin a little sallow. Her gold-flecked brown eyes regarded me with ferocious intelligence. My mouth went dry. A tremor had disturbed the surface of my drug-maintained calm.

When she spoke, her voice was a surprise. It was rich,

warm, cheerful. Even that first time, stoned out of my mind, I know it did me good to hear it.

"It's taken me a long, long time to find you, Daniel. You're the first of us. And you're the strongest. They've treated you badly, but it ends today. It ends now."

I felt a strange stirring, a sensation I couldn't place. It was a feeling I hadn't experienced for fourteen years, and my mind went through such a grating gear-shift to allow it that I felt dizzy. I gripped the side of the desk for a moment, then recognised the odd sensation for what it was. It was curiosity. My brain was very slowly, very painfully, waking up.

I looked at the drip on its stand next to the desk.

"Yesterday's dose was half strength," said my visitor. "The one hanging there now is a saline solution. I need you to be *you*, Daniel. I'm a clever woman, and I have some tricks up my sleeve, but if we're going to break out of Station, I'm going to need you to smash a few things."

I blinked. Moment by moment, I felt myself returning, but it was a nightmarish sensation, bringing with it memories I didn't want to face and a sickening suspicion about the length of my stay in that sterile, windowless room.

"How long?" My voice sounded strange to my ears. Weak, croaky, deeper in pitch than I remembered. I coughed. "How long have I been here?"

She sighed. Her hands were together on her lap, but they were not resting there. Her right hand held the wrist of her left tightly. When she let go, her left hand twitched and spasmed. With an effort, she placed her right hand on mine. Her skin was dry and warm, the pressure on my hand firm. She waited until I looked at her. Her voice was full of sympathy, but I saw strength and determination in her eyes.

"Fourteen years."

She waited. I was far from alert, and I couldn't comprehend what she had told me. I must have looked as blank and as numb as I felt because she squeezed my hand and gave me a small smile.

"We'll talk about it later, Daniel. For now, I've bought us a few hours so you can get your strength up."

I stared back at her. My hand went up to my upper arm, feeling the place where the power button used to be. There was no scar there, but I still felt a lump under the skin.

The door opened, and a nurse pushed a covered trolley into the room. He was unfazed by the woman in the wheelchair. He nodded at us, left the trolley and went out the way he had come in.

My visitor took her hand from mine and tugged at the corner of the cloth covering the trolley. It fell away, revealing two whole cooked chickens, and bowls full of baked potatoes, spinach, peas, carrots, and cauliflower. There was a bunch of bananas and a full fruit bowl with apples, pears, and grapes. There was a jug full of milk and two glasses.

She leaned across and set the two glasses on the desk.

"Would you mind?" she said. I reached over and poured two glasses of milk, my hand shaking a little.

"Thank you." She took three bananas and put them in her lap.

"The rest is for you. You will need your strength, Daniel." She lifted her glass. "Cheers."

In a daze, I clinked my glass against hers, and we drank cold milk together, in a secret government facility buried in the heart of London. A woman in a wheelchair, and a man who had been drugged and kept asleep for fourteen years.

I felt that strange, but increasingly welcome, sensation again.

"Who are you?"

She smiled then, the milk moustache giving her features an impish quality.

"Georgina Kuku," she said. "Call me George. I'm your sister."

28

Georeorge kept looking at her watch. I leaned over.

"What time is it?"

"Five forty-five."

I frowned. "Morning or evening?"

"Evening."

I pictured myself on a summer evening, walking along a street. It was a dream-like image, insubstantial. I turned to George.

"Fourteen years. 2015?"

She nodded and handed me the last banana. The entire trolley's contents had been consumed, and George had done her fair share of the consuming. Considering she looked painfully thin, she could pack away her food. I wouldn't have wanted to challenge her to a pie-eating competition. Maybe she really was my sister. Half-sister. If we shared the same father, had she inherited some sort of power from him, too? I looked at her again. A gust of wind could knock her over, never mind a bullet.

"What month?"

"December. Christmas soon."

I altered the mental picture, making it evening; wintry, woolly hat weather, with coats buttoned up and scarves wrapped round faces. I made the street lamplit and added flakes of snow. Then I looked at the white walls, the drip, the monitor, the hospital bed. I couldn't believe my mental picture had any connection with reality. It felt less substantial than Enid Blyton's magical wishing chair, which could take you to far off, fantastical lands.

I started to pull the needle out of the cannula. If we didn't go now, I was sure my mental image would turn out to be a fantasy, and I would never see the sun again.

"Let's go."

George put her hand over mine and stopped me.

"If that needle leaves your vein for more than five seconds, you'll trigger an alarm. Wait."

She looked at her watch again.

"Ten more minutes. We have to wait until after six."

"Why? What happens then?"

"Change of shift."

She pointed at the banana I was holding.

"Eat up."

AT FIVE PAST SIX, there was a knock on the door. I stood up, fists clenching.

"Don't worry," said George, smiling. "He's part of the plan."

The door opened, and a guard walked in. He was a big, burly man in his thirties. He unclipped his handgun and put it on the table, before undressing, folding his clothes at the end of the bed.

I looked at George quizzically.

"Oh, he doesn't know we're here."

The guard didn't turn at the sound of her voice, just unlaced and pushed off his boots before removing his trousers. He then went to the small wardrobe, took out my spare pyjamas, and put them on.

I whispered, not wanting to break whatever spell he was under. "How? How is that possible?"

"I mess with people's minds, Daniel. In a nice way. Usually."

George dug into her pocket and brought out a sealed packet. She handed it to the guard, who opened it and removed a needle and cannula. Without hesitation, he found the vein on the back of his hand and tried to push the needle in. It took him three attempts to find it, and, by the time he did, blood was dripping from his hand. He seemed not to notice.

"Daniel, transfer the drip, please. Remember, once it's out, you have five seconds."

Still only half convinced this was really happening, I did as she asked with a casual confidence I may not have displayed had I been thinking straight. An idea occurred to me as the guard padded away and got into my bed.

"Are you messing with *my* mind?"

George laughed with open pleasure.

"Of course. Daniel, you've been in a semi-catatonic state for fourteen years. If I wasn't giving you a kick-start, it would take weeks before you would be in any kind of state to escape."

I examined my own mental processes, as far as that's possible.

"I can't...I mean, nothing feels weird. I...what are you doing, exactly?"

George spun her wheelchair to face the door.

"No time now," she said. "I'll explain at the hotel." She gestured with her thumb at the pile of clothes. "Get dressed and let's get moving. I promise I won't peek."

THE CORRIDOR OUTSIDE WAS EMPTY, just as George had promised. I insisted on opening the door, then running through, ready to confront any guards. She followed, chuckling at my frown.

"The guard on duty is now asleep in your bed. We won't meet anyone else on this level until we get to the stairs. Do you mind pushing?"

I took the handles of the wheelchair and walked along the corridor. After a few steps, I realised I was walking strangely. This was the first time I had gone any further than the distance from the bed to the bathroom, and my slight limp was now noticeable. The injury had long since scarred over, but even my enhanced healing ability couldn't grow back my toes.

I looked at the walls. They looked different. They were light grey rather than olive, and there were no coloured lines indicating routes to different divisions. Had they changed the paint scheme, or was I on another level?

As if she had been reading my mind, which she was, George spoke.

"You're two levels beneath the one you used to live in. This area is used for medical facilities. There are operating theatres and traditional hospital wards where injuries can be treated in-house. Mental health care, too. Post-traumatic stress counselling, cognitive behavioural therapy, hypnotherapy - one of Station's specialities, as you know. Physical therapy, too. I had a weekly session here for months."

We still hadn't seen a soul. If this level's layout was roughly the same as the one I knew, we should be a minute's walk from the stairwell.

"You've been here months?"

"Yes, nearly eight months."

"How did Station catch you?"

She chuckled again. It wasn't dismissive. George was amused. She gave off the air of someone who was having a fabulous time.

"Oh, they didn't. I handed myself in."

"You, hold on, *what*? Why?"

She looked over her shoulder as I pushed her around the last corner. At the far end, I saw the security door leading to the stairs.

"I needed something from Station, and I wanted to find out what they knew about us."

"Us?"

"Halfheroes."

"There are more of us? Others survived?"

"Of course."

"What did you need from Station?"

We had reached the door. I came to a halt. The thumbprint and code security protocols were still in operation. I hoped she had a plan.

"I needed help to find our dad."

As I gawped at her, I heard footsteps. I put my hand on the butt of the guard's gun.

"Relax," said George. "Doctor Copson just needs to check his code. He keeps fretting about forgetting it."

A worried-looking man in his sixties hurried up to the door. He smiled at George. It was as if I wasn't even there.

"Hello George, how are you this evening?"

"Very well, thank you, doctor. And you?"

He stared at the keypad and rubbed the bridge of his nose.

"Yes, yes, I'm fit and healthy, thank you. Um..."

George smiled at him. "Four seven seven eight six, isn't it?"

Doctor Copson smiled and punched in the numbers. He put his thumb in place, there was a click, and the heavy door swung open. He took a pace back, and as I pushed George through and the door started to close again, I heard him muttering. "Four seven seven *eight* six. Four seven seven eight *six*."

The door shut behind us with a metallic clunk, and I looked at the concrete stairs, then at George in her wheelchair, then back at the stairs again. She stuck her tongue out at me.

"And here's me thinking you're supposed to be strong."

I lifted the chair onto one shoulder and took the stairs two at a time. George whooped with delight.

"Show off," she said.

I paused at the next level. She shook her head.

"R&D. Which, for sixteen or seventeen years, has meant hybrids. This whole level is where they are kept and trained. I stayed away because my abilities can't touch them. Once, just once, I got close enough to become aware of a hybrid."

She shook her head.

"I can't reach their minds at all. They are so damaged...incomplete. Full of confusion, pain, and rage. Poor things."

I remembered the sound I'd heard when the hybrid had

bitten through my foot. I felt rather less sympathy for them than George did.

I carried her up to the next level and set her down by the door. Another thumbprint scanner, another keypad for a code. But no sign of any help.

George looked at her watch again. "We're nearly a minute early. You're making good time."

The stairs didn't go any further up. This was Station's top level. The central lifts were the only way to the street from here. There were emergency stairs, but they could only be accessed from the same lobby as the lifts. That central hub was bound to be busy. I guessed that was when George expected me to punch a few people. If not there, at the security check on ground level.

"You got it," said George, smiling.

Right on schedule, there was a click, and the door in front of us opened, revealing a woman I'd seen a few times before. Her name evaded me for a few seconds, then I had it. Ward. I had never been told her first name. She was older, of course, her hair grey and cut short, the skin around her eyes furrowed. I remembered sitting across from her in lorry before running across a field towards a barn. Someone had been firing at us...it went hazy after that.

"Good to see you again, sir." She saluted me. "This way, please."

George raised an eyebrow at my expression.

Ward turned on her heel and led us towards the lift. It was a two-minute walk, during which, our chaperone was saluted by half a dozen passing soldiers. She had obviously been promoted while I'd been dozing my life away. I wondered if Hopkins had moved on. Surely he'd be past retirement age by now.

"Still very much in control, I'm afraid," said George,

quietly. Her ability would take some getting used to. "Hopkins has built himself a little empire down here, and since the hybrids have proved their worth in certain deniable military operations, the government won't rock the boat."

We reached the lobby where Ward led us straight to a lift, the doors closing. Catching sight of her, one of two men inside held the door.

The men exchanged nods with Ward as I pushed George into the lift. Not subordinates, then. Not in uniform, either. Specialists of some sort.

"This is where I leave you," said Ward, and saluted me again as the lift doors closed. I had no idea what George had been doing to her, but Ward had obviously not seen me as me. I wondered who she thought I was.

I glanced at our two companions. If they were specialists, I doubted it was medicine or psych. They were both powerfully built and stood with a kind of relaxed readiness that made me nervous. Trained. Dangerous. Something about them reminded me of my handlers. I wondered if that's what they were - but for the hybrids. It would take a certain ruthless, cold efficiency to do that job. They looked just the types.

One of the men was looking at me. He had quite a full beard, despite the fact that he was in his mid-thirties. He was either some kind of eccentric, or fashions had changed since I'd been locked away.

I didn't like his expression. It was as if he thought he knew me, but didn't quite believe it.

I nudged George. Beard spoke.

"Why would Lieutenant Colonel Ward salute a sergeant, *Sergeant*?"

I nudged George harder. She made an odd sound.

"He asked you a question." The second man was taking an interest now. He was clean-shaven and had a conspicuous neck tattoo. Maybe that was a fashion thing too.

I calculated we had about thirty seconds until the lift reached the ground floor. Neck Tattoo was closest to the control panel and the alarm button. Beard was still looking, and I still didn't care for his expression.

"Um," I said, stalling for time and giving George a little shake. I glanced down. She was snoring.

Looked like I was on my own.

Beard's gaze wandered from my neck down to my feet. The guard who'd taken my place had been a big bloke, no mistake, but no one got close to my measurements. The T-shirt under my jacket had ripped when I had put it over my neck, the jacket itself was half open as I couldn't wear it any other way, and—most telling of all—the trousers stopped three inches short of my boots. Which were killing me.

When his eyes flicked up to my face again, I saw the sudden recognition there. He reached for his handgun.

"It's—"

My elbow caught him in the stomach and knocked every last bit of breath out of him. He collapsed to the floor just in time for me to slap Neck Tattoo before he touched the alarm. He slammed into the side of the lift, then dropped.

At that moment, there was a *ting*, and the doors slid open in front of Station's security detail.

Station was very, very determined never to allow any kind of security breach, so they had three layers of defence set up at street level. The first—a long desk, behind which two retired Station operatives boosted their pensions by dealing with members of the public who had wandered in by mistake—was purely cosmetic. There was a large metal turnstile that could only admit one at a time, and an internal wall that hid the rest of the lobby from view. Anyone who approached the desk was filmed, and the feed from the cameras monitored by operatives in a secure room downstairs. They were the second layer.

If the operatives running the second layer thought there was a possible threat, they had two options: soft and hard. I had made a joke about that during my early days at Station, but it had earned me a withering stare from Hopkins. Not that I'd seen him come up with any other stare. As far as I knew, the withering stare was the only stare in his arsenal. Stick to what you're good at, I suppose.

The soft option was two armed soldiers approaching the desk and suggesting the interlopers leave. Station had only used that option twice, and it had proved effective. Both occasions had been provoked by confused foreign tourists who didn't know they were being asked to leave. The international sign of having a loaded gun pointed at you had worked a treat.

The hard option, as yet unused, brought down steel shutters at every door and window, locked down the lift and stairs, and brought eighteen additional armed soldiers to deal with the problem. Should that be insufficient, gas was available. And, as Hopkins always made clear, should that final layer ever be breached, an alarm would go off in Whitehall, a phone call would be made, and Station would be buried under a hundred thousand tonnes of rubble.

There were some State secrets that were never intended to see the light of day.

All in all, Station's security arrangements were frighteningly thorough.

There were two things in our favour: my power, and the fact that the entire security operation was designed to stop people getting *in*. No one had ever considered the possibility that someone hundreds of feet underground in the most secure facility ever built in the UK, surrounded by armed soldiers and hybrids would even consider, for a second, the possibility of trying to get *out*. They'd never make it more than a few feet.

They hadn't counted on George.

I knew I would have to make this quick. I'd only have a few seconds before the alarm was triggered.

If the alarm was triggered.

Perhaps there was another way.

As the lift doors slid apart, I put the side of my foot against Beard—he was still gasping—and flipped him into the side of the lift, where he went quiet as he fell on top of his colleague. I pressed the button to send it down again.

I had never been more grateful for my broad physique as I hunched over George's wheelchair and pushed her out, hiding the inside of the lift with my bulk while the doors slid shut behind me.

There was one man waiting for the lift. He tried to go around me as I stepped out, but I grabbed his upper arm.

"Are you a doctor?" I pointed at George. "She's had a seizure. I need help."

Her snores undermined my case, but by then I could hear the sound of the lift starting its descent.

"No," the man looked at my shoulder, "Sergeant, I am not a doctor. And, according to your uniform, you work for me. But I don't recognise you. What's your name?" He looked down at George doubtfully, and stepped away, his hand moving closer to his gun.

"I shaved, sir," I said, rubbing my chin. "I had a big old beard. Bushy great thing. That's probably why you..."

He took half a step closer, squinting to read the name

badge on my chest. I hit him. A very light uppercut, pulling my punch as much as I dared. Didn't want to kill him. His eyes rolled back. I caught him and lowered him to the floor.

"Medic!" I called. Two armed soldiers ran in from the ready rooms conccaled behind the internal wall.

"What happened?" One of them knelt and took his pulse.

"Some kind of fit, I think. He grabbed his head and fell over."

The other guard talked into his lapel, calling for medical assistance. I grabbed the front of my jacket and read the name badge upside-down.

I pushed George away. The first soldier called after me.

"Sergeant! Where do you think you're going?"

I stopped and shot him a glare.

"You seem to have this under control. Colonel Hopkins ordered me to get his god-daughter back to the hospital, and I have a taxi waiting. Would you like me to stay here with you instead? Perhaps you could help me explain to the Colonel how I let her miss her dialysis appointment?"

He hesitated. No one wanted to attract any kind of attention from Hopkins. Ever. He thought for a second, then waved me away. I'd only taken three steps when he called me again. I turned, forcing an exasperated look onto my face.

"What's your name, Sergeant?"

"Marmagradible," I said. Well, you try reading something upside-down under pressure.

He stared at me.

"It's spelled the way it sounds."

I walked to the turnstile without looking back, holding up my security card as I got closer.

"She's not well," I said.

A security guard trotted over and opened a gate at the side so I could wheel her through.

Ten seconds later, I was outside, hailing a taxi.

George opened her eyes as I eased the chair into the cab.

"What a lovely sleep. Did I miss anything?"

29

Cressida

October 5th, 1979

It's been a while. I half-thought I'd never write in this diary again.

I was transferred to the Ministry Of Agriculture six months ago. I collate data on fluctuations in land supply, and my boss makes recommendations to the minister. It's completely mindless work, but it requires concentration and an eye for detail. To my great surprise I enjoy it. I come home pleasantly tired and never give a moment's thought to what passes across my desk once I leave the office.

I sometimes consider the university education I passed up and wonder what might have been. I've never believed that life follows some sort of plan, that things happen for a reason. No. I was present at the scientific discovery of the century, hence, I missed an education and a more stimulating career. I have regrets, but I can live with them.

I have consciously avoided thinking about Abos, although my dreams refuse to play along with that decision.

As for Father, our relationship has been dented somewhat, but blood is thicker than water. We find other things to talk about. Perhaps, eventually, we will be able to repair some of the damage.

I'm only writing now because of what Father announced after dinner. My head is still reeling. I should have known that what he told me was inevitable at some point.

Abos is about to go public.

Tonight, a press release will land on the desk of every national newspaper, as well as every correspondent from around the world covering British news. Both the BBC and ITV are included. They will be given access so that they can broadcast the event live.

Abos will be presented to a world that has no idea he exists.

They are calling him Powerman. How utterly ridiculous. Father had the decency to look embarrassed when he told me.

Father said I could go if I wanted to. The invited audience includes, as well as the press, ambassadors from the world's governments, representatives of our own government (most of whom were only told of Abos's existence today), and senior figures from the highest echelons of Britain's army, navy, and air force.

And me. Somewhere at the back. In a woolly hat, a thick scarf, and a pair of sunglasses. If he happens to glance my way, he won't recognise me. Maybe he's forgotten me anyway.

Tomorrow evening. Broadcast live across the globe. Powerman. Good grief.

30

October 6th, 1979

The announcement was scheduled for five pm, and all three British TV channels rearranged their schedules so that they could show it live. I travelled with Father in a Station car. We didn't know where we were going until we got there, although as we got closer, it became clear where Abos was making his debut.

Wembley Stadium.

Security was tight, and we passed through three checkpoints before being allowed to enter the stadium itself. A wooden stage had been erected on the pitch, and public address system—the sort they use for rock bands—was stacked in two towers on either side. There was one microphone, but other than that, the stage was bare. The pitch was spotlit.

We filed in and took our places, Father showing me to the back row in the stands before he headed towards a row nearer the front. I was seated with members of the foreign press, most of whom knew each other and were exchanging pleasantries. I saw a few shrugs in answer to the same question being asked, over and over, in multiple languages: "Why are we here?"

There were almost two hundred people present according to my rough count. Ridiculous in a venue the size of Wembley. I craned my neck and looked at the backs of the heads nearer the front. I recognised Hopkins straight away. His seat was central and, as I looked away from him, I caught sight of Carstairs walking along the same row to join him. He looked up, and I shifted to one side, glad that the Irish journalist in front of me was wearing a large bobble hat.

There were only two TV cameras there, one BBC, one ITV, which surprised me at first. Then I noticed that both cameramen were shadowed by a soldier making sure they were filming the stage, not the crowd. They would not be allowed to show the faces of Station personnel.

The buzz of conversation around me faltered as a low rumbling came from the other side of the pitch. There was a large gap in the advertising hoardings and, as we all squinted at the source of the sound, it became a loud, throaty roar, and a Challenger tank burst through the gap. It rolled towards us belching dark exhaust smoke. When it was about fifty yards away from the stage, it stopped, and the engine cut out. A few seconds later, the crew of four climbed out and jogged over to the sidelines.

"Good evening." I jumped at the voice. There was a red-faced man on stage now, standing at the microphone. It was no one I recognised, but I assumed, from the number of medals on his jacket, that he was someone important. From what I remembered about uniforms, a general. I was dry-mouthed and nervous. The assembled journalists and invited guests went quiet.

"Thank you for coming tonight. I apologise for the short notice, but it was in the interests of national security. What you are about to witness has been a closely guarded secret within the British military for three years."

An interesting piece of disinformation. I wondered if anything he was about to tell us would be true.

"The British army, navy, and air force, tasked with defending this nation, have long been associated with the development of cutting-edge technology. Not only weapons, but early warning computerised radar systems, fighter jets, ships, and submarines."

One of the foreign journalists—Italian, judging by his suit—yawned ostentatiously. His gesture garnered a few smirks from his colleagues.

"Tonight, you will meet the culmination of decades of research."

Decades? Of research? Another reason why they get us to sign the Official Secrets Act. They don't want us to point out when they are blatantly lying to everyone.

"The man I am about to introduce will change the way military conflicts are resolved from this day forward. After today, in fact, I don't imagine Great Britain will be challenged, militarily, ever again."

A murmur spread through the crowd at this. I glanced around and saw nothing but perplexed expressions.

"Ladies and Gentleman, this soldier's identity is a matter of national security. However, we all know him by his official army code name. I give you Powerman."

If the general was hoping for a cheer or a round of applause, he was disappointed. He was visibly put out by the chuckles from the journalists present.

Then Abos walked out of the players' tunnel, and everyone was quiet again.

He was flanked by two beefy-looking soldiers, but he made them look like the caricatured weaklings on seaside postcards. He towered above them, and his strides were so long that they had to trot to keep up. Abos was wearing the British army uniform I had last seen him in, with one difference. He sported a Royal Air Force helmet - like the ones worn by fighter pilots. It was painted in Union Jack colours. I felt a pang of embarrassment. He also wore flying goggles like a pilot - tinted black. Hiding those golden eyes. Avoiding any awkward questions. Smart move, I suppose. Shame, though.

Abos stood at attention in front of the stage, facing us. He was impassive. I looked at his cheekbones and mouth, then tried to picture those honeyed eyes, wondering where he was looking. Just then, a little cheer arose spontaneously. I followed everyone's gaze back to the player's tunnel, from which Michael Whiteson had emerged. I'm no fan of athletics, but even I know Michael Whiteson. After winning the four hundred, eight hundred, and fifteen hundred metres at the 1976 Olympics, he repeated the feat at the Commonwealth games in Canada last year. Whiteson is the most famous athlete in the country, always on the television or in the papers. He acknowledged the crowd with a little wave, stripped out of his tracksuit and took up a runner's starting stance at the edge of the pitch. A soldier handed him a silver relay baton.

"Mr Whiteson has kindly agreed to help us with this first demonstration," said the general. "A race around the perimeter of Wembley Stadium. I think you'd agree that it would be unfair to let them both start at the same time, though."

If the general has been considering a move into public speaking, surely today's engagement will have dissuaded him. Everyone was silent while he laughed at what he had considered to be a little joke.

"Ah, well. Of course not. No, we'll give Michael a chance. Whenever you're ready, Mr Whiteson."

He had the crowd's attention now, even if he had lost their respect for his oratorical skills. We all watched the fastest middle distance runner in the world set off at a blistering pace. I'd never seen a world-class athlete up close. It's far faster than it looks on TV. Abos walked over to the same starting position, and we waited. Whiteson got a quarter of the way round, then halfway. Abos didn't move. The chuckles started again.

When Whiteson hit three-quarter distance, Abos set off. This was accompanied by a huge gasp from everyone, even me, and I was expecting it. Swear-words in a dozen languages could be heard as the watchers tracked the blurred figure already rounding the far side of the pitch.

Whiteson finished his lap to find Abos waiting for him, the silver baton in his hand. Whiteson looked from his own empty hand to the baton Abos was holding, his face an almost comical picture of disbelief. I glanced around me and saw the mirror of that expression on the features of every hard-bitten, cynical journalist in sight.

There were a few similar demonstrations as a warmup to the main event. The current heavyweight boxing champion was permitted to spend three minutes punching Abos, who offered no resistance. The boxer started off jabbing politely, thinking, despite the briefing that he must have been given, that this was some strange publicity stunt. He gradually started to mix in a few harder punches, with horrible, painful-looking body shots and powerful blows to the head. Abos was unmoved by everything the man threw at him. It was over in two minutes when the boxer declared himself too exhausted to continue.

Abos rattled through a few more sporting demonstrations - his long jump was at least double the length of the current world record, and he managed it without a run-up. He used a cannonball instead of a shot put. A journalist volunteer could not lift it at all, but Abos casually tossed it over to the far side of the stadium where it broke a row of seats in the top tier. He held both arms out from his sides, and four rotund reporters hung off him - two from his left arm, two from his right. His arms didn't sag at all, and— after thirty seconds or so—Abos took off for another lap of the stadium, the reporters hanging on for dear life. Halfway round, two of them couldn't hold on any longer, and he carried them back, one at a time, at high speed. Their hands were shaking so much that I wondered if they would be able to write up their experience.

There was one more demonstration of strength before the finale. Abos jogged over to the Challenger tank and lifted the front end with one hand while waving to the crowd with the other. There was applause, albeit hesitant.

"It's clever, I grant you, but it's a trick." The Irish journalists in front of me were arguing.

"How is it a trick?" His colleague, a short red-haired woman, had a softer, less nasal accent. "Come on, now. We both saw him run, do you know what I mean?"

"Are you sure?" He was smiling a little smugly. "I don't know about you, Cathy, but I saw him clearly in front of me here, then again at the end of his lap. The rest of the time, it was a blur. That could have been anything. I reckon he ducked out of sight while we looked the other way. Classic misdirection. They might have spent weeks, months, setting this up. It's quite a show, I grant you, but I don't buy this whole Powerman nonsense."

"Ferg, he just lifted a tank, there. Are you facing the right way?"

"Hydraulics under the pitch. They parked it in the pre-arranged spot. All that lanky bloke had to do was to stand there and put his hand on it."

She shook her head, doubtfully. Then the general started talking again.

"Thank you for your time this evening. We will have one more demonstration, and there will be no questions at this time. Press releases with more information will be released within the next few days. Now, I know that representatives of the media have a reputation for being a little sceptical."

He paused. There was no response. He coughed.

"Much of what you have witnessed might seem impossible. You may even believe you have been victims of a bizarre practical joke."

He scanned the faces of the crowd, his manner serious.

"This last demonstration is the reason we invited you here this evening. If you were watching this on television, you would assume it was a camera trick. You cannot dismiss the evidence of your own senses so easily. Powerman, over to you."

The general left the stage, and all eyes turned to Abos, who had lowered the tank to the ground. He took a few steps away, then, without any theatrics, rose to a height of about ten feet. The sound the crowd made was the same shocked gasp you hear when a tightrope walker with no safety net suddenly wobbles. Abos flew towards us.

I looked over at the cameras and saw the soldiers directing the cameramen to remain focussed on the tank.

His arms by his sides, his legs together, Abos flew slowly

over the entire crowd. As he got close to the top rows, I dropped my head, hoping I wouldn't be too conspicuous - the only person not looking up at him.

"Jesus Mary Mother of God," whispered the first Irish journalist.

"I can't see a wire, Ferg," said his colleague. I admired her coolness while watching a man fly. "You eejit."

Fergus didn't respond. The collectively held breath of nearly two hundred people was expelled unanimously, and I cautiously peeped out from under my hat.

Abos was still in the air, but was now hovering near the tank again. He reached out a hand and beckoned.

The tank groaned as if tons of metal were shifting, then rose, ponderously and impossibly, into the air.

Outside Wembley Stadium, life continued as normal. There must have been cars passing, phones ringing, air-brakes hissing, children playing, birds singing, the million sounds of a city. But what I remember is a silence so thick it felt that nothing could penetrate it. No one moved, other than to direct their gaze first at the tank, then at Abos.

When the tank shot over the field and took up a position directly above us, no one screamed, no one moved. We all just looked up at it. There was a clump of mud and grass on the tread of the tank near me. I watched it detach and fall, landing with a wet plop on the smart-suited Italian journalist. He didn't react.

When the tank flew back to Abos, he closed his hand— very, very slowly—into a fist. As he did so, the tank began to groan loudly. Metal folded onto metal, massive machinery began crumpling in on itself in a cacophony of destruction.

Abos crushed the tank as if it were a paper cup.

The noise was horrendous and all the more shocking as it followed that powerful silence.

I don't know how long it took. Seconds? Minutes?

Abos lowered the remains onto the turf and flew into the dark sky, disappearing from view.

We all looked at the huge, roughly spherical, mound of metal on the pitch in front of us.

The Irish journalist turned to his colleague.

"Feck," he said.

October 7th, 1979

The Sunday papers are out. They all used the same photograph: Abos hovering above the pitch at Wembley Stadium, looking down at the crumpled tank. Here's a selection of the headlines.

SUPERSOLDIER REVEALED TO STUNNED WORLD

HE CAN FLY, RUN FASTER THAN A FORMULA ONE CAR, AND CRUSH A TANK JUST BY LOOKING AT IT. BEST OF ALL, HE'S BRITISH!

SUPERHERO ATE MY BUDGIE

The articles go into more depth inside, and there's stunned reaction from the rest of the world. Our allies were given twenty-four hours' notice of what was to be revealed, apparently.

I watched the news this lunchtime, and besides recapping his demonstration over and over and speculating about his origins, it seems the media have not taken to the name Powerman. Thank goodness. From what I saw on television, and from listening to the radio this evening, a dreadful rag that Father won't allow in the house has now renamed Abos. It looks as if this name will stick. The headline read:

REST OF THE WORLD, MEET THE DETERRENT TO END ALL DETERRENTS

That's what they're calling him. The Deterrent.

31

January 1st, 1980

A year has passed since I last wrote. I re-read some of the older diary entries, back when Abos was still a secret. Before Carstairs had brainwashed him. When it was exciting–fun, even—to work with Father at Station.

If I sound bitter, it's because I am. But I'm more upset at my moral cowardice. I made it my business to find out what was going on. And when my worst suspicions were confirmed—when I found out that Abos was being drugged and manipulated—what did I do about it? Nothing. Worse than nothing. I'm still here, living under the same roof as the man who prepares the chemical cocktail that makes it possible for them to keep Abos under their thumb.

My only contact with Abos—The Deterrent—is now shared with the rest of the world. I see him on TV, in the papers and magazines. It's possible to meet him in person at army, navy, or air force recruitment events, but I know I wouldn't be allowed to get close. Applications to join the military have doubled since The Deterrent became the face of the British army. Budgets have swelled, too. That makes no sense. Why spend more on munitions and soldiers when there's a superhero on your side?

The Deterrent has been busy this past year. I suppose his most notable success was the IRA car bomb. That photograph is so iconic now that I've even seen it on T-shirts and printed on children's lunch boxes. Abos is floating above the Thames, a red Ford Cortina held over his head. Tower Bridge can be seen half-open behind him. Seconds later, he flew off with the car and dropped it into the North Sea, where it exploded with no loss of life, other than a huge number of very surprised fish.

The photographer must have been perfectly positioned near the top of one of the office blocks that line the river. It's such a perfect shot, it's almost as if it were planned that way.

Cynical. Cress, very cynical.

Every newspaper wants to interview The Deterrent, but his office (yes, there's a Deterrent office in the Ministry of Defence at Whitehall) refuses all requests. He's a private man, they are told. The strong, silent type.

His physical appearance has been the inspiration for millions of words as well as TV programmes and even a popular cartoon series. The coverage isn't universally fawning although at least half of it seems to be sexual in its subtext. A small minority of commentators have raised the spectre of eugenics and the Nazi blonde-haired superman. I wonder what they'd make of the fact that he only looks like he does because an American scientist called Roger Sullivan bled all over his container?

The Deterrent has been involved in military action, high profile disaster relief work and anti-terrorism missions. But his movements are never revealed in advance, so press access is granted at the behest of The Deterrent's office, who, surely, answer to Carstairs. Is the real Abos still in there somewhere, struggling to be heard under layers of chemical confusion? Station controls his development, stymied his natural progress. Whatever he is today is a result of his freedom of thought being taken from him.

I'm on the sidelines, watching Abos become a puppet.

What can I do about it? Blow the whistle? It's crossed my mind. It might mean a life sentence for treason, but that's not what stops me. It's the letter I received that does that. I know now that no one will believe a word I say.

Just before Christmas, the envelope arrived. A plain, brown envelope with no return address. It contained a psychiatric hospital report from 1969 detailing the treatment of a girl who had suffered a complete mental breakdown just after leaving school. She had experienced delusions, seen hallucinations, and heard voices. After a six month stay in hospital, she was released into the care of her father. He has cared for her since then although she has suffered a few more episodes and needed to be hospitalised on three subsequent occasions. She is not considered to be a danger to others, but her father was advised to keep sharp objects and medication under lock and key for her own protection.

The chief psychiatrist of the hospital had added a hand-written note to the report, commending the government department which had allowed the unfortunate girl to accompany her father into work, even giving her a 'job.' The effect of this on her self-worth was inestimable, he wrote.

It was my name at the top of the report.

I didn't show Father. What would be the point?

They have me where they want me. I can do nothing to them.

32

Daniel

GEORGE HAD PLANNED my escape for a long time. The taxi from Station took us to Stratford International train station, where she gave me the code to a locker containing one big, wheeled suitcase, and a smaller piece of hand luggage. Both very smart. She took the smaller one and headed for the toilet, instructing me to do the same, get changed, and meet her back under the information sign.

It was a good job she had specified a meeting point because the jewellery and dress transformed her. She looked like royalty. As I got closer, trying not to feel self-conscious in the suit, I noticed again how thin she was. She wore tights under the dress, but they might have been made for a child. Both legs were withered and bent, as was her left arm. She let me look, then pulled a cashmere rug over her lower body.

"You look amazing," I said.

She smiled. "You don't brush up too badly yourself. Shall we?"

Stratford International offered a wide selection of connections, and, once Station had been alerted to my escape, they would be quick to trace the taxi journey. They wouldn't be expecting us to hole up less than a mile away.

From Stratford, we travelled by limousine, booked and paid for in advance. George waited in the car while I went into the hotel lobby, confirmed the suite and had our luggage sent up. Then I pushed her into the hotel. Immediately, the hotel staff transferred their attention to her, barely glancing at me. I realised what I was supposed to look like: her bodyguard. As far as it was possible to make a six-foot-four, eighteen-stone man invisible, she'd managed it.

Once in the suite, I ordered from the room service menu. The two members of staff who wheeled enough food for ten people into our room acted as if it were perfectly normal behaviour.

I gave them a fifty-pound note each from the roll George had handed me, and they glided away.

I was starving, but I still kept drifting back to the huge window. I could see the London Eye across the river. St James Park was a minute's walk away. I wanted to be out there, breathing the air, seeing normal people doing their Christmas shopping, walking dogs, standing outside pubs, stamping their feet against the cold.

"You can go out the day after tomorrow," said George. "Mid-morning. When the streets are packed. You're probably the most wanted man in London. No point taking unnecessary risks. Once the first twenty-four hours have passed, they'll look further afield. But they will be out there tonight. Checking hostels, B&Bs, cheap hotels, squats. We should be safe though. There's no way someone as unimaginative as Hopkins would ever think of looking here."

I looked around the suite, from its chandeliers to its two enormous bedrooms, both with en suite bathrooms bigger than my old bedroom. One wall in the drawing room was dominated by a flat-screen TV - technology I hadn't even known existed. Every piece of furniture, from the chairs to the chaise longue, sofas, and enormous dining table was unique, supplied by different designers. Somehow, they all tied together and gave the whole place an air of understated, expensive elegance.

It was a stunning hotel. For three and a half thousand pounds a night, it had bloody better be.

I looked over at George. Her hair was now pulled back by what I would describe as a hairnet, but—since it was studded with diamonds and constructed of white gold fili-gree—the word hardly seems adequate. She wore a simple black dress.

I was wearing a dark grey suit by a designer I had never heard of. I had a Breitling on my wrist and a pair of beau-tiful Church's loafers that made my feet feel as if they were being kissed. Mainly because they fitted.

"Come on," said George, lifting a silver cover to reveal the biggest steak I'd ever seen. "Let's eat."

I poured us each a glass of red wine I couldn't begin to guess the price of and started eating. George matched me, bite for bite, and when I pushed away my third plate, defeated, she started on two huge desserts.

"What is that?" I said, as she demolished the second bowl.

"Jam roly poly and custard." She shovelled the last mouthful in, sighed, and dabbed at the corner of her mouth with a napkin. "I had them make it specially."

She wheeled herself back from the food and headed for the first bedroom, burping as she went. She called out over her shoulder.

"Bedtime. I've ordered breakfast for seven-thirty."

I tried to speak, but she got there first. Again.

"I know you have questions. We'll be here a few nights. I'll—"

She stopped talking. I went to her. Her eyes were shut, her lips pressed tightly together, and she was gripping her left hand with her right.

"Are you okay?"

She didn't speak for a while, then the grip she had on her hand loosened, and she opened her eyes, looked at me, and shook her head.

"That's something else we must talk about," she said. She reached up and put a hand on my cheek. "Just not right now. Now go to sleep."

She closed the bedroom door behind her.

I went to the window and looked out at the city. When I stepped out of my shoes, my feet sank into the soft, deep carpet. Nothing seemed real.

I went to bed as instructed.

The last thought I had before my eyes closed was that there was no way I would be able to sleep.

THE NEXT DAY, we talked. Or, rather, George talked. I listened, asking the occasional question.

My life up to this point had been fairly tough. A lonely childhood, a mother who didn't love me, no father. At seventeen, an amazing few months when I thought my life was about to change for the better. Then Station, and four years of believing I was making the world a better place. Being a hero. Until that last mission when the illusions Station had put in place crumbled away. Having robbed me of my innocence, they took away everything else. They stole fourteen years from me.

Like I said, a fairly tough life. Compared to George, though, it had been one long party.

33

Georgina Kuku was born in London in May 1982. Her mother was married to a Nigerian diplomat. He had thrown her out when he discovered she was pregnant, despite not having sex with him for almost a year. Alone in a strange country, George's mother had tried to get home, only to learn her husband had revoked her passport. Her access to their bank accounts had also been blocked. When she called him, begging for help, he informed her that, should he hear from her again, he would have her family back in Nigeria killed.

Reverting to her maiden name, Mrs Kuku looked for work in London, but no one was interested in taking on a mother-to-be, despite her qualifications. Eventually, through a tenuous connection made at a dinner party months before, she found a job in a country house just outside London.

Mrs Kuku was expected to cook, clean, and look after the rich couple's two teenage children. She had one afternoon off per week and was not paid at all, just given board and lodging. When she had brought this up, her employer—a man who had inherited his wealth—asked if she'd rather he call her husband and ask him to take her back. Mrs Kuku had submitted to her fate, for the sake of her unborn child.

For twelve years, George's mother had been a slave, bringing up her daughter in the single room they'd been given. There were no playmates for George, and no school when the time came. As far as the state was concerned, Mrs Kuku and her daughter didn't exist.

George's education was piecemeal, using books borrowed from the children's room, and from the well-stocked library no one else ever visited. A quiet, bright child, used to spending most of her time alone, George made the most of her mother's attention and love in their few hours together each day.

Once or twice a week, George was allowed to watch TV for a few hours in the basement. At the age of eight, she'd gone to look for her mother when a power cut stopped her cartoons. She found Mrs Kuku's employer pushing his body against her mother in the pantry, his hands pulling at her blouse. Thinking she was being attacked, George hit the man's legs until he turned and slapped her away, leaving her stunned on the cold kitchen tiles.

At the age of eleven, while his wife was away for the weekend, Mrs Kuku's employer visited George while her mother was cleaning at the far end of the house. When she screamed, he left, but promised he would be back.

That night, George's mother took the largest knife from the kitchen, went upstairs and buried it in her employer's chest.

They took his car and drove away, George's eyes wide as she left the gates of the estate for the first time. When her mother stopped outside a police station and told her to get out, George did as she was told, before shouting in fear and disbelief as her mother drove away.

George found the letter at the bottom of her bag. Her mother revealed the identity of her real father and begged for forgiveness. George would have given anything to be able to tell her that no forgiveness was necessary, but she never saw her again.

A few days later, a tired-looking lady from Social Services patted her hand and told her her mother was dead.

George spent the next two years in an orphanage. The other children bullied her at first, then, when she started screaming whenever they came near, avoided her. She spent her days alone, apart from the hours she was forced to attend school.

The British education system held no interest for George Kuku. When it came to English, History, Geography, Philosophy, and Languages, both classical and modern, George had already progressed well beyond her classmates thanks to the superb library she and her mother had used.

Just like me, puberty came late to George. She was nearly sixteen when blood on her sheets coincided with the worst headache she'd ever had. She cried out in pain and, when the orphanage staff couldn't calm her, an ambulance was called. Hospital tests confirmed a rare condition that attacked the body's nervous system. She could expect progressive muscle wastage, deterioration of the respiratory system, and, eventually, death.

George's prognosis suggested she might live into her fifties, but she needn't worry about saving for retirement. A children's facility for those with untreatable long-term conditions accepted her, and she moved once again.

Alongside her illness—linked inextricably to it, according to George—was a major change in her consciousness. As the months wore on, George became clumsy, then struggled to walk. But a new world was opening in her mind. By the time she first used a wheelchair, at the age of sixteen, she had begun to embrace her birthright, the genetic gift from her father.

George had started her second life, as a child of The Deterrent.

She had researched her father as much as she was able, but no useful information was in the public domain. She intended to find him. She knew it was likely there were other children. For a girl as alone as she was, the idea of finding a family must have been powerful.

Her power was different from any ability officially attributed to The Deterrent. This excited and fascinated her. She had watched the footage of him with the Challenger tank—who hasn't?—but that was a demonstration of his power over inanimate objects.

George was different. She could look into other minds. More than that, she could plant ideas there.

She took a few years to develop her skills. At first, she experienced it like white noise. Wherever she was, whatever she was doing, it was in the background. It dropped in intensity at night when most minds were asleep.

One night, she woke up in the ward she shared with five other girls, experiencing three distinct mental states: her own, the matron's on duty, and a cleaner who was mopping the hall outside. It wasn't that she could hear their thoughts, exactly. George found her ability difficult to describe. She had once tried writing how it felt, but hers was an ability no one else shared. Words couldn't get close. It was like describing the sound of a bassoon to a deaf squirrel.

After that night, she slept as much as possible during the day so she could hone her new talent at night. A few weeks was all it took for her to be able to identify individual mental states and link them to the staff members or children producing them. Soon, she was able to do the same thing during the day, aware of dozens of people simultaneously.

She discovered the other side of her ability by accident. The director of the facility had been sitting in her car, wondering how much longer she could risk embezzling the charity that paid her wages, before she could escape with her young lover. George watched her thoughts with disbelief, as the director had always seemed devoted to her work.

What George did next wasn't accomplished in a completely conscious way, it was a mixture of instinct and intelligence. She pictured the director coming to her bedside, handing an envelope to her containing a bank card and chequebook in her name, giving her access to a new account containing twenty thousand pounds of the stolen hundred thousand. George had no idea how to open a bank account or transfer money. She just imagined the end result - the director handing her the envelope. And she made that image as bright and clear as she could, sealing it in place with a kind of white-hot mental weld.

The sleep she fell into immediately after this event was so deep that a nurse thought she had lapsed into a coma and moved her to the intensive care room. Two days later, she woke up and asked for toast. She ate three loaves of bread.

Ten days later, the director walked into the ward, pressed an envelope into her hand, and left without a word.

George knew she had made it happen. She also knew her subsequent collapse was the price she'd paid.

She was still wondering how long she should wait before leaving when the director was arrested.

Three days later, George moved to London and put down six month's advance rent on a tiny flat in Putney. She was eighteen.

~

GEORGE SET herself to uncovering information about The Deterrent. She could discover truths hidden to others. She could sift through minds, one at a time, find out what she wanted to know. It might take a little time.

It took fifteen years.

The problem was the toll her power took on her body, and the effect it had on her physical condition.

George had identified three separate abilities. The first was looking into the minds of others. The second was the ability to place suggestions so strong they became commands. It was this that drained her and placed a strain on her immune system. As she learned how to use this aspect of her power, she suspected she was directly, and adversely, affecting her projected lifespan.

She needed an income. By frequenting cafes in the financial district, she found that embezzlement was far from uncommon in the city of London. There were plenty of minds to choose from, and she selected a dozen from the greediest. They each set up monthly payments to her account of a few thousand pounds. Because of the punishment it inflicted on her body, she forced herself to take her time and allow a few weeks to recover before moving on to the next candidate. True financial independence took five years to put into place.

By then, George suspected she might not make it into her fifties after all.

Her speculation about her lifespan wasn't pure guesswork. It was backed up by her third ability.

More nebulous in quality than other aspects of her power, this third ability gave George a window into the future. Her future, specifically, but also a more general picture. The white noise of millions of London minds was like listening to a vast orchestra playing a discordant symphony. Sometimes, a flurry of notes concentrated in a certain area would suggest violence about to erupt. Occasionally, a theme barely audible at first would swell and gain traction, and she would start to pay attention. Living near the City meant she picked up on the dotcom stampede early, made hundreds of thousands as stocks rose, then sold it all months before the tech bubble burst.

Her own future began to define itself in ways she hadn't anticipated. When she started her research in earnest, when she began seeking out those who might know something about The Deterrent, she began to see details about moments in her future. It was as if she were on a plane beginning its descent through thick clouds. At first, there was nothing to see, then a glimpse, abstract and unformed, of fields, a lake, with few details. Then more glimpses, maybe long enough to pick out a building, cars moving in queues, sunlight glinting on their roofs. A break in the clouds, and the aircraft banks, revealing the lights of the runway towards which, inexorably, the remainder of your flight will take you.

As George's research started to produce results, she saw that destination more clearly. And yet she continued.

TWELVE YEARS after moving to London, George got the break

that led her to Station. She had scaled down the hunt for a few years, making sure she had enough money to be truly independent and enough skill with a computer to write her own tailored search programs. She also made connections within the city's criminal underworld. Her abilities meant she could ensure the few people she contacted face-to-face were left with no memory of their meeting. But, as a wheel-chair user in a city that sometimes seemed designed to be an architectural obstacle course, her progress was frustrat-ingly slow.

George was a patient and determined woman, but she came close to giving up more than once.

She spent months trawling through the newsgroups and chatrooms springing up daily as the internet's reach spread in the first decade of the century. There was no shortage of information about The Deterrent, and plenty of speculation about his children. A superhero, a real superhero, as powerful and unlikely as any that had ever appeared in a comic book, had been part of British national life for two years. Follow that with the disappearance of the seven-foot flying man, and the internet was the perfect breeding ground for millions of pages of speculation. Most of it was wild, unfounded, or plain stupid.

George sifted through the stream of garbage. She built up a slim folder of comments, news items, and correspon-dence that slowly led her to four carefully considered conclusions.

1) The Deterrent was not a product of a secret genetic engineering project. A quarter of a century after his disap-pearance, cutting-edge science was still nowhere near that level of sophistication. Sticking an ear on a mouse was hardly in the same league. The Deterrent's actual origins

had been concealed behind a smokescreen of national security.

2) He hadn't died in 1981. Despite the day of national mourning a year later, there was too much circumstantial evidence suggesting that the military had continued searching for The Deterrent. The British government believed he was still alive.

3) Of the children left behind, a documented thirty-seven had died at puberty. Messily. An elaborate and expensive investigation by a talented computer hacker had provided photographs and post-mortem reports. Whatever power had kicked in was, in most cases, too much for their human bodies. But, since no one knew how many pregnancies could be attributed to the promiscuous superhero, there must be other children. Some of whom might have survived. Which led her to

4) Me. Daniel Harbin. The lurid tabloid accounts of Mandy Harbin's encounters with her super-lover were a matter of public record, as was the disappearance of her only son at seventeen. Combined with the rumours of a supersoldier during the years following, the circumstantial evidence was compelling.

I was George's most promising lead. She was convinced I was out there somewhere, and she suspected I had been picked up by the same government department responsible for my father.

She didn't want to draw any more attention to herself than necessary. With the help of the country's top forger, George constructed a fictitious personal history, leaving a paper trail, and altering online databases. By the time she was ready to emerge from the shadows, she was Georgina Carlton-Marshall, orphaned heiress to a Zimbabwean property magnate.

In 2011, she made more overt enquiries about The Deterrent and his children. She emailed government departments, wrote letters, telephoned and, on a few occasions, presented herself at the British army press office, asking to speak to anyone who had been directly involved with the superhero.

She was variously ignored, fobbed off, or handed information already in the public domain. George increased the frequency of her calls, getting exasperated at how long it took for someone to respond to her persistency.

Finally, someone, somewhere, started to pay a little attention and an automatic email alerted her to the fact that her forged records had been accessed online.

A few days later, she received an invitation from a Major Harris.

Ushered into a Whitehall office the following week, George found herself opposite a middle-aged woman who had met The Deterrent. The Major answered her questions in such a helpful way, while simultaneously avoiding giving her any information, that George wondered why Harris hadn't ended up in politics.

Then the Major asked questions of her own. George had noticed the security cameras on the way in. She knew she was being recorded. And, from the impressions she had already gathered from Harris's mind, she knew the date of birth she had chosen for Georgina Carlton-Marshall's birth certificate—only a month earlier than her own—had been identified as a point of interest. She fell neatly into the age bracket that made her a possible child of The Deterrent. They'd wanted to get a good look at her. She wondered if her wasted body had disappointed them. Harris had certainly already dismissed her, but she knew now that the Major was just a pawn in the game.

By this time, George was well practised in engaging with people on two levels. She could hold a conversation while probing a mind.

Major Harris was a disappointed woman. Far from rising through the ranks as expected, an early clash with a senior officer left a blemish on her record she'd never been able to expunge.

As George sifted Harris's memories, she saw The Deterrent—her father—for the first time, through this woman's eyes. Harris had taken him out of...a station?...to a park where he had saved a man from being run over. George remembered the story from her own research. It was an early, unofficial sighting reported in a London paper. Now she knew it had happened on Harris's watch, which was why, thirty years later, she was a major, rather than, as she had hoped, a general.

To George's mounting excitement, she found three names still clear in Harris's memories from that time. One of them, a Professor McKean, was long dead. The other two were far more intriguing. Colonel Hopkins had been the superior officer who had, in Harris's eyes, ruined her career. The last name, along with some clear memories, was half familiar to George. The surname had come up again and again in her research and was filed in the *deceased* folder along with McKean and a handful of others. But the Christian name was different.

Who was Cressida Lofthouse?

34

Cressida

February 13th, 1981

The Deterrent's office finally softened its approach to PR and let a journalist from the New Musical Express meet Abos. I guess they're worried The Deterrent is not as popular with the younger generation as the old. Daily Mail readers love him - a big, white man with a Union Jack on his head, how could they not? The left-leaning papers are a little less enthusiastic, but they still praise the amazing work he has done, the lives he has saved.

I doubt Carstairs and his cronies care a jot if Abos is popular with anyone, but since their golden boy is officially sanctioned by the British government, his public image may be more of a concern to those whose jobs might go at the next general election.

My personal theory about the NME piece is that it's a reaction to the appearance, late last year, of The Detergent, a punk band from North London, who had a Christmas number one with Cleaning Up Crime (With My Pants On The Outside).

So maybe The Deterrent's PR people want to make sure Abos is perceived as 'cool', rather than a superpowered figure of fun.

Whatever their reasons, they let Tony Moorhill, a self-confessed 'cocaine socialist' (whatever that is) accompany Abos on a carefully stage-managed visit to a sixth-form college in Ipswich. A month ago, a building had collapsed, trapping a teacher and six students. The Deterrent had cleared tonnes of rubble and lifted a pre-fab classroom to let them out. It had looked great on TV as the dusty figures emerged into the light. As usual, selected members of the press were there to cover it.

The day with the NME journalist didn't go quite to plan. Makes for fascinating reading. Particularly because I think Abos mentions me. And it gives me hope. Perhaps Station's hold over him is not as secure as it was. That description right at the end...it gave me goosebumps.

UNDETERRED: TONY MOORHILL MEETS THE MOST TALKED ABOUT MAN IN HISTORY

A seven-foot question mark with no answer. That's The Deterrent. Like most of you, I first saw him back in October 1979, dropped my vodka onto the carpet and shouted, "What the f— is that?" at my TV. The whole thing was too bizarre to be a hoax, but, really? A giant flying soldier who can trash tanks with telekinesis?

Since then, I've watched him stop robberies, put out fires, and rescue victims of a pile-up on the M1 by peeling back car roofs with his bare hands. Fires, explosions, train wrecks, landslides, fallen trees, he's always there for the photo op. Last week, in the 'And Finally' bit of the news, he rescued a dog from a river. A seriously cute dog. He returned her to her owner, a seriously cute little girl with pigtails who cried when she was reunited with little Fido. Aaaaaaah. Seriously?

Anyone else starting to get the feeling we're being manipulated? Just a teeny tiny bit? Injustice, racism, sexism, and poverty are still rife. Our 'ruling classes' continue to ignore our pain because they're doing very nicely, thank you. Very nicely indeed. (They forget that they'll be just as dead as you and me when the nuclear holocaust levels their mansions and turns their Bentleys into lumps of charcoal. I digress) But, hey, just as it seems the seething masses might get pissed off enough to take action, a 'superhero' appears, everyone screams, 'ooooh' and everything else fades into insignificance.

Have you looked at the newspapers lately? Can you remember a day when The Deterrent didn't get a mention? One single day? I'll save you the trouble: it didn't happen.

Thatcher halves benefit payments to striking steelworkers; who cares? Look at this picture of The Deterrent lifting an ambulance out of a traffic jam.

American nuclear missiles to be housed in Berkshire and Cambridgeshire? Forget about it, look over here, where our home-grown superhero has played a charity cricket game and hit the ball into orbit!

What did the papers lead with today? Dead civil rights activist? Industrial action planned on the railways? Or flying man joins the Red Arrows for a display? I'm not giving you three guesses.

So when I was offered exclusive access to The Distraction, sorry, The Deterrent for a day, I jumped at the chance.

I wasn't given any info up front, just told to be at Liverpool Street Station at seven last Saturday morning. My protests that there was only one seven o'clock in the day for me, so couldn't we make it, say, noon, fell on deaf ears.

I want you to know that I took this assignment very seriously. The first journalist to interview the big man! I was determined to be professional, prepared and clear-headed. But then Mordo from the Bombs called me that Friday night and invited me to a party. A party. With Mordo. From the Bombs! Obviously, it would have been extremely unprofessional of me to even think about going.

Six hours later, by standing in the middle of the road and waving wads of tenners in the air, I made a cab stop for me. Unfortunately, I had forgotten my address. But I did remember I was supposed to go to Liverpool Street. I arrived before dawn and attempted to sleep off an unlikely amount of drugs and alcohol on a passing bench. A copper shook me awake at six-thirty. I made a beeline to the nearest bog and shoved some wake-up powder up my nose.

I checked my reflection. Unshaven, hair sticking up everywhere, bloodshot eyes with pupils like pinpricks. Perfect. I breathed into my hand. After gagging for a moment, I fished a can of deodorant out of my bag and sprayed my entire body, then necked a whole packet of polos.

Good to go.

After being mistaken for a tramp, which wasn't the best start, I was escorted onto a platform by The Deterrent's assistants, a couple of charmless chumps called Tomkins and Smith. Or Smithkins and Thompson. Tomcat and Smeg. Whatever. They didn't like me, I didn't like them.

They stuck me into a first-class carriage (I took one for the team, comrades, and I want you to know that I didn't even so much as glance at the free biscuits), stuck a black coffee in my hand, and directed me to the seats at the far end. Not that I needed directions. Hard to miss a seven-foot man squeezed into a British Rail seat. Two middle-aged, scary-looking stuffed shirts in army uniforms were sitting at a nearby table, watching me. I waved cheerily at them.

I eased into the seat opposite The Deterrent and wondered why a man who can fly was taking the train to Ipswich.

"Why would a man who can fly take a train to Ipswich?" I said.

"Flying is tiring," he said. "And I like the train. It means I can travel with my colleagues." I looked at the sinister blokes in the seats opposite and looked over my shoulder at Smithy and Tonka.

"That's nice," I said.

Up close, he's quite something. I wasn't sure what to call him at first - Powerman is definitely out, although they seem to have quietly dropped that idea anyway. The Deterrent is a mouthful and sounds ridiculous in conversation. He admitted he has a name, but wouldn't share it. I suggested TD, and he was happy enough with that.

He is bloody massive. I know you've all seen pictures. Some of you might even have seen him at one of his press calls. But you've never sat opposite him. He's intimidatingly large. His head is enormous, but it has to be, otherwise it would look stupid sitting on that huge neck leading to those oversized shoulders. I'm all out of adjectives. He makes normal people look like little kids in comparison.

He wasn't wearing the stupid helmet. Before you get excited and want details ("TD shook his mass of blonde curls, and winked, his eyes the piercing blue of a movie star."), I should tell you he was wearing a bandana. Plain black, covered his hair. I can't help you. If I had to guess, judging from the hairs on the nape of his neck (swoon), I'd say dirty blonde. He was wearing dark sunglasses, but I interview musicians for a living, so I'm used to that.

We talked for about ten minutes before he said he needed a nap. And he actually used the word 'nap,' too. My granddad used to have a nap. And my nan. Cats nap. Since when do superheroes nap? I should have asked him about that, I suppose, but—between you and me—I was bloody delighted to get my head down myself.

Next thing I know, we're at Ipswich, and the platform was lined with people hoping for a glimpse of the big lad. He was wearing the goggles and helmet now. He got off the train and was instantly mobbed, men shaking his hand, women hugging him, people passing him flowers, choco-lates, books, babies - as if he were a cross between a rock star and the pope.

The rest of us disembarked and elbowed our way through the crush while TD was posing for photos and signing breasts. I saw one of his lackeys nearby.

"He'll be there all bloody day," I said. He shook his head and pointed. I looked back, and TD was flying over the station building towards us. He landed by the college minibus, and we all got on board.

All right. I admit it. The flying thing is impressive. I've listened to scientists try to explain it on TV, I've read through, skimmed—okay, glanced at—the articles with theories about how he does it. They all say something differ-ent. No one has a clue really. I will say this: it's bloody cool. The man has style.

"What do you think about the adulation?" I asked. TD

had to stand - none of the minibus seats could accommodate him.

He looked blankly at me. Then something unexpected happened. Thommo or Smippy leaned across and said, "What do you think about all these people liking you so much?"

TD had blanked at the word 'adulation.'

So, I've discovered his weakness. Every superhero is supposed to have one. Well, The Deterrent's weakness is a limited vocabulary. Apologies to any supervillain reading this paragraph with mounting excitement, hoping he could eliminate his nemesis and take over the world. Nah, you're not going to do it by hitting him over the head with a dictionary. Sorry, buddy.

It's interesting, though. Hard to judge TD's age with any accuracy, and that's one of the questions he wouldn't answer, but he looks anywhere between mid-twenties and mid-forties. But he doesn't know the meaning of 'adulation.'
 In the interests of research, and not because I was taking the piss or anything, I threw in a few long words during that journey and was rewarded with that blank look for most of them. I got in 'supercilious,' 'credulity,' 'Machiavellian,' and 'purview,' but Thomlinson and Smedly threatened to stop the bus and throw me off by the time I got to 'discombobulation.'

Perhaps TD's not that bright, and his entourage are there to cover for him. He wouldn't be the first amazing physical specimen to have found himself at the back of the queue when they were handing out brains.Somehow, though, I don't think that's it. TD seems intelligent. Slow, yes, careful with his words, but not thick. There's something else going on, and it wasn't until I finally got home and wrote this up that I realised what it was.

I'll tell you later.

The visit to the college was utterly devoid of any interest. TD had his photo taken with the principal and some of the students he'd rescued. Don't get me wrong, he did an amazing thing, but ceremonies bore me. I've been thrown out of four weddings when I tried to liven them up. I dutifully kept my mouth shut this time, as TD lifted a massive stone with his bare hands and laid it on the spot where the foundations for The Deterrent wing are due to be started next week. I didn't know whether to yawn or puke.

It was just as the polite applause was dying away that the day got interesting. One of the stuffed shirts from the train hurried over to TD and showed him a message on his pager. They hurried into the college in search of a phone. I gave them a few seconds, then followed.

When I got close to the office they were using, the army bloke was on the phone. I couldn't quite make out what he was saying, but he saved me the trouble by summarising it for TD.

"Single Anchor Leg Mooring System, seven miles off the coast, east of Lowestoft. There's a diving bell conducting repairs. Two men trapped underwater - the winch is snagged. They have about three hours before they run out of air but hypothermia—exposure to cold which will cause their bodies to shut down—could become life-threatening within the next hour."

As he spoke, they all came out of the office and hurried back out, paying no attention to me. As I burst through the front door, the army bloke was giving TD coordinates. TD looked ready to go.

"Wait!" I shouted. "The interview. I was promised the whole morning."

That was when something unexpected happened. I

didn't anticipate it, and the entourage was totally gobsmacked.

TD nodded, took three huge strides over to me, wrapped a massive arm around my waist and picked me up.

"Close your eyes," he said. I don't know about you, but when a seven-foot bloke wider than my freezer who can crush steel just by thinking about it tells me to close my eyes, I close my eyes.

I didn't know what had happened until I heard the word, "no" being shouted. It sounded a fair distance away. And it was coming from below.

I opened my eyes and looked down past my dangling trainers. The college was far below, the people around it tiny specks.

If it hadn't been for the fact that I hadn't eaten, an embarrassing incident might have occurred in my underpants. Instead of which, I passed out.

I couldn't have been out long, because when I looked again, we were still flying over land, a yellow ribbon of beach below us as TD followed the coastline north.

I made a quick mental deal with myself to treat the entire episode as if it were a trip brought on by something slipped into my drink at Mordo's party. Everything was easier after that. I even managed a friendly nod at a passing seagull.

I was bloody glad of my trench coat. It was freezing up there. I risked releasing one of my hands from the death grip I had taken on TD's forearm, which was wrapped around my chest. I dug into my bag and found another journalistic essential: the woolly hat. I jammed it on my noggin with one hand, saving my ears from falling off from frostbite.

Within a few more minutes, we were descending

towards a red-hulled ship. I'm no nautical expert, so if you want to know all the details, go and read the newspaper reports. It was big, red, it floated, and it had lots of machinery on it, and hefty bearded men who wore Arran jumpers un-ironically.

At the blunt end of the boat, there was a winch carrying a metal cable thicker than my arm. It had been pulled back in, and I could see the frayed end where it had snapped, leaving two poor bastards in a metal ball five hundred feet below us.

TD didn't waste any time, just set me down and talked briefly to the bigger, most bearded man of all. Beardy was evidently a Scot.

"The umbilical cord connecting them to the ship has been completely torn away. We tried to winch them to the surface, but the winch must have snagged on the same point as the umbilical. Can ye reach them, man? If ye cannae, they're doomed."

In the interests of journalistic integrity, I admit that he didn't actually say that last bit. It's just that he sounded just like Private Frazer in Dad's Army. Sorry.

TD took three long, loping strides to the side before throwing himself overboard. There was a splash, then silence.

The big, bearded man looked at me. I looked at him and sniffed. I wondered how hard it would be to chop a line of coke in the bog if the ship kept moving around this much.

"Tony Moorhill, NME," I said. "Watcha." Then I threw up on his wellies.

Beardy and his slightly shorter colleagues sorted me out a tin cup of water while they ran about doing boaty things, shouting into radios, and looking at a sonar screen, which made bleeping noises just like in the movies. It was all very tense, I suppose, but I was mostly concentrating on not puking again.

The bloke standing by the sonar screen suddenly made a funny noise, halfway between a gasp and a choke. He was jabbing at the screen while making noises like a sexually aroused seal. Don't ask me how I know what that sounds like.

The 'bippy' blob on the screen was moving, and the bips were getting louder and higher in pitch. All right, I'll move on. Like I said, read the newspaper reports if you want the factual stuff.

Everyone ran onto the deck. I joined them at the rail where they were watching the grey, rolling water, despite how boring and potentially puke-inducing that promised to be.

The top of the diving bell breached the surface. To my surprise, it looked similar to the way I'd pictured it - a white sphere with portholes. It was contained within a metal cage which supported it and, as became clear moments later, allowed it to sit upright on a flat surface. It carried on rising as if an invisible winch was in operation.

We all variously gasped, swore, or screamed like a girl (it was exciting, all right? don't judge) when TD appeared underneath, lifting the entire structure into the air. He didn't waste any time posing, which was a good job as I'd forgotten I was supposed to bring a photographer. He placed the diving bell in the middle of the deck and stood aside.

There was a second where everyone looked at him, then all the bearded ones, large and small, ran to the bell and started unscrewing things and twisting valves. Soon, they were reaching inside and scooping out what initially looked like giant caterpillars. I moved closer and saw they were the two divers, tucked into some kind of special thermal sleeping bag. They were both talking and seemed okay. They had beards, too.

Later, I found out they had been rescued before hypothermia had set in, and they made a full recovery. Ta-da.

I moved back to the rail and hung on. Now that the drama was over, the constant motion of the sea was again making itself known to what was left of the contents of my stomach.

I hate the sodding sea.

"What's wrong?"

TD was at my side, dry as a bone. Clever trick. I realised that this was the first question he had asked me all morning. It made him seem, for a moment, normal. Almost.

"Seasickness," I said, and gave him a practical demonstration.

"The helicopter will be here in about thirty minutes," he said. I responded with a dry heave.

He looked at me for a few seconds saying nothing. Hard to read someone when you can't see their eyes, but I think he was making a decision.

"Come with me," he said, and picked me up again. Flying without the comforting surroundings of a plane with, well, actual wings and an engine, is terrifying, but I felt so much better once we'd left the see-sawing ship that I could have kissed him.

He saluted the beards, and they cheered back at him. I hate the salute. I know it's a trademark, but its quasi-military nature is one reason I've never bought into Deterrent-mania. Makes my skin crawl.

We flew over a stony beach on the east coast, then up to a cliff top where he set me down. Outside a pub. Good work.

"Pint?" I said.

There were only half a dozen punters in there. They variously spat out their pints, dropped cutlery or coughed up pieces of scampi.

"Two Adnams." The barman took it all in his stride.

I didn't know how long we would have until the rest of the gang joined us, so, once he'd sunk the first pint and I'd ordered another round, I tried talking to him properly.

It was a fascinating, if frustratingly short, conversation. In my defence, I would definitely have bought him an orange juice if I'd known this was his first experience of alcohol. Scout's honour.

He dozed off after about ten minutes. The helicopter arrived five minutes after that. I was shouted at, accused of gutter journalism and left to find my own way home after they'd carried the big fellow out.

It was only after I had started on a plate of chips that I realised I didn't have a clue where I was.

Lowestoft.

Took me three and a half hours to get home.

Here's our conversation in full. I've edited out the long silences. He doesn't rush his answers. I felt like he was in there somewhere, lost in the fog. The booze made him talk more, but it definitely confused him.

TONY: TD, you're a good-looking bloke. Is there a girlfriend in the picture? Or a boyfriend? You've got all these powers, I assume you can work wonders in the sack, right?

TD: The sack?

TONY: Bed. In bed.

TD: Bed? Sleep?

TONY: Sex, mate, sex. Are you getting some? You'd bloody better be, I mean, if you can't score, what chance do the rest of us have?

TD: Oh. Treats?

TONY: Treats? What do you mean?

TD: Are you married?

TONY: Me? No, mate. Maybe one day. Who knows?

TD: Peter and Jane have a mummy and daddy. They are married.

TONY: Peter and who? Are you talking about your parents?

TD: I saw her room.

TONY: Who? Whose room?

(THIS WAS the longest pause in the conversation. I gave up in the end and changed the subject.)

TONY: Where are you from?

TD: (slurring a little, hard to make out): Before...not...station...station

TONY: The station? That's where I met you today. But where do you come from? You mentioned Mum and Dad. Do they have powers too?

TD: Tony?

TONY: Yes, TD?

TD: Are you happy?

TONY: God, no. Bloody hell. Are you sure you're British? We don't ask each other questions like that. All right, all right. I'll tell you the truth. Sometimes I'm happy. Sometimes I'm sad. On balance, I'm probably sad more often than

I'm happy. It's called the human condition. What about you? Are you happy?

TD: No. No. I am not happy, Tony.

TONY: Why not?

AFTER ANOTHER LONG SILENCE, he started snoring softly. I was wondering what the hell to do when I heard the helicopter. Minutes later, I was alone with my chips, waiting for a taxi to the station.

And that was the end of my day with TD. Was he referring to sex as 'treats?' Whose room was he talking about? And why isn't he happy? Your guess is as good as mine. My advice? Buy him a beer and see if you can get clearer answers. Say hi from me.

I promised to share my theory about the big chap. I liked him, despite deciding in advance that I wasn't going to. And I know why I liked him. Because no one can resist a child. And that's what I think he is. Underneath all those super muscles and power, he struck me as a kid. And not a very happy one.

If I'm right, and I am of course, then that raises a number of questions. I'll leave you with one. The one I think about in the middle of the night.

What happens when he grows up?

35

Cressida

April 12th, 1981

Friday evening and all yesterday, there was unrest in Brixton. Last night, it became a riot. I watched the events unfold from the comfort of our living room, but even subdued lighting and soft furnishings couldn't diminish the shock of seeing such rage and violence boiling over a few miles away.

Father took himself off to his office to work, but I kept watching. A reporter—keeping a careful distance from the rioters—read out a government statement reassuring the public that The Deterrent would help "uphold the law and restore order," but that's not what happened.

That's when I saw him.

The police ranks parted like the Red Sea as he walked through to the front line, where officers in riot gear, carrying plastic shields, were trying to hold their ground.

The crowd stopped throwing bricks when Abos walked out in front of them. He stood between the opposing sides, silhouetted in front of a burning car, the flames reflected in those dark goggles.

Someone shouted, "Whose side are you on, white boy?" Abos said nothing. He looked back at the police, then turned towards the mob again, scanning their faces. Abruptly, I felt as if I was seeing the scene as he was: an organised and trained police presence, uniformed and predominantly white-skinned, facing off a disorganised crowd full of passion and anger, mostly dark-skinned. He stood there, and he did nothing.

Finally, someone lobbed a bottle at him, which bounced off his chest, and that seemed to act as a catalyst. Seconds later, the air was thick with flying objects, most of them aimed at Abos. The howl of rage from the crowd was terrifying as they rushed him.

The police hung back and left him to face them alone.

The rioters hit him with their fists, and with baseball bats and broken bottles. Their anger was like a living force, making the crowd a roiling mass of rage. They saw The Deterrent as a symbol of authority, and authority had betrayed them. They accused the police of targeting black men, stopping and searching them because of their race. I'm ashamed that I hadn't known about any of this until it erupted in violence. How could this situation have reached such a crisis without me knowing anything about it? I'd read a couple of newspaper articles suggesting government policy was encouraging institutional racism, but the government is always being blamed for one thing or another, isn't it?

Abos let them hit him. He stood there and took it. He

only acted when someone doused him with a petrol can and set him alight.

He rose into the air, the flames spreading quickly. Two men who had hung onto him dropped away, one clutching his boots for a second, then screaming as he fell and hit the street.

The camera followed Abos as far as it could, a flaming beacon heading for the Thames.

I waited for more information, but none came. Finally, I went to bed. I know he can't be hurt, but why did he just stand there?

I lay awake, thinking about him, feeling useless. Abos has never been far from my thoughts since the day he opened his eyes, but since reading that article, I haven't been able to get the idea out of my mind that he misses me too. That it could only be me he was talking about when he said, "I saw her room."

Eventually, through sheer exhaustion, I slept.

I woke an hour later. Something had disturbed me, but I didn't know what. I had fallen asleep outside the covers with the bedside light on, this diary with its glued-in NME article in my hand.

I turned off the light. Then, for no reason I can explain, I walked to the window and opened the curtains.

Abos was there, floating outside, looking at me. His trousers were burned, as was one side of his green jumper, but the flesh beneath was unmarked. He held his goggles and helmet in his right hand.

I looked back at him, hardly daring to breathe.

We stayed that way for what seemed like hours, but was, in fact, seven minutes according to my clock.

He didn't smile, he just looked at me. There was soot on

his face and his charred clothing had been torn by knives and broken bottles.

I started to open my window. As if waking from a dream, he looked around, then back at me, before shooting upwards so fast it was if he vanished.

When the tears had dried on my face, I went back to bed.

36

Daniel

GEORGE ORDERED afternoon tea for us in the suite. Whatever the staff thought was going on with this profligate woman and her bodyguard, they were far too discreet to even raise an eyebrow.

It had taken George all day to tell her story. Just before the tea arrived, she produced an old journal, placing it in my hands.

I opened it. A photograph fell out and fluttered to the carpet. I picked it up. It was black and white, a man in his fifties and a younger woman. She was striking, giving the camera a frank, direct and intelligent smile. The man looked more guarded and serious.

"Cressida and her father," said George.

I turned the photograph over. There was writing on the back.

September 1st, 1969. Our first day working together!

I tucked the photograph back and turned the page.

George shook her head.

"Uh-uh. Tea first and I'll tell you how that came into my possession. Then I'll go down to the lobby bar, where I shall sip dry sherry and enjoy the pianist's repertoire of popular show tunes. A few hours should give you enough time to read Cressida's diary. It's a lot to take in, so don't rush. When I come back, you'll know almost as much about our father as I do. We'll get a good night's rest, then tomorrow I'll tell you what I've been planning, what I've stolen from Station, and how we can destroy that god-forsaken hellhole once and for all."

It sounded good to me.

GEORGE TOLD me she knew her visit to Harris would set wheels in motion. Within twenty-four hours, thorough checks were made on her fabricated personal history. She wanted the extra attention. It was all part of her plan. If she could infiltrate the organisation who had worked with The Deterrent, she hoped to find out the truth about me, and any others like us.

And she could steal three decades of information gathered during the hunt for The Deterrent.

Harris's mind had given her the break she needed, possibly a shortcut. Now, she had to find Cressida Lofthouse.

37

Cressida

November 22nd, 1991

After Brixton, I saw Abos once more. Ten years ago. Ten years ago tonight.

This is the first time I've even looked at this diary since then. I brought the bottle of J&B upstairs, prised up the floorboard under the rug, brushed the dust (and three dessicated spiders) off the box, poured my first glass and started reading.

Now I'm a little tipsy. And sad.

If anyone ever reads this and blows the whistle, there'll be such a scandal. I'd love to see Hopkins' and Carstairs' faces. It almost certainly won't be during my lifetime, unfortunately, so I doubt they will be around to face the consequences.

Every year, I think about what happened, remember that night a decade ago, go over everything that was said and done.

Afterwards, no one ever saw Abos again.

The official story is that he disappeared in the storms. Missing, presumed dead, was how the military spokesman put it. We've all seen that clip a hundred times.

And we've all read the articles and books, watched the documentaries, heard the radio shows. So many theories, some of them advanced so forcefully and plausibly that I find myself half-believing them. None of them anywhere near the truth.

I know it wasn't the storms. He's not dead.

I live here alone now, diary. Father died in his sleep six years ago. After Abos had gone, Station paid him for twelve months before pensioning him off and closing the department. Well, it wasn't closed completely. Mike Ainsleigh is still there. Some kind of research continues.

Roger went back to America, leaving his wife and child. McKean returned to Scotland, where he took a research post, only to drown in a fishing accident within six months.

As Father's next of kin, I have the house, a small government pension, and the savings he and Mother had built up. I have enough to get by. I don't work anymore, but I volunteer at the local library. A spinster librarian at forty-one!

I could be rather wealthy if I were paid royalties for the book based on my reports when I was at Station. When it was first published, in 1983, it was the fastest-selling book in history.

The Deterrent: The Inside Story Of Britain's Superhero, by HT Bowthorpe is a bestseller even now. As the only 'official' account written by someone attached to The Deterrent's scientific team (the mysterious HT Bowthorpe, whoever that is), it's considered the most accurate account of Britain's only superhero.

The whole thing is poppycock. A fabrication. A tissue of

lies. Like all good lies, it's partially based on the truth. Most of the descriptions of the inside of Station, the laboratory, and Abos himself, are lifted word for word from the notes I handed in every week to Hopkins. The location and name of the facility have been redacted, naturally.

When it comes to The Deterrent's origins, the book is one big red herring. The heavy hints about genetic research leading to the development of a superwarrior? I suppose Hopkins thought it would be more believable than the truth. And I doubt the British government wants anyone to know that they found their superhero lying around in the middle of London. They want every other nation to believe, even now, that we might create an army of Deterrents to replace Abos. After ten years, I wonder if anyone is still falling for that.

This is the story told by HT Bowthorpe.

In 1976, a British soldier, badly wounded in an explosion, was flown to a secret facility where new genetic and bio-mechanical techniques had been developed after the Second World War. The brightest and best scientists from the country had come up with ways of enhancing physical strength and mental capabilities but the techniques were unproven and potentially dangerous. They had not yet reached the stage where they would be prepared to test anything on humans. The dying soldier's arrival, an individual with no family, gave them that opportunity. Without their intervention, without attempting to use a combination of these untested procedures, the man would die.

They operated. The description of the operation lasts a whole chapter in the book which is impressive since it never happened. The book is written for the general public, so scientists studying it hoping to find a hint of how the human brain might be rewired to enable it to move objects as big as

Challenger tanks must have been disappointed. It was full of meaningless twaddle such as,

"The chief surgeon, after twenty-eight hours without rest, faced surely the most delicate procedure ever attempted on a human brain. Doctor G needed to manipulate synaptic receptors in such a way that they could forge new, unique connections between parts of the brain that had previously been unable to communicate with each other. Epigenetic creation is still a field which remains unknown outside the secret labs of the Miltech team."

Synaptic receptors? Epigenetic creation? Drivel and tosh. Miltech is a fantasy, too, doesn't exist. Still, on the face of it, a hidden rural laboratory seems more plausible than an underground complex so close to the Liverpool Street Underground that, in some of its corridors, you can put your hand on the walls and feel the vibrations of the tube trains as they pass.

The rest of the book is mostly nonsense. National security is invoked on page one. Details have been changed, locations moved, real names concealed, blah blah blah. Hilarious, really, as that means everything that follows could be fiction. Which, for the main part, it is. The patriotic jingoism really got my goat, I must admit. The Deterrent of the book is such a bore once he starts talking, full of awful soundbites about queen and country. I skimmed those parts.

They used my notes about teaching sessions almost verbatim although there's an extra chapter detailing the months when he couldn't yet speak at all. Their fictional injured soldier suffered such extensive brain damage that he needed to learn to talk again. I (or rather HT Bowthorpe) gradually drew out his latent abilities over the course of about sixty pages, introducing him to the Peter and Jane books and taking him out for occasional walks. It's all very heart-warming.

The bulk of the book is a celebration of all the amazing feats performed by The Deterrent between October sixth, nineteen seventy-nine and November twenty-first, nineteen eighty-one. Most of these are in the public domain already, but the book adds little details and tedious quotes from The Deterrent. "I was proud to lend a hand to the air force and locate the terrorist group which was violently opposed to our entire way of life. After eliminating the threat, we celebrated with a flask of tea. A taste of home out in the desert!"

Only one sentence about the Brixton riots. "I helped police control the rioters and looters before being called away by MI5 to deal with a far more dangerous situation which, even now, I cannot reveal."

Hmm. As far as memory serves, the "far more dangerous situation" in question involved Abos hovering outside my bedroom window. I can see why MI5 wouldn't want to reveal that.

As for the events of November twenty-third, nineteen eighty-one, the last, comparatively short, chapter covers that. A well-documented night of freak weather provided Station with enough of a smokescreen to suggest why no one has seen The Deterrent since that night.

In a five-hour period, the United Kingdom was hit by the highest amount of tornadoes ever experienced by a European country. None of them were particularly strong, but, during the evening, the middle of the country, from North Wales across to Norfolk was visited by a hundred and five reported tornadoes.

As this is a matter of public record, it's easy enough for the book to hint that such a freak occurrence in our national weather system may not have been entirely natural.

According to the book, The Deterrent left London at seven pm to investigate the tornado reports. He flew north-east to Norfolk, where the highest confluence of storms had been reported. He never returned.

Bowthorpe leaves it to the reader to extrapolate. In the years following The Deterrent's disappearance, a deluge of books and magazine articles, plus Hollywood's various attempts to tell the story, have advanced many fantastical theories. All choose between the same three possibilities. The Deterrent is either:

1) dead
2) held by persons unknown, or
3) intentionally missing

2) is surprisingly popular, considering the fact that Abos has superpowers. If a group out there had the wherewithal to defeat him, surely the world would have heard more from them since.

The books suggesting alien intervention sell remarkably well.

1) and 3) are the only options that make any kind of sense, really.

According to the book, the last person to see The Deterrent alive was one Corporal Evan Todd. Corporal Todd had this to say.

"He told me he would be back by nine-thirty, as some of the boys were showing The Great Escape in the Mess, and it was one of his favourite films. He was in good spirits. Positive, motivated, full of energy, as always. We exchanged salutes at the door, then he took off. I watched him go. I never got tired of watching that. Seeing a man fly. Incredible. When he didn't come back for the film, I knew something was wrong. We still haven't got over it, any of the squad, we're all gutted. I still can't believe I'm the last person who ever saw that fine soldier alive."

That's because you're not, Todd. I am. And, trust me, he wasn't planning on going anywhere near any hurricanes. What actually happened was far stranger, far more disturbing than that.

And far sadder.

I SUPPOSE part of the reason it's taken me ten years to write about that night is because it nearly ruined my feelings about Abos forever. I took a long time to even start thinking about what happened. And it wasn't as if I could speak to anyone.

I don't want to go into detail about everything, even now. I know it's supposed to be cathartic, that we're supposed to face our traumatic memories in the interests of good mental health. I've read the books. But, at heart, I'm an old-fashioned kind of girl. Some things are better left locked away.

This account will be the only time I'll look back fully. I'll make myself remember everything that happened, even if I won't share all of it. Not even with you, dear diary.

There's one last reason I've hesitated to write what I'm about to write. If...*when* this diary finally comes to light, it will confirm the truth of a particularly lurid thread of newspaper stories that dogged The Deterrent. Stories that were ignored by some papers, but that proved irresistible to the tabloids. I'm sure most people dismissed them as nonsense, given the clean-cut, old-fashionedly gallant image always enjoyed by Abos.

I remember the first story clearly. It was on the A-board outside my local newsagent early in nineteen eighty.

MY SUPER-SEX SESSION WITH THE DETERRENT

I walked into the shop in a daze and bought the paper, sitting in a coffee shop to read it. Large photographs of the 'lady' in question dominated the story. Mandy Harbin was pictured in various stages of undress, doing her best to imitate the pouty models who appeared on other pages of the same rag.

Her story seemed to be nothing more than a transparent attempt by a busty young girl with no prospects to make money and perhaps launch a career at the sordid end of the modelling business.

Ms Harbin claimed that The Deterrent had singled her out while signing autographs after rescuing a crane operator from almost certain death. A photograph reprinted in the paper, clearly shows Mandy Harbin holding out her arm for Abos to sign. They had met. There was no doubt about that. The part of the story that stretched credulity was the subsequent late-night visit to her maisonette (she claimed to have whispered her address to him), where they, in her words, "made love first on the bed, then in the shower, then on the stairs. It was romantic."

The bed, the shower...and the stairs. Romantic indeed.

I remember stuffing the paper into the first bin I saw. It never occurred to me that there might be even a grain of truth in it.

Even when other women came forward, I refused to believe it. Their stories were remarkably similar - The Deterrent had visited them at night after he had met them at one event or another. Some of the women took the same

route as Ms Harbin, appearing in tabloids in their underwear, but others kept their clothes on, perhaps in an attempt
to seem more credible. None of them had witnesses to
collaborate their stories. Apparently, this seven-foot man
could get into their bedrooms without being seen by a single
neighbour. One memorable claim came from a student who
lived in a house shared with five others, none of whom saw
anything.

Since the main newspaper printing the stories (which I
still can't bring myself to name) was offering cash for
women to come forward, The Deterrent's press office didn't
even bother responding to them. But the claims didn't
go away.

SUPERSTUD KNOCKED ME UP!

SUPERBABY DUE IN SEPTEMBER

EVEN THE PILL COULDN'T STOP HIM!

The paper followed her through each trimester to its
inevitable conclusion. In September, we were treated to the
sight of a bonny baby in the arms of a proud-looking
Mandy. A healthy, completely normal baby. The press
looked in on her now and then in the years following, but,
in the absence of pictures of the toddler flying around the
house or lifting cars over his head, they lost interest. Mandy
gradually disappeared from the magazines and the chat
shows, as did the other women who had claimed The Deterrent to be the father of their children.

It all looked like a publicity stunt by the gutter press,
involving the exploitation of some desperate women.

Never, not even for a moment, did I suspect it was true.

Then Abos came to me.

I've sipped too much whisky writing this. I'll continue
tomorrow with a clearer head.

38

November 23rd, 1991

That's better. It's wonderful the positive effect a bowl of porridge and a strong cup of Assam can have.

No more prevarication, Cress. Today marks the tenth anniversary of the last time I saw him.

I imagine a lot of people remember that night for another reason: the unnatural weather. London was expecting a few of the freak tornadoes, so I had decided on an early night with a good book and a mug of cocoa. There's nothing better than curling up in a warm bed while a storm rages outside.

I must have fallen asleep while reading because when I woke up just after midnight, the book was in my hand and my bedside light was still on. I went to the bathroom and cleaned my teeth. As I was about to get into bed, I had the same feeling I'd had that night in April, the night of the Brixton riot. I stood still for a few moments and convinced myself I was being silly. I got into bed and turned out the light.

I lay there with my eyes open and my heart thumping. Then I got up again, crossed the room and, before I could think too hard about what I was doing, drew the curtains apart.

He was there.

Eventually, I opened the window.

"Hello, Cress." He looked like an angel floating there, his golden eyes turned silver by the moonlight. He smiled. A small, tentative smile.

"Hello, Abos." I didn't know what to say. If Station knew he was here, I was likely to spend the rest of my life locked up in an institution. But I couldn't send him away.

"Wait there," I said, "I'll let you in."

I went to close the window, intending to go to the back door. He stopped me, turned sideways and entered the room headfirst as I backed away in surprise.

Abos landed lightly on the carpet, his head close to the ceiling. I put out my hand. His smile deepened, and he shook it. I smiled, too, remembering how I had taught him this most British form of greeting.

"Cress, I—I have waited so long."

I took his hand again and held it, looking up at that face I remembered so well.

"I'm sorry, Abos. I was not allowed to see you."

"I know. Mr Carstairs said you were too busy. He said I could have other treats. He let me have lots. But I still asked for you. He got angry, and I had to stop asking. I pretended to forget you. That made him happy. But I didn't forget, Cress."

It was the longest speech I had ever heard from Abos. Much of it didn't make sense. Treats? And it seemed he wasn't just respectful, but afraid of Carstairs. Father's drugs had been used to place Abos in some sort of dependent relationship with that twisted man. I bristled at the idea and decided it was time to tell Abos the truth.

But what he did next stopped me.

He let go of my hand and pulled his jumper over his head. He was bare-chested beneath. I suddenly became very aware that I was only wearing a cotton nightie. He took my hand again and placed it on his chest. His solid, muscled chest. I swallowed hard.

"Abos, listen to me. The way Carstairs has been teaching you, the life you lead, it's not—"

I stopped speaking because Abos was kissing me. For half a second, I felt myself respond, a physical reaction to this beautiful man. But I, of all people, knew he was far from human. For most of a decade, I had watched scientists try to take readings and get samples from what looked like a large glass cylinder with some mouldy soup inside it. I had seen him change from his mushy pea state and become a superior copy of Roger. I had watched him learn our language and our ways, then seen how he was manipulated and controlled by the very people who should have been helping and supporting him.

There was no way I could let this happen. My body wanted to respond, but I knew it would be a huge mistake.

I put both hands on his chest and pushed him gently, but firmly, away. He took a small step back and looked at me.

"No," I said.

I looked into his eyes and saw something that scared me. I knew he had heard me, but it was if what I had said hadn't registered.

"No, Abos," I said, more loudly this time. I knew where

I'd seen that look before. It was the same look Roger had given me outside the pub that night. The same look Abos had given me in front of Carstairs that one, excruciating, occasion when he had stared at my body rather than my face. It was a look of pure sexual desire.

Abos reached forwards, took the top of my nightie in his hands and tore it in two. I stumbled backwards, naked, beginning to panic. He followed, picked me up and lay me on the bed. His hands were on my breasts, then he was climbing onto the bed next to me, undoing his belt.

He bent over me and kissed me again. He tried to kiss me with his mouth open, his tongue darting straight into my mouth. I'd been kissed like that just once before. At school. Behind, would you believe it, the bike sheds. The memory of that bit of adolescent fumbling came into any mind as Abos's knee forced my legs apart.

Something had just become very clear to me.

I slapped Abos as hard as I could across his face. He paused for a second and looked at me, the tiniest bit of confusion registering along with his lust.

"Abos, stop this! Do you care about me? Do you care about me at all?"

He pushed himself up and off me.

"Of course, Cress. Yes. You know I do."

"Then you must stop this. If you care about me, you need to stop and we need to talk."

He looked crestfallen. The glaze of lust faded, then disappeared as he looked at my expression and the way I was holding my arms across my breasts. I remembered his early lessons when he talked about the language of the body. If he was as good at reading it as he claimed, he could hardly miss the signs I was giving off now. He began doing up his belt.

I walked quickly to the door and put on my dressing gown, before sitting back on the bed. I patted the space next to me, still trembling with shock and adrenaline. I attempted to control my breathing and settle my mind. My own feelings about what had just happened could wait until later. Right now, I wanted to make a dent in Carstair's conditioning. I was determined to prevent Abos becoming a superpowered sexual predator. For the sake of women everywhere. And for his own sake.

"Put your clothes back on and sit down, Abos."

He did as he was told but still looked puzzled about what was happening. He had obviously been expecting me to respond positively to his sexual overtures and was confused by my adverse reaction.

An intuition came to me.

"Abos. These treats and rewards you mentioned. Are they women?"

He nodded without a hint of guile. "Yes. Mr Carstairs says I deserve a treat because I work so hard."

"So when you go on missions, how do you find these treats, these women? Does Mr Carstairs find them for you?"

He nodded. "Usually. Sometimes women ask me to visit them."

It wasn't hard to believe that women would throw themselves at him.

I tried to marshal my thoughts, wondering how long the drugs Carstairs administered were effective. According to the chart I'd seen, Abos took his 'vitamin mix' daily at eight am. It was now twenty-five minutes past midnight. Sixteen and a half hours since his last dose. Seven and a half until his next. If he still slept for four to six hours a night, it was possible that, this late, he might be more clear-headed. I couldn't hope to undo two and a half years of chemical and psychological interference, but I might sow a seed of doubt.

What actually happened was something I hadn't anticipated.

Abos happily admitted to having sex with hundreds of women. When I asked about Mandy Harbin's baby, he looked blank. A few more gentle questions, and it was clear that he didn't really understand that sexual intercourse could lead to pregnancy. In Mandy's case, if she was now to be believed, despite the fact that she was on the pill.

How many other women might he have impregnated if contraception couldn't stop him?

I moved the conversation on to consent. This was an utterly unfamiliar concept to Abos. In his opinion, every woman wanted to have sex with him. He had no doubt about it. All his experience had confirmed it. Then he admitted something that made my blood run cold. I wasn't the first to resist him, but Carstairs had assured him that a little physical foreplay was sometimes to be expected.

I felt sick. Had he raped women?

Carstairs had objectified the opposite sex so thoroughly in Abos's mind that he regarded them merely as vessels for his pleasure after he had fulfilled whatever task his masters had asked of him.

The only reason, it seems, that Carstairs hadn't succeeded completely in his attempt to ensnare Abos's mind entirely, was me. Or, rather, the attitude towards me embedded in Abos's consciousness long before Carstairs turned up. As far as Abos was concerned, I was the equal of all other human beings he had worked with.In some ways, he deferred to me, as I was his teacher. My authority had been diminished when our meetings were stopped, as

Carstairs formulated his scheme to control Abos, but he had underestimated the strength of that initial connection.

Sitting on the end of my bed, Abos admitted that he had indulged in all the sexual rewards offered to him hoping they would one day lead back to me.

Rather drily, I pointed out that his ultimate superior—the head of our government—was a woman. Did he consider her to be inferior, available as a 'treat' perhaps, despite the fact that she was Carstair's superior? He visibly struggled with the logical disconnect between what had been strongly suggested under the influence of mind-altering drugs, and what I was telling him now. That all women should be treated the same as men, that explicit consent, and mutual respect, must be present before any sexual relationship can begin between adults.

When he was at his most confused, literally holding his head in his hands, I told him about the drugs Father had formulated to control him. I knew this was likely to lead to me being permanently sectioned by Station, but I had to tell him he was being chemically manipulated, that his freedom was an illusion.

He was silent for a long time. I told him my theory.

"Abos, when I met you, you were a baby. An infant. Not a human infant because your body was fully grown and you could reason and speak. But an infant of, well, what-ever species you are. While I was teaching you, you showed a capacity to learn, you were curious, you began to mature. But, even if your mental faculties develop far faster than humans, I believe, emotionally, you were like a small child. Now the way you're behaving, the way you've been encour-aged to behave, is like a male adolescent. An exaggerated, more selfish version of an adolescent. You act as if the world exists for your gratification, your view of life centres around yourself. That's very common in a thirteen-year-old human. But it's not a true picture. Everyone has the same rights as you - the right to live, learn, be happy. The right to choose."

He lifted his head and looked at me, his golden eyes full of tears.

"Cress. Don't you want me?"

I squeezed his shoulder in as close to a maternal way as I could manage.

"That's not the point. You assumed I did. You didn't respect my right to a choice."

He stood up.

"I'm sorry, Cress." He looked the model of a repentant adolescent. I half expected him to stick his bottom lip out. I felt a wave of sympathy for him. Whoever, whatever, he was, Abos did not deserve the treatment he had received.

"No," I said, "it's I who should apologise. On behalf of my Father, my government, and my country. You should never have had to suffer this."

"What do I do now?"

He looked at me and waited. The most powerful being on the planet. The mystery Station was no closer to solving than it was when we retrieved the cylinder from Marsham Street in 1969. Asking me what he should do.

"Abos," I said, looking straight back at him, "you need to grow up."

He didn't look away.

"Cress, you are my teacher still. I will learn this from you."

He turned, then seemed to change his mind.

"May I kiss you, Cressida? Just kiss you?"

Diary, I kissed him. That's all I'm saying. Don't judge.

When he left, I knew it was forever. I watched him from

the window as he flew east, quickly hidden from sight in the darkness.

THAT WAS A DECADE AGO. No one has ever seen him again. Station paid me one visit in the weeks following his disappearance. It was an officer I had never seen before. He asked a few cursory questions. Carstairs had long since dismissed me as a threat. His mistake.

One day, someone will read this. My fervent hope is that it won't be anyone from Station, but someone who can use the information to expose what happened.

I'm sure Abos will never allow himself to be controlled again if he ever does reappear. But what of his children?

One last secret, diary. Before he left, Abos asked me for a gift, one that I gave willingly. A gift that I will not reveal, even in these pages.

Good luck, Abos. I miss you.

39

Daniel

WHAT GEORGE HAD FEARED MIGHT TAKE her weeks, actually took minutes. She found information online about Cressida, even a photograph of her awarding prizes at a library in Clerkenwell.

She dropped a message in the dark web to a hacker who seemed to live online. Within seconds, a response pinged back with Cressida Lofthouse's address.

Ten minutes later, George was in the back of a taxi.

She reached the leafy Clerkenwell street at dusk, on a Spring evening in 2013. As she approached the house, the front door opened, and a woman hurried down the steps. George slowed, but the woman was much too young to be Lofthouse. As they passed each other, George let her mind reach out, absorbing a little information. The woman was a military nurse, completing a shift. She had just handed over to a colleague. Cressida Lofthouse was inside. Dying.

George continued past the house. The impression she had just received was clear. There was no room for misinterpretation. Lofthouse was in the final stages of a rare disease. She was asleep, or in morphine-assisted unconsciousness much of the time, and was rarely lucid. George felt a flutter of panic. To have come this close to her best lead and have so little time to do anything.

She reached the end of the street and paused. She knew she couldn't afford to wait. The risk of Lofthouse dying was too great. Even now she might find nothing useful in the poor woman's mind.

She turned her chair and headed back the way she had come. She eyed the elegant stone steps leading up to the front door of the house. Round the back as usual, then.

She got as far as a locked gate. She looked up and down the street. It wouldn't be fully dark for a couple of hours, and a woman in a wheelchair sitting outside a gate was sure to be noticed, even on a street as quiet as this.

She shrugged. It would take some effort, and she would undoubtedly feel the consequences for the next couple of days, but she couldn't be sure of ever getting another chance.

She closed her eyes and let her mind drift. When she was in this state, she had to open her field of attention at first, encompassing as much as possible. That meant that anyone within half a mile might add a note to the music George was hearing. Once she had settled into this phase, she had a choice. She could widen the field, in which case, far more minds contributed to the noise, but the information she received became more general. Or she could narrow it, capturing one or two minds and bringing a finer focus to bear.

George found the new nurse—Andrew—and, more

faintly, and less coherently, the fevered ramblings of Cressida Lofthouse. They were both on the ground floor, which was an unexpected piece of good luck. Cressida's illness must have forced her to move her bed to the front room.

George honed in on the nurse first and planted a simple idea. The more complicated an idea was, the more energy it demanded of her. She could have convinced the nurse there was an emergency which required him to run to the gate and let in a doctor. Or, as George chose to do, she could plant the idea that he had forgotten to leave the gate open for a delivery he was expecting. A simpler idea, using less energy.

It took twelve minutes for him to act on it. While she waited, a man walking his dog paused and looked at her with the beginnings of concern.

"Waiting for a cab," she called, waving her mobile phone as if that corroborated her story. The man walked on. Thirty seconds later, George heard the sound of a bolt being drawn back.

She waited another minute, then opened the gate and followed the wall around to the French doors at the back of the house. There was a small step to negotiate by the door, but George pulled the wheelchair over it backwards. Her left hand had been getting weaker during the preceding months, but there was still enough strength left in it for her to complete the manoeuvre.

As she waited in the kitchen, the door to the front room opened, and Andrew emerged, crossing to the sitting room where, thanks to George, he had decided to spend an hour lost in a book.

George entered the front room. The curtains were closed, but a bedside light and a standard lamp made the room seem warm and comforting. A large bed dominated the space. Propped up against the pillows, her complexion so pale she almost disappeared against them, was Cressida Lofthouse.

George had seen others close to death. There was an atmosphere around those whose ties to this world were stretching and breaking. George knew others felt it too, but it presented her with a problem. Cressida was lost in memories and dreams, rarely coming back to the world she would soon be leaving. George would have to interpret what she found in her mind and hope to glean something useful.

She closed her eyes. After a few seconds, she reached out and took Cressida's hand. There was no need to establish a physical connection, but, according to Major Harris's memories, this dying woman had been close to The Deterrent. A friend, even. Holding Cressida's hand seemed like it was the right thing to do.

Images, smells, sounds. A man pushing her up against a wall, his breath beer sour. An older man crying, pouring whisky from a green bottle. A woman dying in this house, a daughter holding her father's hand, not knowing who was supporting who. A pair of eyes, opening. Golden eyes.

With a start, George looked at Cressida. She was awake. She was looking straight at her, her expression a mixture of surprise and awe. Cressida wet her lips, tried to speak. George took the glass of water from the bedside table and held it to her cracked lips. She sipped, then spoke, smiling.

"You have his eyes."

George blinked, the gold flecks in her deep brown eyes catching the glow of the lamps.

Cressida's head fell back on the pillow. George reached into her mind and saw The Deterrent floating outside a window, his helmet and goggles removed. She saw him put his hand on the trunk of a tree, heard him read words from a children's book. Then she felt him rip her nightdress...

...and then, as if Cressida knew she was there, she was suddenly presented with a pin-sharp series of images. A hamster in a shoebox, being lifted into a cage. Cressida as a child, playing with the hamster, feeding it sunflower seeds, talking to it while she sat by her bedroom window. Then a tiny, furry body in a biscuit tin, and a wooden cross with a name laboriously carved into it in a child's hand: Mr Biffles.

A cough from the sitting room brought George back, and she backed out of the room, through the hall and kitchen and into the garden, closing the door before Andrew crossed to the front room.

Mr Biffles? What could be so important about a dead hamster that would cause Cressida to fixate on it? The last few minutes had just been the same few images over and over on a constant loop. The hamster, the cross, the name...the biscuit tin. The hamster, the cross...something wasn't right, something about the memory didn't quite ring true. George felt exhaustion starting to claim her as she sat in Cressida Lofthouse's garden, trying to work out what the dying woman had shown her.

It was as she had turned back towards the gate that she realised. It was the biscuit tin. It was much too big. Why would you bury a tiny creature like a hamster in a biscuit tin?

George swung around and went back to the garden. On the far side, just next to some rose bushes, was a tiny cross. From that distance, and in the failing light, George couldn't make out the letters carved there, but she didn't have to. Mister Biffles.

FIFTEEN MINUTES LATER, after Andrew had experienced an uncharacteristic urge to do some gardening, George was in the back of a taxi, so tired she could hardly keep her eyes open. She was clutching an earth-encrusted biscuit tin. She prised the lid open and took out the book inside. Unable to wait, she clicked on the internal light, opened the first page, and started reading.

March 22nd, 2013

To whom it may concern.

The notebooks you are holding comprise the diary I kept during the years since the discovery of Abos - The Deterrent.

40

I had put the diary down and was staring out of the window again when George came back to the suite.

She eased herself out of the wheelchair and onto the sofa, propping herself up against the cushions. Her smile was unforced.

"You know, I think I needed that. Station didn't even have muzak playing. I'd forgotten how lovely it is just listening to music. And it wasn't all songs from shows, thank goodness. He sneaked in a Dr John number, so I was happy."

I had no idea who she was talking about.

She pointed at Cress's diary.

"Well? What do you think?"

I didn't know where to start. My father—George's father, too—began as a blob of slime in a cylinder buried in London. He hadn't been born, he'd *grown*. What did that make the pair of us? Halfhero made us sound cool. Half-blob, not so much.

"I feel as if someone's answered a bunch of my questions but given me twice as many."

She nodded. "That's pretty much how I felt when I read

it. And, judging from Cress's account, even Abos may not have all the answers."

"You think he's alive, then? The Deterrent?"

"I do. So does Station."

"How can you be so sure?"

"Because they've been looking for him for thirty-five years. I got myself into Station to break you out and steal all the information they had about Abos. All their theories, all the dead ends they'd already investigated and rejected."

"And did you succeed?"

"Better than that, I copied the algorithmic program they've been running for the past five years, based on their best guess at how Abos has been hiding. My guess is better."

My leg was twitching. I knew my pulse rate was up.

"What do you mean?"

"Can you bring me the laptop?"

I handed it over. She patted the seat next to her. I sat down while she clicked some keys. The screen showed a male face which changed to another after a split second. Then another man replaced that, followed by another. I had to look away after a few seconds as dozens of faces flicked by at a nauseating speed.

"What is that?"

George clicked again, and the images disappeared.

"That's Station's program. During the first decade of searching for The Deterrent, they came up with a theory that might explain how the man with the most famous face in the world could hide."

I said nothing, but she saw my expression and laughed.

"I'm getting there, Daniel. It's a facial recognition program. They rolled out an early version in the 1990s, but it was only three years ago that processing speed became fast enough to make it useful. You remember who Abos looked like? In the diary?"

"Of course. That arsehole, Roger."

"Exactly. His blood gave Abos enough genetic material to make a superior version, based on Roger Sullivan's DNA. They reasoned that to enable him to disappear, Abos might have pulled the same trick."

I looked at her, my eyes boggling. I didn't know eyes actually did that. My mouth was dry.

"You mean, he might look like someone else now? Someone in the team?"

"You've got it. They scanned photographs of every man who had worked with Abos. There was no record of any other opportunity for him to get blood, but perhaps a shaving cut, or even a discarded plaster might have been enough."

"But...couldn't he have got blood from someone outside Station?"

"Yes. They are still adding faces to the database based on everyone they have records of him meeting."

"Everyone? But that could take..."

"Years? Decades? Quite. They started with those who had the most contact with him, then widened the search. It's a long shot, Daniel. But they will keep exploring every possibility, however remote. Station is terrified Abos might reappear as a superhero affiliated to another country. They'll do anything to prevent that. One reason Station is so keen to find and capture us—The Deterrent's children—is that they hope Abos might come looking for us one day."

"Do you think he will?"

"I think Station is clutching at straws. They can't unravel Abos's motivations any more than we can. If they hadn't kept their pet superhero drugged...well, who knows? Maybe they would have understood him a little better."

George grimaced as if in pain, but waved me away when I offered to help.

"It took ten weeks for Abos to grow first time round, and he was in the cylinder then - whatever that was. No one knows if he can repeat the trick without the cylinder. If it was just providing him with nutrients, then maybe he can. They've been running those faces through the program, but morphing the features, making them more symmetrical, removing blemishes. They've also artificially aged the faces. When Abos copied Sullivan, he appeared younger, as if he were in his twenties. If he did the same, and then aged as normal, he might look like he's in his fifties now."

I had only known George for a couple of days, but the expression she had on her face could only be described as mischievous.

"What?" I asked. "What is it? What aren't you telling me?"

"Come on, Daniel, you read the diary. All the clues are in there. She practically spells it out."

I groaned. "Come on, George. Put me out of my misery. Where is he? What does he look like?"

"You're asking the question all wrong."

For the first time in my life, I understood how siblings could fall out.

"George. Please."

Her expression became more serious.

"I'm coming to it, I promise. Daniel, I spent three weeks in Station. I let Harris bring me in. She told me she wanted to help. She asked me why I was spending so much time investigating The Deterrent. I told her I thought I might be his daughter. Then, as I'd hoped, they imprisoned me.

Invited me to a meeting in a building near Station, drugged me and took me in."

"You planned for them to abduct you?"

"Of course. They had to think they were in control. To them, I was an intriguing opportunity that had dropped into their laps. I couldn't let them suspect for a moment that I had any kind of power. They ran every test conceivable. They were desperate to find something, I think. Station is still looking for children like us, the ones who survived puberty. You're the poster boy. There must be others out there, but Station hasn't found them."

I thought of the so-called terrorist cell I had been set loose on, the blood on my hands from that day. I said nothing, but made a silent vow that if Station somehow recaptured me, I would kill myself before letting them use me again. I remembered my hands, wet with blood, round the throat of the red-haired woman who must have been my half-sister.

George saw the look on my face and put a hand on my arm.

"I know what happened that night in Shoreditch."

I couldn't have replied even if I'd wanted to.

"You feel terrible guilt and shame. I can't stop that. No one can. Intellectually, you know you are not responsible for their deaths. Station is."

She waited until I nodded.

"Emotionally, though, you still feel responsible. Even though you were brainwashed and drugged, even though you were in a chemically induced state of rage, you still carry that guilt. Use it. Turn it into anger and use it against those who still want to control or kill us."

I nodded again. There was a long silence. I asked what had happened to her inside Station.

"I didn't need to be a mind reader to see how excited the scientific team were to meet me. It took about ten days before the disappointment set in."

"They didn't find your power?"

"No. By the time they had concluded the tests, they thought it was likely that some inherited ability may have begun to manifest at puberty, but my body had been too weak to withstand its onset. They think my illness is the result. They all felt a bit sorry for me."

"Nice of them."

"Yes. Well. By then, I'd had time to sneak into a dozen minds. I was planting ideas in various brains for weeks, leading up to your escape. Shifts were rearranged, a few people called in sick, and security staff looked the wrong way while we walked out. I also had a data guy drop me an email with a link to the online search program. He included details of the backdoor he'd programmed. I was able to copy and adapt it. Well, not me, my hacker."

"You're amazing," I said.

"I'm constantly underestimated," she said. "Station underestimated Cress, too. Hopkins has built an appalling patriarchy down there. It's his greatest weakness. Well, that and halitosis."

"And The Deterrent? Abos? You were about to tell me..."

"Nearly there."

"George!"

"Wait. This is important."

I took a deep breath to stop myself banging my head against the wall, which would have wrecked some very expensive wallpaper. Was that real gold flake in the design?

"The hybrid programme hit a limitation years ago. They can't get hybrids to live past one or two missions before their bodies collapse. Their physical development is accelerated through growth hormones from the time they're foetuses, but even an enhanced physique can't withstand the damage when they are sent into action."

"They're berserkers," I said, remembering my encounter with the Tweedles. "They run on pure rage. They want to kill everything in their path."

"Their lack of predictability, and their short lifespan, makes them a bad bet for the military. The funding is being withdrawn next summer. I got that from Hopkins himself."

"You were in his mind. Ugh."

"Not somewhere I ever want to revisit. But I needed information, and I planted an urgent appointment on the other side of town the day we escaped. Daniel, he's not shutting down the programme. He's contacted some private investors."

"Hopkins? Going against orders? He wouldn't."

"He's convinced himself it's in the best interest of his country to keep the hybrids. He plans on breeding an army. He thinks he'll be seen as a hero, not a traitor when the truth comes out."

"He's delusional."

"Yes. But he's also persuasive, and dangerous. He sees this as his legacy. We need to close down the hybrid project before he moves all the research and data elsewhere. His paranoia will come in useful for once - everything is held in Station, and the computer network is a closed system. We destroy that, we destroy the project."

She stopped talking. Finally.

"George!" I was almost shouting. "You still haven't told me. You've found our father, haven't you? Where is he? Who is he? What does he look like now?"

She gave me an odd look.

"What?"

"One more thing. You're going back to Station, Daniel. Tonight."

"I'm what?"

"You're going to destroy it."

"I, er, excuse me? What?"

"You know the layout, you know where the hybrids are. Hopkins will be there, but this evening, he's sending half of Station's staff to help flush out a suspected terrorist organisation in Kent. That will help."

"Your work?"

"Of course." She looked even more frail than she had the day before. If using her power exhausted her physically and shortened her lifespan, the past few months of pursuing Station, getting in there and arranging my escape, then setting the stage for tonight...well. It must have taken a hell of a toll. She would need a long rest after this. Especially as I was about to let her down. I don't think of myself as a coward, but walking back into Station would be suicide.

"George, I can't fight hybrids. I took on two of them fourteen years ago, and I only just survived. They will be stronger, faster, tougher now. And there will be more of them. They'll tear my legs off and use them to crush my skull."

"But you won't be alone. Abos will come with you."

At last. I felt my heart lurch.

"Where is he?"

George handed me a piece of paper with an address on it. My hands were shaking.

"What's this?"

"My flat. Take a taxi. Abos should be there by now. Go have a chat. Come back after the two of you have wiped out that horror show Hopkins is running."

I brushed imaginary dust off the collar of the gorgeous

suit, feeling suddenly terrified. This was it. I was going to meet The Deterrent, the disappearing superhero. My father. And, assuming he still had the same powers, taking Station down suddenly seemed eminently possible.

"George - what about you? Come with me."

"I don't come with you," she said. It took me a few moments to work out what she meant.

"Your power? I thought you couldn't be that specific."

"This time I can be. What happens today has been very clear for a long time. I don't go with you. I wait here. There's something I need to do, too."

George fell silent for a second, then spoke so quietly I could barely hear her.

"It has to happen the way I saw it if we're going to win. If I change anything, we might fail."

She held out her arms, and I hugged her for a few seconds. She was crying.

"I'll bring him to see you," I said, giving her as gentle a squeeze as I could manage. "We can have a family meeting."

She laughed a little at that, still choked with sobs. Then she lightly pushed me away and waved towards the door.

"See you later," I said, as I walked out, all my thoughts focussed on the meeting ahead. Much later, I thought back to that moment and remembered that she hadn't replied.

George was the one who could see the future. Me, not a chance, even when it's blindingly obvious.

I went downstairs, got in a taxi, and drove off to meet my dad.

41

George's flat was on the ground floor of an imposing Edwardian terrace within sight of Putney Bridge.

I paid the taxi driver with a fifty and let him keep the change. He was gruffly grateful, eyeing my suit and probably assuming money meant little to me.

My generosity was down to expediency. If I waited for change, I might lose my nerve.

I was shaking, my mind skipping from half-formed thought to half-formed thought like a butterfly on crack.

I found I could only function if I allowed myself to complete one simple task at a time. Open the taxi door. Step onto the pavement. Close the taxi door. Walk across the pavement to the front door. Push the buzzer on the door. Stare at the door as it swings open under the pressure of my finger on the buzzer.

I could smell freshly baked bread.

I stepped into a wide hallway with a tiled floor. A reproduction of Picasso's Guernica hung on the wall. There were four doors off the hallway. The two doors on the right and the door on the left were shut, but the one ahead, at the end of the hall, was open. It led to a brightly lit kitchen, where a figure moved across my line of sight.

I willed my feet to move, or my voice to speak, only to discover that my brain was the victim of a coup. I remained dumb, rooted to the spot.

A voice called out from the kitchen.

"You must be Daniel. Come on in. I'm just making a cup of tea, and George has got some of that posh honey that costs a fortune. You have to try it on toast, it's smashing."

My feet belatedly accepted my earlier instruction and started to move as my brain clunkily processed what was *wrong* about the voice. Two things. A Welsh accent was one of them. The other, which was confirmed as I walked into the kitchen, was that it belonged to a woman.

I went straight to the table and put both hands on the back of a solid oak chair to stop me falling over.

Standing with her back to me was a tall woman with short, grey hair, wearing dark jeans and a thick blue woolly jumper. She was cutting bread into slices. A teapot sat on the counter, steam curling from its spout, two mugs next to it.

She turned and smiled at me.

"Hello, Daniel."

She looked to be in her mid-sixties. Her face was lined, her brown eyes surrounded by creases that deepened as she smiled. It was a kind face, a gentle face. A maternal face. It was also, unmistakably, a face I'd seen in a photograph a few hours previously, although she had been nineteen or twenty in the picture.

It was the face of a dead woman.

"Hello," I said, because I didn't know what else to say.

It was Cressida Lofthouse.

WE DRANK TEA, and I tried the toast. She was right, the honey was excellent.

Eventually, I found my voice.

"You're not...?"

"Cressida Lofthouse? No, love, I'm not. George told me she had died. I was very sorry to hear it. Cressida was a very special person."

"Then you're...?"

"Yes. Yes, I am."

The woman who looked like Cressida took a small case out of the bag at her feet and put her hands up to her face. She removed her contact lenses and placed them in the case before looking back at me.

Her eyes were golden.

"Abos," I said.

"Yes. Well, I've been known as Amy since 1981. But, yes, your father. Or mother. Maybe 'parent' would be easiest. Pleased to meet you."

We shook hands. In a life not devoid of surreal moments, this one took the proverbial biscuit. I was sitting in the kitchen of the mind-reading half-sister I had never known, shaking hands with my father, who was now a woman, although not really, as she wasn't human.

"George emailed me a week ago," said Amy. Abos. Dad. The Deterrent. Abos was a non-gender-specific name. I decided life would be simpler if I used it.

"How did she find you?"

"She told me, and I quote, that 'those prats at Station have spent years looking for a man just because it happened to be Roger Sullivan's blood that spilled on your cylinder in 1978.'"

"But how did she know you'd look like Cressida Lofthouse?"

"She told me she'd read Cress's diary, and that Cress had mentioned the gift she'd given me that night."

"Oh." I felt my face redden. That wasn't the gift I had imagined. I gave myself a mental slap for being so stupid. There was no way Cress would have had sex with Abos after what had happened between them. I can be so dense sometimes.

"She gave me ten millilitres of her blood. I found a long-abandoned cottage in Scotland and started the process. It was faster than the first time. It took three days."

"The first time? You mean you went back to being, er, you returned to the state of, er, you became a..."

Abos smiled. Those creases around her disconcerting eyes deepened again.

"Amorphous Blob Of Slime. Yes, I know what it stands for. George sent me a scan of Cressida's diary. It's a good name. Yes, I returned to that state, then this body grew. I'm about six inches taller than Cress, but that's the only major difference."

"Where have you been all these years? And why come back now? Why not before?"

Abos looked into my eyes and, for a second, I felt as if I had become unmoored from reality. Her eyes were so truly *other* that her non-human origin was abruptly, unavoidably apparent. It was a chilling sensation, and I looked away. Whatever Abos was, I was its child. What did that mean?

Abos stood up and poured more tea.

"For the past thirty-six years, I've lived in a tiny village in North Wales. I turned up on a freezing, stormy night in 1981, knocked on the door of the vicarage, and, until this afternoon, that was where I stayed."

"Who did they think you were?"

"I told them I had escaped from an abusive relationship."
She brought the two mugs over and set one in front of me. "I
wasn't lying about that. I just didn't go into specifics. David
and Mary never asked. They were good people. They helped
me find work at the primary school. I took a distant learning
course and started teaching. Like most teachers, I learned
more than any of my pupils. They'll never know how
much more."

She sipped her tea, cradling the mug in both hands.

"What Cress told me in 1981 came as a terrible shock.
The drugs, the brainwashing...but, much worse, my
behaviour. That night, for the first time, she made me aware
that other people didn't exist for my pleasure. I saw that I
was being used, and that I was using others."

Something about the way Abos was speaking sounded
off-kilter to me. Almost as if she was describing something
she didn't actually remember. I asked her about her memories of that time.

"I remember that life, the life at Station, as if it were a
story I'd read in a book. A story I know intimately. I feel
connected to those years, but it doesn't feel as though *I* was
there. I know it *was* me, but there's no strong personal
connection. In some ways, I'm grateful for that. I behaved
like a sex-mad adolescent. I can't blame everything on
Station."

I coughed.

"You read Cress's diary. Roger Sullivan was a sexual
predator. You don't think...?"

"Yes, it has occurred to me. Perhaps the DNA in the
blood partially forms my character as well as my body. Cressida was my teacher, and look at what I've been doing for
the past three decades."

I opened my mouth, but she pointed at the clock.

"We'll have time for questions later," she said, putting her contact lenses back in. She considered what she'd just said before adding, "I hope."

That sounded a bit ominous.

WE TOOK A TAXI TO STATION. I was wearing an outfit George had left at her flat for me. Combat trousers, a thick jumper. A pair of army boots.

Abos spoke quickly as the meter ticked up the fare, and we drew closer to the one place in the world I never wanted to see again.

"George gave me instructions for tonight," she said. "She knows what we need to do."

George was an amazing individual, a force of nature, but I still struggled to think of her giving orders to a superhero.

Abos looked at me and answered the question I couldn't bring myself to ask.

"I knew there were children. I read the newspapers. But I didn't feel any connection to them. To you."

She was stating a fact, but I still felt cold hearing it.

"I was a child myself," she said. "My body was that of an adult, but my mind was comparatively unformed. I didn't know what sex was, just that I enjoyed it. There was nothing in the Peter and Jane books about the human reproductive system. Your mother...is she okay?"

I realised I didn't even know if my mother were alive or dead.

"We don't really talk."

Abos looked out at the London streets, the busy pavements.

"I wish I had understood what I was doing. The hurt that I caused. I have spent many years now with children, with mothers and fathers. I am sorry, Daniel."

I had a flashback to George telling me I wasn't responsible for crimes committed while under Station's control. Why was it I was able to forgive anyone other than myself?

I turned to the woman in her sixties who had been my father, but was now a new person. If she could be described as a person, that is.

"You have nothing to apologise for."

"I was used. As were you. And now Station breeds creatures without the intelligence to challenge their conditioning. Did George tell you what Hopkins is planning for the hybrid project?"

"The private investors? Yes."

"It ends tonight. We will follow George's instructions. She is remarkable. Her power is fascinating."

"You can't do what she does? With people's minds?"

"No. I cannot. The combination of human DNA with, well, whatever I am, may, somehow, have produced this ability. Perhaps it is latent in humans, and my genes triggered it. There is so much I want to talk to her about."

She looked out of the window again. I saw a sign for Liverpool Street.

"Now, let me tell you exactly what we are going to do."

She told me. I didn't much like it.

When we drew up a few streets away from Station, she took her bag and went into a cafe toilet while I waited. When she came out, she was zipping up a black quilted jacket. Her handbag had gone. She was carrying a black balaclava. She put it over her head.

"Well?"

I wouldn't have known who she was, even if she was

male or female. I told her so. She nodded, satisfied. I pointed at the balaclava.

"Don't I get one?"

"Nope. We want your face on every security camera, Daniel. They know you, but we don't want to give them any clues about me. You ready?"

Ready to return to a subterranean prison that had robbed me of most of my adult life?

"Ready."

42

W
e walked in the door as if we owned the place.
For once, I had abandoned my hunched
posture, instead striding forwards like a boxer
on his way to the ring for the fight of his life. I was terrified,
but there was no way I would let anyone see it.

Beside me, Abos hurried to keep up. Having expected to
be dwarfed by a seven-foot tall man, I was secretly enjoying
the fact that I was now about six inches taller than The
Deterrent.

The guard behind the desk looked up from the sports
pages, then made a strange noise before going for the alarm.
I expected that and put on a burst of pace, ending with a
double-handed push on his chest. His chair had wheels, and
he rolled backwards at speed for a few yards before hitting a
cupboard. He was still accelerating as the back of his head
made contact with a wooden panel, and he slumped.

I kicked open the gate I had wheeled George through
just two days earlier. We had almost reached the lift when
the shutters came down around us, the alarm sounded, and
twenty soldiers came our way. Ignoring them, I kicked open

the door to the stairs. Well, that was what it would look like when the video footage was reviewed. In reality, there was no way even I could break through a steel door that size. Abos did the real damage, using the same trick he'd once pulled on the Challenger tank, lifting the buckled door off its hinges the moment my foot connected with it.

As soon as we were in the stairwell, I replaced the door, off-centre, wedging it into the space to block it. With Abos's help again, of course.

We jogged down to Station's second subterranean level. The hybrid level.

We burst through the security door. Being back there was enough to make my last meal curdle in my stomach. We turned and followed a thin white line on the wall.

As we jogged, I heard a series of sharp, electric fizzing sounds as if someone were pressing a buzzer. I turned to Abos.

"Cameras," she said. "I'm shorting them."

I looked up at the next tiny camera as we approached it. Another fizz, and the blue light winked out.

We passed a door marked *Coms*. Abos stopped.

"After you," she said.

I kicked it in and stepped through. Two men leaped to their feet, one staring at us in shock. The other followed his training, drew his weapon, shouted a warning, then—as we ignored him and kept walking shot me twice in the chest. The ricochet from one shot caught the second soldier in the upper arm, and he yelped. The first guy, choosing pragmatism over potential pain, threw his weapon away and put his hands up.

"Get your friend to a doctor," I said. They headed towards the door, and I called after them. "Not here. Get out of Station. How many more people are down here?"

He hesitated. I was punching holes in the video control console as I spoke to him, reducing it to an ugly tangle of metal, shredded cabling and crushed circuit boards.

"Anyone left here after the next twenty minutes or so will die. I'm giving you the chance to save them."

He displayed a touch of bravado.

"What, you two are taking on the whole of Station?"

Abos turned towards the wrecked console. The cameras were all out of commission now.

The console lifted from the floor, rose a few feet, then smashed back down, destroying anything that might have survived my pummelling.

I turned back to the soldiers.

"Yep," I said. The injured man looked up at his comrade.

"Can we go now?" I answered with a slow nod.

They left. We followed, but turned away from the exits and headed for the hybrid lab.

The first surprise was that the hybrids weren't locked away behind five inches of solid steel and an airlock. There was just a double door.

The second surprise was that the room, which was the size of an aircraft hangar, was full of beds. There must have been over a hundred of them, all occupied, with tubes snaking out of wheeled drips next to each one. As we walked into the room, we saw the misshapen heads, the heavily muscled bodies. Hybrids.

At the far end of the cavernous space, on a raised platform, was the man who had once asked me to serve my country.

Hopkins.

∾

ABOS and I walked through the chamber towards the Colonel. For the first time, I wondered if that was really his rank. Outside of Station, he would surely have been promoted. Perhaps he didn't care. He was top dog in his underground fiefdom.

"I must confess, I was surprised when I saw who had triggered the alarm," he said.

I hadn't laid eyes on Hopkins in fourteen years. I realised he was an old man now. The cane he now kept by his side was not decorative; he leaned heavily on it when he stepped up to the rail at the edge of the platform.

"Who's your friend, Daniel?"

Abos removed her balaclava, and Hopkins stopped dead, staring in disbelief as we got closer.

"Miss Lofthouse? Impossible. I saw your dead body."

Abos removed the contact lenses. When he turned his golden eyes on Hopkins, the old soldier stared in disbelief. Then he said pretty much the stupidest thing I've ever heard. I wished George had been there to hear it.

"But you're... a woman."

Abos replied, playing up her Welsh accent, which confused Hopkins still further.

"Well, you haven't got any brighter over the years, have you, boyo? Now, be a good lad and give yourself up. We're closing Station down."

Hopkins stared at the being he had seen grow from a blob of slime into a superhero he had been able to manipulate. I wondered if he had realised he could have found The Deterrent years ago, if not for his catastrophic assumption that Abos was male.

We were halfway along the rows of beds now. Hopkins took something out of his pocket and pointed it towards us, pressing something.

"You're too late. We are building an army here that will make this country truly great again. And we couldn't have done it without you.

"You realise what they are?" Hopkins waved an arm to take in the whole room. I saw what was in his palm. A power button. Like the one they had used to trigger me. On the 'missions' when they needed me to kill whoever they pointed me towards.

In my peripheral vision, I caught a small movement in one of the beds. They were waking up.

"They're monsters."

"Maybe," said Hopkins. "Maybe you're right. You should know, Daniel. They're your children. Meet the family."

There was more movement around us as hybrids sat up, pulling the needles out of their arms and swinging their legs round. That horrible, dull, rage-filled glare was in evidence as dozens of pairs of eyes swivelled our way.

Hopkins' words echoed in my mind. I already guessed Station had used my blood and skin samples to help them manipulate genes and produce hybrids, but now I realised the whole truth. It was much simpler. And much more devastating.

The women. The women who had come to my room, apparently unable to resist me. Dozens of secret visits to relieve their sexual tension. Always using a condom. Never staying afterwards. I was such a fool.

Hopkins wasn't lying. These misshapen, tortured killers were my biological children.

"We still can't work out how to make them live beyond twelve or thirteen," said Hopkins. "It's a shame, really. But their mental limitations make them easy to programme and the growth hormones we use mean they are perfect for situations where extreme violence is necessary."

I felt despair and rage rise inside me. As the hybrids surrounded us, Abos put a hand on my arm.

"There's no other way, Daniel. I'm sorry. But I won't let you do it." I felt myself lift into the air as she looked at me, then I was flying towards Hopkins, who watched my approach with disbelief. It was a strange feeling, the air rippling around my body like a heat haze as I rose and crossed the room, about twelve feet from the floor. I landed next to Hopkins and pushed him sprawling into a corner where he wheezed in pain. He looked like a frail old man. It would give me no satisfaction to kill him, despite part of me wanting to do just that.

I turned back to the main room. I couldn't see Abos at all, just a seething, bloody mass of bodies, fists, and feet flying as they tried to reach their prey and tear it apart. The hybrids just kept coming, doing their best to drag others out of the way and get to the stranger in their midst.

Hopkins dragged himself back towards the railing, trying to breathe normally. We both watched as the mass of bloodied bodies moved, a living ball of arms, legs, torsos, heads, writhing as it rose, slick with blood, into the air, like a child's balloon. If the child was in a modern take on Hieronymus Bosch's vision of hell.

There was a noise, a muffled boom I felt in the pit of my stomach. The ball of hybrids exploded outwards, each individual body hurtling away from the centre. For a moment, the figure in the middle, the nucleus of their bloody atom, was visible: Abos, her clothes torn, her skin slick with her own blood and that of her attackers.

Hopkins grunted in satisfaction when he saw that his protégés—my children—could hurt the superbeing who had defied him. He was watching with fascination, and his mask had, temporarily, dropped. His expression was not that of an officer doing his job, however distasteful it might be, it was the that of a man addicted to violence and death, who had allowed his humanity to wither. I wondered if he was still telling himself the lie that he was serving queen and country.

Hopkins was the real monster, not the poor twisted bastards who could never be anything other than pain-filled, rage-fuelled killers.

I looked back at Abos. Below her, snarling hybrids tried to reach up as she hovered above like a bloody angel sent to deliver them. She spread her arms and, accompanied by the scrape of metal on concrete, a hundred or more beds flew up from the floor, drips still hanging from them. The hybrids were still braying for her blood.

"Daniel." Her voice rang across the hall, clearly audible above the howls of the hybrids. I looked at her. Those golden eyes, so odd, so alien, seemed to look right into the heart of me. I heard the sorrow in her voice. And I heard the decision.

"Look away. Please."

The beds had converged around her, hanging directly above the hybrids.

Abos lowered those golden eyes, and I turned away from the railing, hauling Hopkins with me.

I didn't watch what followed, but I heard it; metal hitting flesh and muscle, bones snapping, snarls turning to screams or howls of pain. A brief respite then the same sound again, this time wetter, fewer howls, some awful, unforgettable weeping. Then a third, final, crushing blow followed by the silence of death.

A pair of feet walked into my field of vision as I knelt there, doubled over. I had one hand on Hopkins' collar, forcing him to look away. Abos waited for me to move. She didn't speak. Sensible shoes. Black, sensible shoes covered in blood.

A siren sounded before I could speak. It was a siren I had heard once a week during my years at Station as part of a regular drill. A siren that would sound familiar to anyone who had lived through the Blitz in London or—like me— had spent hours listening to *Two Tribes*, by Frankie Goes To Hollywood.

In this context, the siren didn't mean bombers were approaching, or that nuclear war had broken out.

It meant that the protocols around a critical breach of Station security had been initiated, and all personnel had three minutes to evacuate. Everyone in Station knew their chances of living beyond the next three minutes had just dropped. If you heard the siren while at ground level, you'd get out. If you were anywhere else in the entire complex, you were dead.

In about two minutes and fifty seconds, a series of linked electric charges would be automatically detonated, and the office block above Station would fall, burying its secrets it in a concrete and brick tomb.

I looked up at Abos, then down at Hopkins.

"I'm an old man," he said. "I have done my duty. Now it will fall to others to carry the torch."

What a pile of crap. Especially as Station was about to be buried forever. Hopkins settled himself against the wall and waited for the ceiling to fall in.

I wondered how he would react if I ripped his moustache off.

"Let's go," I said to Abos.

Hopkins pulled something out of his jacket. It was another power button. Before I could stop him, he pushed it.

AT FIRST, I looked around, half-expecting a superhybrid to emerge from a secret room. All the platform games I ever played in my bedroom or in arcades featured a boss level, a tougher enemy that offers a real challenge to the dedicated gamer. I waited, moving my feet into a fighting stance.

Then I felt it begin, and the horror of what Hopkins had done became clear.

My arm still carried the drug release system Station had surgically placed there when I joined them. Hopkins had just triggered me.

I turned on him. He was still smiling. I could feel a cold sensation travelling down my arm. I remembered it from the missions I had run, but there was something different this time. Something about the world felt suddenly, and utterly, wrong.

"What is it?" Abos put a hand on my shoulder. I looked at the hand. It was changing, becoming more like a claw - reptilian, covered in scales, blood crusted on long, vicious talons.

Hopkins spoke.

"I was beginning to think we'd never get close enough to trigger you again, Daniel. Your escape caught us all napping. Still, spilt milk and all that."

"You need to get out," I hissed at Abos, trying not to look at the talons. "Now."

"This is the really good stuff," said Hopkins. "A triumph of psycho-pharmacy. I've only seen results on hybrids, but your performance should be remarkable."

"*We* need to get out, Daniel. I won't leave without you."

Hopkins spoke again. He said a meaningless word which I don't remember. It sounded like a random assemblage of consonants and vowels. But I felt something change. I heard a noise I knew was internal, a rushing surge like a hurricane building up power. The recorded announcement sounded like it was miles away: "Two minutes, thirty seconds."

"The Deterrent is your enemy," said Hopkins, in a voice that seemed to write commands directly into my brain's software. "Abos has killed your children. She wants to kill you. You must kill her first."

43

F ights—physical, brutal, hand-to-hand fights—-are ugly. They are an upsetting reminder of the animal still lurking behind our civilised veneer. The vast majority of fights are unplanned, beginning when emotions have escalated, and control has been lost. Some are entered into by mutual agreement, from an after-school playground brawl to a heavyweight title bout. Still others begin with no such agreement, when one participant launches her or himself at the second party, who is forced to mount a defence or succumb.

The fight between Abos and me was of the last variety. Looking back, it must have represented an incredible challenge for her. Physically, I am incredibly strong, and my body can withstand a great deal of damage. I inherited both qualities from my opponent: my parent. She is equally tough, equally strong, but she has additional powers; of flight, greater speed, and the mental manipulation of physical objects.

In relation to the battle that followed, although it lasted only a fraction over two minutes, the word 'epic' would not be an exaggeration. And Abos had to fight as if she had one hand tied behind her back. She didn't want to hurt me.

I, on the other hand, was under the influence of powerful hallucinogenics, adrenaline, and God knows what else. And I did want to hurt her. Very much.

I wanted to kill her.

I can only describe what happened from my point of view, as warped and fantastical as it seems now.

It started when I turned and looked at Abos. I didn't see Cressida Lofthouse, or a golden-eyed superbeing. What I saw was no longer a *he* or a *she*, but an *it*: a genderless demon, stripped of its human likeness. What I believed I was seeing at that moment was Abos finally revealed in its true form.

It was naked. Its body was like an anatomy picture in a medical encyclopaedia, shiny muscles clearly visible, ligaments and tendons flexing, stretching and contracting, near-black blood flowing through thick, wiry veins. The face was the worst. It was hairless, misshapen like the hybrids, the forehead prominent and swollen. Yellow eyes the colour of sickness fixed on mine, a forked tongue emerging from dark, cracked lips to flick towards me.

I hesitated for a moment, reeling in shock. Abos had vanished, replaced by this hideous monster. A tiny part of my mind protested that what I was seeing couldn't be real, but it was swiftly drowned out by the tide of insane rage sweeping through my psyche.

The fact that the demon, despite being given ample time, didn't attack me, in no way slowed me down once I'd recovered from the initial shock.

I punched with both fists, stepping forwards and putting all my weight behind the blows. The demon took the impact on its chest and was knocked off its feet, ripping the railing away from the platform as it fell, landing on a dead hybrid.

Before it could get up, I leaped after it, legs coiling under my body as I jumped, ready to kick out and crush the creature as I landed on it.

I roared my frustration as the demon rolled to the side to avoid me. It retreated fast - faster than I believed possible, running across the corpses of its victims, heading for the exit. I started to sprint, then slowed when I looked ahead to the entrance. A steel security door had slid into place. Rooms could be sealed in the event of an emergency. This must have been Hopkins' work. And he'd done me a favour.

We were trapped. Together.

I jogged, trying to avoid the bodies around me. I didn't see hybrids any more. I saw children. Children butchered by the demon up ahead. I screamed in rage and felt power filling my body, white-hot, incandescent, a pure blinding rush of energy that had to be satisfied before it consumed me.

I ran. The demon had its back to me. I raised my hands above my head, visualising my fists coming down on that skull, cracking the bone, driving through and crushing the foul brain within.

A second before I reached it, the creature broke through the steel door. It was standing a few yards away, but I saw the surface of the metal buckle and give, the sound of it as it tore away from the entrance momentarily louder than my scream.

The demon moved as the door imploded, meaning my punch landed on its shoulders, losing much of its impact. Nevertheless, the creature staggered and fell to its knees, crying out in pain.

I roared in triumph and kicked, lifting the demon off the

ground and into the corridor wall, leaving a dent in the concrete when it fell. It rolled onto its side, its breath coming in gasps. I knew I'd hurt it.

I stepped forwards, intending to stamp my boots on the foul thing, over and over, until no one would even recognise it as ever having been alive.

The demon made noises, almost as if it were appealing to me, although there were no words, just grunts and snarls. Then I saw that its yellow eyes were focussed on something behind me.

I looked over my shoulder just as the steel door knocked into me, carrying me over the demon and pinning me against the wall, wrapping itself around my arms. I howled and squirmed, shifting my body, trying to get into a position where I could free myself.

As I struggled, I heard the demon move away. I redoubled my efforts and managed to raise my head. The demon was at the far end of the corridor. One more corner and it would be at the stairs.

I carried on thrashing and twisting, refusing to accept I had lost.

Close to my ear, I heard the sound of metal being forced out of shape, bent and torn. I felt the pressure ease in my shoulders. I looked back down the corridor. The demon was looking at me, its hand raised.

It was doing this. It was releasing me.

Once again, a tiny internal voice tried to make itself heard. *Why would it free you?*

The steel door dropped to the floor. I was free.

The demon was gone, leaving a trail of blood. I threw myself after it, a vision of its foul eyes closing in death driving me forward.

As I came round the second corner, I saw the thing enter

the stairwell, dragging one leg behind it. The creature was moving slowly. I knew I could catch it.

I ran hard, bursting through the doorway with the bloodlust pounding in my ears, ready to deal the final blows.

The stairwell was empty. Confused, I looked up and saw the terrible, bloody body rising up, a pair of leathery wings barely missing the stairs as it powered through the air.

I took the stairs two at a time in pursuit.

I emerged in the lobby in time to see the beast drag itself through the one shutter that had risen when the countdown had begun, allowing any Station staff at ground level to escape.

I gave chase and found myself in the fresh air as the last few seconds of the countdown sounded through the speakers in the building behind me.

At that moment, a cold certainty struck me, breaking through the blood-thirsty delusional mess filling my mind. A thirty-floor office block was about to fall, and I was standing directly below it.

I felt, rather than heard, the first explosion. The detonation made the ground shudder, and I stumbled and fell. The ground shook violently as the chain of explosions did their work.

I got back to my feet, weaving like a drunkard, and ran, the instinct for survival proving stronger than the fact that I couldn't outrun a falling building.

I had only covered five yards when a stronger, deeper, rumbling explosion lifted me like a child's toy and smacked me back to the ground. My left arm took the brunt of my fall, and I heard my wrist snap.

Grimacing with pain, I propped myself up on my elbow and looked up at the office block above as it toppled. Still functioning instinctively, I scrambled backwards as I watched bricks fold inwards, windows explode, and clouds of dust pour from the base of the building.

There was a movement in the sky nearby, and I turned my head to see the demon sink to the ground, then crawl away. I realised there was a possibility it might escape. I changed course. If I could get my hand around its ankle, we could both die here together.

As I neared my goal, the demon turned its head and saw me. Its yellow eyes seemed different somehow, almost golden, and its wings had vanished. Its face was changing, sometimes looking almost human. It looked exhausted. It raised its hand, and I flinched in anticipation of its final attack.

Then it spoke, and this time I understood it.

"Come back, Daniel."

And I saw Cressida Lofthouse's bloodied face, Abos's golden eyes locked on mine, and I knew who I had been fighting.

Before I could react, she grunted with effort, and I was lifted into the air, thrown away from the falling building.

I twisted as I flew, finally hitting the wall of a building across the street from Station. I dropped, my head hitting the floor.

Fighting to stay conscious, I looked back as the office block collapsed with a roar that must have shaken every building within a square mile.

The sound of that roar reached me a fraction of a second after I saw the massive cloud of grey and yellow dust billow out from the spot where the entrance to Station had once stood.

Then I saw her. She had crawled a little further away. For a moment, I thought she would make it, but the cloud of dust also carried debris. I saw a chunk of masonry the size of a car land on Abos with a sickening thud, crushing her body.

The last shred of awareness I was clinging on to slid away, and I welcomed the blackness that followed.

I NEVER FOUND out the name of the woman who helped me. She must have worked in one of the buildings nearby, maybe even the one Abos had thrown me into. The explosion brought everyone outside.

The first I knew of her presence was her voice, gentle but insistent.

"Hello? Hello? Can you hear me? You've been in an accident, but help is coming. Can you hear me?"

I don't know where she found them, but she pulled heavy, soft blankets over me, and kept talking until I opened my eyes.

"Can you hear me? Can you - that's right, it's okay now. No, don't try to move, just lie still. Here, have some water. Can you raise your head a little? That's right, here we are."

I sipped at the bottle she held to my lips, then gulped as the cool liquid spilled into my mouth and down my throat.

My vision was clearing. I looked towards Station. Or, rather, towards the huge mound of rubble beneath which Station was now buried. And I located the place where Abos had been hit. The chunk of masonry hadn't moved. Nothing was moving anymore.

I leaned to one side and threw up. My benefactor rubbed my back.

"The ambulance will be here soon."

She held the bottle to my lips again, and I drank until I had drained it.

"Do you want some more?"

I nodded my thanks, and she walked back into the building behind me.

I could hear the sound of sirens now, getting louder. There must have been hundreds of people on the streets, looking at the devastation, exchanging meaningless but comforting remarks in whispers, as if anything louder might be disrespectful. They were glad to be alive. At that moment, I didn't share their happiness.

Using the wall behind me for support, and being careful not to move my broken wrist, I pushed myself to my feet and, before the woman returned, I limped away into the darkness.

44

It took two hours to get back to the hotel. There were two reasons for this. First, I was a six-foot-four man built like an industrial fridge-freezer, covered in dust and blood, cradling a broken wrist. To avoid attention meant using back streets and alleyways and growling at anyone who got too close. Second, I didn't want to go back, didn't want to tell George what had happened. I had killed our parent. How do you tell someone that?

There was one piece of good news. Station was no more. And the hybrids were gone. My children.

I stopped for a few minutes in a dark, wet yard behind a restaurant. Crouched next to a trade bin, I wept for the lives of the children whose lives had been so horribly manipulated. Treated like battery chickens, pumped full of growth hormones and only ever allowed to feel the sun on their faces when they were being sent to kill someone. Like dogs bred to fight, then shot in the head once they had outgrown their usefulness. And Station had used me to launch their programme.

I vomited until there was nothing left in my stomach.

Then, drained, dizzy and in shock, I walked along the last few streets to the back of the hotel.

I wanted to sit down in the dark and close my eyes, but I fought the urge. I forced myself to shuffle over to the fire escape. I gritted my teeth and pulled on the metal rungs with my good hand. My left wrist was throbbing, already healing. I welcomed the pain. I crawled up the eleven floors to our room as freezing rain began to fall.

GEORGE HAD LEFT the window open an inch for me. I slid it up and half-climbed, half-fell into the room.

There were candles burning, and the fire had been lit. Music was playing. New Orleans piano music. George had been trying to educate me a little, broaden my tastes, but I was still an eighties electronica fan at heart. Maybe I could win her over with some Yello, or Vangelis. If she still wanted to spend any time with me after what I had to tell her.

"George?"

I slumped into one of the wing-backed armchairs beside the fire. I rolled back my left sleeve and looked at my wrist. There was some colourful bruising. There were limits to what my rapid-healing body could fix. My foot was evidence of that. But a broken wrist shouldn't present much of a challenge, and my superficial injuries would look much better in the morning.

"George?"

I poured myself a glass of whatever was in the decanter on the table beside me. Sherry? Madeira? Port? I didn't know enough to tell the difference. It warmed me up, that was what mattered. I peeled a banana and ate it in three mouthfuls.

"George?"

For the first time, I felt a twist of concern in my gut.

I stood up. The dizziness was still there, but not as bad. I peeled and ate two more bananas, and my head settled down into a slow, thumping ache.

I looked around the room. The surface of the table was covered in dishes. I lifted the metal dome over one of them, and the delicious aroma of a rich fish stew drifted up. My stomach groaned in anticipation. My body's survival instinct is unflappable. Mentally, emotionally, I was so traumatised, that I felt as if I would never want to eat again. But my body told me otherwise. Shock, grief, and regret were all allowable, just as long as I shoved an enormous quantity of food into my mouth as soon as possible.

I fought the urge to bury my face in the stew. George's bedroom door was shut. Mine was ajar, and there was an envelope stuck on it.

I walked over and picked it up, before returning to the fireside and tipping the contents onto the table in a kind of trance. There were two more envelopes inside, one with a single word on it: *instructions!*

I picked up the unmarked envelope first. After reading the letter inside twice, I opened the *instructions!* envelope and read that.

I didn't know whether to laugh or cry, so I did both.

45

Two months later

I arrived in Cornwall seven weeks ago, the bus dropping me a few miles outside Newquay. A small cottage, just off the main road. I plan on staying until autumn, the longest I've been in one place for years. Well, more accurately, the longest I've stayed *voluntarily* in one place for years.

I used one of the credit cards George had set up for me. The cottage is a holiday let, but it's far enough out of town to make it a poor choice for surfers or families hoping to hit the beaches every day. The owners reduced the weekly amount when I said I'd take it for six months. I shop online and have my groceries delivered. It's amazing to think I can live like this, rent a house, get my food, without meeting another human being.

I'm not a recluse. Trying to avoid drawing any attention to myself might produce the opposite result. It's unlikely a few locals muttering about the new hermit in the cottage will alert the media, but you never know who might be listening. It's better to avoid the risk. So, once a week, I head down to the Dog and Duck and sink a few pints. I take the newspaper with me. I've mastered the art of the Multi-Purpose Grunt, a sound which can be used to give the appearance of answering questions without doing anything of the kind. I occasionally accompany the Multi-Purpose Grunt with a Meaningless Hand Gesture. That tends to deter those who attempt to pursue the conversation past the first M-P G.

"So, enjoying the quiet life, are ya?"

M-P G.

"Not here for the surfing, then?"

M-P G plus MHG.

Financially, my stay here will cost far less than you might imagine. By the time I leave in October, I will have spent around fourteen thousand pounds total on rent, food, and so on. Well, I say "spent," but really it will cost me nothing. My monthly credit card bill is a few hundred quid shy of three grand, and I only pay the minimum payment when the bill comes in. On month one, that's only about fifty notes, but it soon shoots up. By the time the sixth months rolls around, I'll be looking at a minimum monthly payment of nearly three hundred pounds.

I mentioned how brilliant George was, right? Well, this was her scam. Designed to keep me afloat until the terms of her will take effect, and I inherit what her solicitor informs me is a 'considerable amount.' As the solicitor in question charges three hundred pounds an hour, I can only imagine what he means by the word 'considerable.'

My first transaction was a cash withdrawal of a grand. That's enough to cover every month's minimum payment for six months. Once a month, I pop into the local bank, fill in a giro slip and pay my credit card bill with the cash I took from the same credit card in month one. George called it robbing Peter to pay Peter. By the time the credit card company comes looking for Hugh Charse (George's sense of humour, don't blame me) I'll be long gone.

I have another three credit cards set up to abuse in a similar fashion.

The first day I was here, I took all the fresh fruit and veg from my food delivery upstairs, placing it all in the bath, along with various chemicals George had believed would be helpful.

That same afternoon, I ticked off the last item on George's list of instructions. I called the phone number and gave this address. Two hours later, a motorbike courier arrived with a temperature-controlled medical package. I took it upstairs and, after pouring the contents of the tea urn I'd brought from London into the tub, I opened the package and added that, too.

Then I waited.

Two mornings later, I checked on the bath and its soup-like contents. Something had changed. I looked closer, then went downstairs, opened a beer, and sobbed like a baby for about an hour.

It was working.

~

WHEN I WOKE up this morning, I couldn't remember where I was for a moment. I'd been dreaming about Abos, about the moment Station was buried. By the time I had clicked on the light and remembered I was in Cornwall, I was too wired to go back to sleep.

I got up. It was just beginning to get light. I jogged across the fields to the sea.

I've found a beach with a treacherous path from the cliffs down to the sand that only an idiot would risk taking. Assuming the idiot could read, the big signs with red letters warning of rockfalls were enough to put off all but the most suicidally reckless. Or someone who could survive a rockfall.

I stood and watched the waves.

Every so often, once, sometimes twice, a week, I wake up ragged, raw, the pain clear and urgent, the bad memories demanding I give them their due. I have to get outside, feel the air on my face, remind myself that the world is still turning, oblivious to the fact that the god of shame, guilt, and impotent rage (he's a multi-tasking kind of god) is currently taking a dump on my head.

The memory of the night I killed the halfheroes is still there to remind me of who, and what, I might have become. The fight with Abos, that's there, too. The knowledge that I had been the biological father of possibly hundreds of tortured souls bred to be monsters. I doubt the memories will ever completely fade. That's okay.

The waves crash over the wet, black rocks twenty yards from where I'm standing. They carry all the power, patience, and inevitability of natural history. Over time, the force and weight of the water will wear the rocks away, change the shape of the coastline, and reclaim the land.

I find solace watching the sea wash tirelessly against the rocks.

It may take years, but I'll keep bringing every last, bloody splinter of memory into the light.

I remember that last night in the hotel.

I READ George's letter through twice before I moved. The sound of *gospel-tinged piano blues seemed oddly appropriate, and I knew she had chosen it deliberately. People play carefully curated music while they're giving birth.*

Why not do the same when you are dying?

Finally, I put the letter back on the table and walked into George's bedroom.

I knew she had gone. Her absence was as powerfully apparent as her presence had been.

The wheelchair was next to the bed. George was lying on top of the covers. She must have taken a shower in the wet room, as her hair was still slightly damp to the touch. Her eyes were closed, and she looked like she had fallen asleep while listening to the music.

When I stroked her cheek, her skin was icy.

I sat on the bed and took her hand. According to her letter, she had known for nearly a year that she would die in this hotel room, on this evening, alone. She had seen the events leading to her death, and—because of the other futures inextricably entwined with her own—she had pursued the path leading to this night.

She did not directly say so, but I imagined other scenarios where she lived longer but I died, or Station had survived our attack.

She had chosen instead to embrace the series of events that led to this moment: Station's destruction, the loss of Abos, and her death.

At first, I thought she had sacrificed too much, that she had chosen badly.

Then I read her instructions, and I began to understand.

As I stood on the beach, the salt slap of the wind-driven

waves cold enough to hurt, I thought about a nature documentary I'd seen a few nights previously.

On another beach, thousands of miles from this one, the documentary showed baby iguanas hatching and having to avoid the attention of predators. As they ran across the beach, heading for the safety of the rocks, thousands of snakes tracked their movements, closing in to kill and eat them. The documentary focussed on one iguana who, somehow, against all the odds, escaped. As the camera lingered on it scrambling up the rocks to safety, I had a sudden revelation.

I am not a sodding iguana. But I might as well be since all I've done so far is run. And, like the poor scaly bastard on the TV, I had avoided the predators. Up to now, at least. If I had to be an iguana, I wouldn't be just any iguana. I'd be superiguana, a reptile with...okay, maybe I was stretching the analogy a little too far.

It crystallised a decision that's been lurking in my brain for the past few weeks. I've run for long enough. I don't have to be the prey. I don't have to be the predator, either. I can live without fear, without violence.

POLICE TAPE MARKED out a perimeter by the time I got back to the site of the explosion. It wasn't yet dawn, and only a handful of onlookers were there being discouraged by the authorities from getting too close.

I carried a tea urn George had left for me in the hotel room. It was unwieldy and, with my broken wrist, hard to manage, but she hadn't known how big a container I'd need, so had plumped for a twenty-litre version.

I ducked under the tape and made my way to where I last saw Abos.

The piece of masonry was large enough for me to squat behind, hidden from the uniforms swarming ant-like over the pile of rubble where Station's entrance had once stood.

I took the lid off the urn, and placed it on its side, as close to the huge chunk of concrete as I could. Then I lay on my back and got both feet against the massive block that had crushed Abos.

At first, when I began pushing, it seemed like nothing was happening. I had eaten all the food George had ordered and had even managed three hours sleep. Her letter had insisted I would need it.

I grunted with effort, sweat stinging my eyes. Just as I felt I could push no harder, I thought of George lying there, dying alone so that this could happen, and I found an extra reserve somewhere.

Something shifted. There was the sound of smaller stones falling as the concrete lifted. I took a breath, held it, then hissed an exhalation while channelling all my strength into my legs, the muscles screaming. The concrete lifted more, inch by inch, until, finally, I locked my legs underneath it.

I looked at the patch of ground I had exposed. It was dark, my eyes were struggling to adapt, but, as the first grey hint of the day to come brightened the scene, I saw it.

It was just as Cress's diary had described, a kind of blue-green slime.

I found myself thinking back to the moment, just hours before, when I had walked into George's bedroom. In the same way that I had immediately felt her absence, I now felt a presence. The slime was unmistakably alive.

"I came back," I whispered.

I tried to reach it, but my fingers could only get within about two feet of the edge of the puddle of living soup. I stretched, tried twisting my upper body a little to get closer, but nothing worked.

I couldn't help myself. I started to laugh. It was a giggle at first, then it got louder, and I slapped a hand over my mouth. There was a tinge of hysteria to it that threatened to take over. If I allowed that to happen, I would howl with laughter until everyone within earshot came to take a look.

Just as I was biting my hand to stop this happening, I thought I saw the slime move. I choked back the next gulp of laughter and looked more closely.

It was definitely moving. The Amorphous Blob Of Slime was sliding across the rubble, picking its way through the concrete, stones, and twisted metal. When it reached the edge of the urn, it slid inside.

Praying that I wouldn't let it drop too heavily, I lowered the huge block back to the ground, put the lid back on the urn and, crouching, ran back the way I had come, crossing the police line.

"Oi, what are you up to?"

I froze. Turning, I saw an army officer approaching, a further half a dozen soldiers a few paces behind him. There were more of them in a camouflaged transport vehicle parked another twenty yards along the perimeter.

"Me?"

"Yes, you, the suspicious looking giant with a battered face and a tea urn. Come here."

I walked towards him, forcing a smile onto my face.

"Can't help me face, mate. Got into a minor disagreement in the pub last night."

The army guy looked me up and down.

"Really? Care to explain why you're sneaking around the scene of a massive gas explosion at six in the morning carrying a tea urn?"

I kept the smile on my face and put the urn on the floor before giving it a little tap.

"Soup," I said, "for the homeless. On my way to Liverpool

Street now. We set up every morning there. St Crispy's soup kitchen."

"St Crispy?"

"Crispin. Um, don't mean to be rude, but I'll be in trouble if I'm late. I'll leave you to do your army stuff, all right?"

"No," said the officer, "that's not all right," and I wondered what my chances would be like if I decked him and ran. Not good, I suspected.

"No?" I said.

"We're hungry," he said, jerking his thumb back at the soldiers behind him. "Let's have some of your soup."

"Oh. You wouldn't like it. It's cold."

"I don't think we're that fussy." He turned to the nearest soldier. "Davis? Are we that fussy?"

"No, sir. Not fussy at all."

"There you are, then." He called to the soldiers in the parked vehicle behind. "Anyone got a mug? Chuck it up here. Pronto."

A few seconds later, he was handing me a chipped enamel mug. "Fill 'er up, pretty boy."

Shit.

I held the mug under the tap and turned it. A splash of slime came out, followed by another. I stopped when the mug was half-full. The officer took it from me held it up to his face and inhaled.

"Jesus!" He whipped his head away, angling his chin up in an effort to get as far from the offending liquid as possible. "That is absolutely foul. Rank. Disgusting. How can you even—?"

He went to throw the mug's contents onto the ground. I stepped forward and grabbed his wrist.

"What's your game?" he said, but let me take the mug and tip its contents back into the urn.

"There are homeless people out there who need this, sir." I handed back the mug.

"Well, they're bloody welcome to it, the poor bastards." The men behind him chuckled as he shook his head. I breathed again.

"I told you it wasn't nice cold," I said.

"On your way," he said, dismissing me, *"and don't let me catch you hanging around again.*

"No, sir," I said, cradling the urn under my good arm. *"No sir, I won't."*

I CLIMBED the crumbling steps up the rock face and sat near the edge of the cliff. Turning away from the water, I looked back at the cottage, clearly visible on a slight rise.

Just when I was beginning to think I was wrong, that it wouldn't happen today, a figure walked through the open door.

I got to my feet, raised both arms in the air and waved.

The figure waved back and began to walk towards me.

SHE WALKED SLOWLY, cautiously, picking her way across the open field leading to the cliff path.

I remembered the moment I opened the medical package and saw what it contained. George's blood, drawn from her veins the same night Abos and I destroyed Station. Kept refrigerated since then in a private medical facility, waiting for my call. Then the motorcycle ride from South London, the container plugged into a USB port on the bike, keeping the temperature constant.

Abos needed blood. George could provide it. Maybe, in some sense, she could live on.

I had poured the blood on top of the blue-green slime,

which floated on a decaying, stinking mass of rotting fruit and vegetables.

I had felt faintly ridiculous as I stood there. I had thought of the moment in Frankenstein, when Victor grabs a sceptical fellow scientist with a fervour bordering on the demented, saying, "It's alive...it's *alive*!" as thunder roars and lightning flashes around the lab. Somehow, pouring blood into a bath full of slime didn't have the same drama.

But it had worked.

She climbed over the stile and made her way along the path towards me.

She was wearing the trainers, jeans, and jumper I had bought for her. The jeans were too short. I had guessed her height at about five-foot-eight, but this woman was closer to six-foot, leaving a fair amount of skin exposed at the ends of her trouser legs.

She stopped when we were about two feet from each other.

I was looking at George, her brown skin as unblemished as that of a baby's, her smile broad, her eyes the deep gold of liquidambar in autumn.

"Geo—," I began, then stopped myself. "Abos."

"Hello, Daniel. Thank you. For coming back."

We walked together and sat at the cliff's edge.

"Thank George," I said. "She saw all of it."

There was a long silence. As well as her physical body, Abos seemed to have changed in her mannerisms. As we talked, I noticed that even her speech patterns were different. There was no Welsh accent. Abos now spoke with George's voice.

"She was a remarkable person," said Abos.

"She was."

"What now? Do you have places to be? Things to do? Super stuff?"

I mimed a flying superhero taking to the sky. Abos laughed.

"No. Well. I don't know. There's so much I don't know. About myself. About you."

"Tell me about it."

Abos put a soft hand on my cheek.

"What I do have is time I can spend with you. If you'd like that?"

I nodded.

"Yes. I would like that."

She got up, stripped off her clothes, and stood at the very edge of the land, toes curled on the precipice.

I'm standing on a cliff edge, watching a woman fall. She falls backwards away from me, her eyes never leaving mine. There is very little wind, but as she spreads her arms, it's as if a breeze has caught her, twisting her body around like a leaf in autumn.

She's naked, her dark skin silhouetting her against the turquoise waves.

I think of my father, and of my dead friend. I think of the future and wonder, for the first time, if it might be utterly unlike my expectations. I wonder what this feeling is, this feeling that has crept up on me and finally surfaced; fresh, unknown, and impossible to ignore.

As she drops towards the rocks, I start smiling.

I name this new feeling and wonder where it might lead. It's hope.

I watch George's doppelgänger wait until her body almost touches the tips of the waves. She must be able to taste the salt water as she turns the momentum of her fall into a horizontal glide a few feet above the surface. Her speed increases smoothly, and within a few seconds, she is a black speck, rising from the sea and heading towards the clouds.

She vanishes, then the speck reappears in the distance, and, in seconds, she's back over my head, waving before turning and rocketing away once more. A few seconds later, I hear the sonic boom.

I stand there for a few more minutes, then pick up the pile of clothes she left and walk along the cliff path back to the cottage.

AUTHOR'S NOTE

Join my mailing list for book news, and I'll send you the unpublished prologue for The World Walker series: http://eepurl.com/bQ_zJ9

Email me: ianwsainsbury@gmail.com

My blog is ianwsainsbury.com and I'm on Facebook too - https://www.facebook.com/IanWSainsbury/ I'm also on twitter, but still haven't got the hang of it.

Well.

I wrote the words THE END Thursday, 9th November 2017. The last month has been a blur, writing six days a week, between 2,500-5,500 words a day. For me, that's fast. As I got into the final third of the book, it was as if I was trying to write it as quickly as I wanted to read it.

As I type this, I'm about twenty percent through the

editing process. The manuscript goes to a pro first (thank you Phil Owens), then gets proofed and cheekily (and very usefully) criticised by the talented Mrs S. Next, beta readers get their hands on an unedited copy and come back with their comments. At that point, I re-read and start cutting, fixing and polishing, then the whole thing goes off for another paid proof before publication. All this happens while the book is available for pre-order. That focusses the mind. Nothing like a deadline to force me into this chair every day.

Superheroes. I've always liked their stories. Modern myths, often morality tales, our superfolk bound over tall buildings, catch bullets, pick up buses, outrun express trains, and fly about the place wearing outfits they surely bought online while drunk. They're fascinating creatures. I love the origin stories best of all. Bitten by spiders, subject of a dangerous experiment, an orphaned alien, a rich psychopath, a mutant, the list goes on.

I had an idea for a flawed superhero who was as much a mystery to himself as he was to others. Then I wondered what his children might look like, what challenges they might face. After that, things fell into place and, about halfway through writing Children Of The Deterrent, I realised I knew where Abos had come from, and what might be waiting for him along the road (that's part of the next book.)

I had originally been considering writing a different book, with a gender-fluid main character, but found it too hard to get started. When I got to the end of Children Of The Deterrent, I found I had done it after all. Abos is not male or female. That gives her, um, him, er, *herm* (someone suggested *ze* as a pronoun - I like that) a unique perspective. If a person is without gender, then the whole idea of gender-bias is moot. It also brings its own problems. Even if you have superpowers. And it shines a light on some of the unconscious attitudes we're gradually growing out of as a species. I read The Hobbit to my youngest daughter last year. She loved it, but when we got to the end, she said, "Where were all the girls?" Fair point. We're reading Skulduggery Pleasant by Derek Landy now. Feisty female protagonist *and* a smart-mouthed wizard skeleton detective. We're both happy.

Halfhero Book Two is in the percolation stage. There are lots of ideas sitting in the coffee grinder of inspiration, waiting to be placed in the filter paper of possibility, awaiting the hot water of graft. Or something. What I'm saying is, I'm thinking, I'm daydreaming, and I'm waiting for the right moment to sketch out the next book.

And, obviously, I need more coffee.

Now, I know I've said this before, but I used to read Stephen King's author notes and feel a spark of kinship, a feeling he was part of a club to which I might one day belong. Now, I accept that he's president of the club and I'm outside parking everyone's cars for them, but I'm finally in the neighbourhood. I know there are readers who want to write, who feel that same spark reading this. To you, I say this: I'm no different to you, I just got down to writing. It's a crazy thing to do, 100,000 words take a while to produce. There's no way around it, there are no shortcuts. But if you don't write that first book, you'll never know if you have it in you to write a second, or a third. And writing a book will teach you so much. It could teach you that you don't want to be a writer. Or it might open a door you half-remember seeing in a dusty attic in your childhood, a door you once believed led to a different world.

There's a dash of magic involved in writing. I'm hesitant

to admit that, but all five of my books have been helped by a strange, hidden process that works alongside my conscious, planning mind. Oh, bugger. This is a fine line I'm walking. Writing about this kind of stuff can be useful, interesting, and revealing, but I do risk sounding like a pretentious twat. All I can say is, some powerful weirdness occurs that I am unaware of until the whole book is done. Right, I'll shut up about that.

Where was I? I was about to thank you. I've been a reader all my life, from the battered copy of Little Plum I remember my mum reading aloud, to the heaving bookshelves and fully loaded Kindle I have now. I remember a hospital stay when I was nine. My parents brought me The Lion, The Witch and The Wardrobe on my first day, then the next book in the series the next day, and so on. All I could do in hospital was read. Bliss! Then I discovered A Wizard Of Earthsea, Asimov's Robot stories, Heinlein, Mervyn Peake, Dickens, John Irving. My early teenage years were full of Philip José Farmer and Ray Bradbury.

I remember a kid at school sneering at me. "You don't understand anything. Everything you know comes out of *books*."

He intended it as an insult. That's not the way I took it. That was thirty-three years ago. I haven't changed much. I'd say I now understand virtually nothing, and *almost* everything I know comes out of books.

I want a story to sweep me up, show me worlds I could never have seen without the magic of fiction. There are readers who live, breath, *inhale* stories and, while immersed in a book, live a divided life. Part of them is always waiting in that fictional world for the story to continue, suspended at the moment the page was last bookmarked. That's who I write for, that's the prize. I hope I've got close to reaching you with this book and, trust me, I will keep trying.

A quick appeal for your help if you've enjoyed the book. Please review Children Of The Deterrent on Amazon - reviews help level the playing field for independent authors. Link here: Children Of The Deterrent

More stories to come. That's a promise.

Ian Sainsbury

Norwich
November 15th, 2017

ALSO BY IAN W. SAINSBURY

The World Walker (The World Walker Series 1)

The Unmaking Engine (The World Walker Series 2)

The Seventeenth Year (The World Walker Series 3)

The Unnamed Way (The World Walker Series 4)

Printed in Great Britain
by Amazon